MURDER UNDER REDWOOD MOON

SHERRI L. DODD

Black Rose Writing | Texas

ISBN: 978-1-68513-388-7
LIBRARY OF CONGRESS CONTROL NUMBER: TXu 2-367-023
PUBLISHED BY BLACK ROSE WRITING
www.blackrosewriting.com

Printed in the United States of America
Suggested Retail Price (SRP) $21.95

Murder Under Redwood Moon is printed in Minion Pro

*As a planet-friendly publisher, Black Rose Writing does its best to eliminate unnecessary waste to reduce paper usage and energy costs, while never compromising the reading experience. As a result, the final word count vs. page count may not meet common expectations.

Praise for
Murder Under Redwood Moon

"There are a few characters that any reader might find themselves relating to and that is not an easy thing for an author to achieve with one character, never mind more... I found it an extremely enjoyable read from start to finish and quite frankly struggled to turn my laptop off."
–Anne Brownlow, Professional Beta Reader and Retired Criminal Investigator

"I definitely recommend this book for any who enjoy the murder-mystery genre, as well as those who are fans of witchcraft and esoterism: after all, this is the only story I've read which blends the two so wonderfully."
–J. Flowers, Editing and Beta Reading Specialist, Star Reviewer on Fiverr

"There was never a moment of forced dialogue, something that would not serve the story, and I thoroughly enjoyed the way it made the manuscript engaging and dynamic. And that ending that leaves us wondering and, URGH! Yes, the resolution of the main plot is satisfying, but you leave enough crumbs for us to WANT to get the sequel."
–Liljana "Lili" B, Freelance Writer, Alpha Reader (first round draft) and Beta Reader

"I did like this thriller, and I loved the way you worked supernatural with a murder mystery, I haven't quite seen it handled like this and I think you have all the right instincts for what goes where."
– Maddy D., Beta Reading and Editing, Star Reviewer on Fiverr

To my wonderful husband, Edward, for his dedicated work ethic to our business, enabling me to focus on writing and my sons for their encouragement and inspiration to pursue something other than the ease of an empty nest. And thank you to Donna, who has pushed, pushed, pushed me to write a fiction book since high school!

MURDER
UNDER
REDWOOD
MOON

CHAPTER 1
IT STINGS

The dim-lit room beckoned Ian from the far end of the hall. He felt claustrophobic, floating along with only the center of his view, sharp enough to proceed. The outer edges blurred to black.

As he neared, he felt a strong odor beginning to irritate his senses. He identified tobacco, cacao, sandalwood, and the resins of dragon's blood from the southeast Asian tree that bleeds red sap. The scent was dark magic.

He entered the warm glow of the room and saw thirteen crimson and black candles dotting the space. Five of the largest dripped their wax in clumps over a distant altar. In front of it, his brother-in-law, Fergus, busily worked on an object draped in black velvet. He tinkered with a glass vial before reaching for his ceremonial blade, then holding it upward, he chanted.

He drew nearer as Fergus lowered his athame and could smell the oil on the steel beginning to heat from the candle's flame on the altar. Dread began to clutch him, and the pit of his gut drew to a knot.

Now upon Fergus, he sensed the overbearing presence of his brother-in-law. He peered over his shoulder. It was a father's worst nightmare. He watched as the blade sliced deliberately deep into his daughter's stomach, releasing a gushing, deep red tide of her lifeblood.

An ear-piercing banshee scream, primal and agonizing, spiraled him out of his dream world.

He awoke with a yell, jarring Keira, who lay asleep beside him.

"Oh, God! He's doing blood magick on her!"

He sprung out of bed and rushed down the hall toward Arista's room, Keira hurrying behind him while hastily fumbling with her robe sash.

"What Ian?! What is it?"

He burst into his seven-year-old daughter's room. "Arista!" Finding her safe, he bent down and stroked her cheek, but still distressed, he awoke her. "Riss. Honey, wake up."

"Ian, calm down!" Keira reprimanded. "Please … what is it? What did you see?"

Arista sleepily opened her eyes. He had found it harder to awaken her these past couple of weeks.

"I'm so sorry to wake you up, Riss, but I've got to ask you some questions about Uncle Fergus."

"Okay," she said, squinting her eyes from the brightness of the hall light.

He flipped the switch on her small, yellow, sunflower-painted lamp, now bringing a spray of dimmed, warm lighting about the room.

After she tried, and failed once more to gain his attention, Keira sat at the foot of the bed and, with great concern, held on to Arista's blanketed knee.

"Riss, when you go to your uncle's house after school, what do you do?"

Arista rubbed at her eyes.

"Does he hurt you?"

"No."

"Has he ever talked about magick with you?"

"No."

"What do you usually do over there?"

Arista looked scared and whimpered. "Why?"

"Honey, you're not in trouble and I'm sorry that we are doing this so late, but it's very, very important that you tell me the truth."

"I am." Her bottom lip beginning to quiver.

"Ian, you're scaring her." Keira laid down behind Arista and draped her loving arm over her.

He softened his tone. "Riss, what do you do when you're at uncle's house?"

"We play board games and I fall asleep."

"You fall asleep?"

"Yes, and play games."

He looked at Keira. This unfolding story did not set well. He was thankful that he had acted on his gifted aunt's recent phone call. She had alerted him to the alarming prod of her intuition and the danger that Arista was facing. Now he could see that his decision to astral travel into his own dreamworld, a gift he had abandoned long ago, was correct.

"You go to sleep in the afternoon?" Keira said, asserting her first question. "You never do that here."

"I always get sleepy during games."

"Does he give you candies or drinks?" His anxiety grew.

"He gives me a cup of almond milk."

The anger boiled inside of him.

"Okay." He took a breath, trying to keep his cool, and not wanting to frighten her. "So, he's never talked magick with you?"

"No."

"Riss, I had a dream just a few minutes ago. I was in uncle's house and went into his room at the end of the hallway. Do you know which room I mean?"

"Yes, but he doesn't let me go in there."

"You've never seen that room?"

"No, the door's shut."

Keira stroked Arista's hair, as he feared the implications. Fergus had promised Keira he had changed back to the loving brother he once was. He was clean again, and not associating with criminals anymore.

"Riss, can I look at your tummy for just a minute?"

"Yes."

He squatted to the floor as Arista lay down flat on her bed. Keira helped her daughter with her nightgown, pulling it up to her midriff to expose what he hoped was the flawless flesh of a child's belly.

But, as soon as the shadows of their fussing had cleared, he saw it, and clenched his jaw, holding back the rage.

"How did your tummy get hurt?" He pointed at a two-inch gauze bandage covering her abdomen.

She looked down at the bandage. "I don't know."

"When did this happen?"

"At Uncle's house."

He flashed a hostile look over at Keira, who was welling up with tears.

"Do you mind if I take a quick peek?"

"Okay."

But as he reached for it Arista changed her mind. "No, Dad, don't! It stings."

Keira silently cried while stroking Arista's hair. She wiped away her own tears that fell upon her daughter's abdomen.

He took notice and knew the betrayal was too profound for her to bear.

"I promise to be gentle."

Keira continued to comfort Arista as he peeled off the bandage. The sobering proof was immediate. While it was not the gaping fatal slice in his dream, an inch-long dotted scratch tainted his daughter's precious flesh. It was still fresh, only days since Fergus had picked her up from school.

Arista looked at the serrated scabbing, rimmed with reddened skin and her eyes widened with shock. "Oh, no!" She hyperventilated as the confession came forth. "When I woke up, he said I had an accident ... but not show you or you would blame him and be mad."

"Oh, please no." Keira shook her head and lay back down behind Arista, pressing her cheek to her daughter's head, trying to soothe her rising anxiety. "You're safe now," she told Arista, squeezing her in a mother's embrace.

"Like mom said, you're safe now. We will never let him hurt you again."

He tenderly ran his finger along the scratch. He could see faded markings from red ink, suggesting that it was to frame the cut. Still terrorized by what he had seen in his dream minutes earlier, he found solace that a true ceremonial draw had not yet occurred.

But his dreams always came to pass.

"Riss, this looks like it may have hurt. Do you remember what happened?"

"No."

Hopefully, she truly had no recollection of the encounter.

"It looks like it had a design. Do you remember the design?"

"Not really."

"Not really?" He looked into her eyes.

"No."

Keira sat back up to look at the scratch. She squeezed Arista's hand and placed her entire palm lovingly atop the wound, while desperately looking at him.

"Okay, well, I'm not mad at you, and this is not your fault. Thank you for telling me."

Arista relax, but her look of shame remained.

"Remember! Not your fault. You hear me?"

She nodded and looked into his eyes.

"And please *always* tell me or your mom … or both of us … everything. Especially if you get hurt. Even if someone says that we'll get mad. No matter who it is. " How else could he make the point without coming across as angry with her?

Arista stayed silent, but finally after encouragement peeped out an agreement.

Disguising his coursing rage, he cupped his daughter's cheek with his hand. "Well, mom will give it true *TLC*, and put a better wrapping on it. We'll take care of this. Okay?"

"Okay," she whimpered.

He had mixed emotions from her trusting gaze. Of course, she could trust him, but he had failed her. He had not kept her safe from Fergus. He would never forgive himself that he let this offense befall her.

Keira hustled back from the medicine cabinet and held up bright pink medical tape, salve, and a forced smile. "Let's put it in pink."

Arista gave a half-hearted smile, and Keira lovingly redressed the wound.

Afterward, he apologized for the late-night disturbance, and Keira gave the last goodnight kiss while they cozily tucked her back into bed.

But with the flip of Arista's light switch, he knew he had a critical decision to make. As he and Keira walked back to their room, his conflicting thoughts overwhelmed him—violence, legalities, heartbreak, and regret.

A thick tension suffocated any of their small talk, and Keira plopped down on the bed in surrender. "I hate him. I'll never … never trust him again!"

As she rubbed her crying eyes, he held his breath and paced, the fury percolating within him. *What to do now?*

He sat down at the edge of the mattress next to Keira and put his hand on her thigh. He simmered in the tension, the ticking of their hall clock pricking at his frayed nerves. It was not Keira's fault. She did not know her once-beloved brother practiced the dark arts again, and especially not with Arista.

Unable to find the right words, he looked at their wall photo of the beautiful Santa Cruz redwoods. It presented evergreen trees rising into the rich blue sky, a hint of serenity during this moment of fury. The framed photo had been a gift from his Aunt Bethie. It depicted the tranquil mountain region where she lived, and she had frequently encouraged them to come stay in her second small cottage down the street from her own.

"Boulder Creek," he soberly said.

"What?" Keira glanced up at the photo.

He looked at her, her expression a mixture of sadness and anger. His empathy was quickly swallowed by the memory of Fergus lording over Arista on his altar, and the harm that had befallen his innocent child, only days from her eighth birthday. He soured again.

"Ian," Keira whimpered.

He shook his head, trying to detach from the vision, but he could not. This dream carried the ultimate price if left unaddressed.

His chest heaved and he could no longer deny it.

"I'm going to fucking kill him."

CHAPTER 2
AN EVERGREEN WINTER MORNING

At twenty-three, Arista loved the independence and quiet solitude of her small inherited mountain cottage in the redwoods.

She beckoned from her bedroom. "Where's my kitty?"

Her roommate, Royal, a lumbering Siamese cat, was a source of feigned codependence.

"I know you can hear me."

She heard the small tinkling of his collar charm on the stainless-steel food dish as it traveled through the hallway from the kitchen.

"Roy-al!" She singingly called out to him and waited for his appearance.

Nothing. She knew once he was eating, there was no hope of getting him to come until finished.

She walked over to her small standing vanity area, her improvised and very cherished altar. Picking up her astrology candle, she drew in the fragrance, and lit the wick.

"*Leo—Fearless, Confident, Passionate*," she read from the candle's parchment label. "Well, it's what I strive for." She insecurely laughed. "Good morning, Ghost. Though I don't suspect you are here." She paused, wondering if there would be an answer this time. "I didn't think so, but a respectful hello to you, wherever you may be at this hour."

After all, it was mostly at night when Ghost appeared, making the air grow heavy, causing faint flickers, and she heard the creaking of her wooden floors. She had felt the presence since her divination skills had progressed in the late teens, and picked up the intricate crumbs of paranormal activity that others would surely miss. In fact, it was a spooky game and a unique type of fun to have adrenalizing moments in touch with the Otherworld.

Ping.

"Well, the day is starting, Royal," she said, followed by a stern beckoning. "Get in here. I'm tired of talking to myself."

Hustling over to her phone, she grabbed it from the bed. Instead of info about the day's start time from Analina, a text from her friend, Maddie, drew her concern.

'Let's meet up! My uncle and I had a run-in with freaks last night.'

"Oh, no."

Maddie had been her best friend since she had arrived in Boulder Creek, so being there for her was crucial, especially for an occasion like this. Yet, she prioritized being reliable at work and could not let Analina down.

"Hmm, a decision best made with a cup of tea."

She selected her music for the morning, waited for the resonance to come across her speaker, and tossed her phone on the unfolded pile of clean jeans. Further, her spirit lifted with her morning refresher of a piping-hot wet wash cloth, wrapped over her dry and sleep-worn face. She delighted in the sensation.

In a moment of confusion, a flash of an image struck her mind's eye, interrupting her ritual. A grubby hand, the heel of it meaty with a design on it. Only a split-second had lapsed before the vision vanished.

"What the … that was wild!"

She shrugged it off, wrung and hung her washcloth, then headed to the kitchen.

"Royal!" She playfully reprimanded him by his dish before swooping up the sated, chunky feline. "Into my arms, like a baby. Why didn't you come?" She kissed his shiny black nose and gave his furry, muddle-colored belly a fluffled scratch before setting him down again.

Royal impatiently laid back his ears, pondered a moment, and cleaned his haunch, agitated by the abrupt human scoop tactic.

The glow of the morning sun made up for the clutter in her rustic kitchen. A silver fairy with its crystal orb hung in the sunlit window, filling the room with circular rainbows.

The oak-plank floor creaked as she sleepily trod over to her dinette table. It was a beautifully handcrafted assemblage of reclaimed materials that had been in her family for generations. Antique railway spikes and an old rod supported its bulky, gnarled wood. Her great-great-grandparents had built it together, and it stood as the most dignified item in her quaint cottage. Though she was never sure of the practicality factor based on its size. Nevertheless, Auntie, her paternal great-aunt, and her legal guardian since the age of eight, was adamant that the piece stay put, and asked her to keep the wood clean, waxed and protected.

She grabbed the pitcher of her favorite tea—a marvelous homemade blend of green rooibos, hibiscus, and rosehips, with dried flowers of lavender and sweet blackberry leaves. The latter two ingredients, she would macerate herself with mortar and pestle. She had prepped it the prior night, and let it bathe in the moonlight, drawing in the feminine energy of her celestial goddess, Mother Moon.

Settling her time constraint for a moment, she took in the appealing sweet scent. On this morning, she filled her mundane life with magick—the sight of prismatic circles, the softness of Royal's coat and now the aroma of this delightful beverage.

With herbal tea in hand, she keyed in Maddie's number.

"My uncle had some guys come at him last night by the shop." Maddie poured into her story without a proper greeting. "I think they were loitering around our house later, too. And they're dark, Arista, like, super dark … hooded and lurking … like grim reapers! All black clothes and just a real creepy feeling to them."

"That's awful!" Her heart began to race, feeding off of Maddie's anxiety. Every time her bestie's emotions flowed, so did hers, and she worked hard to minimize her empathic tendencies, with the fine line between extremes and empathy creating inner conflict. Maybe she could fit in a face-to-face after work.

"Can Auntie handle creeps like that? She talks about how nothing can penetrate her protection spells."

"Yeah, she has said that a time or two ... or ten!" Auntie had told both of them stories about her defensive abilities. She had also taught her countless spells that would keep her safe from harm's way. In doing so, she also taught the importance of their greatest belief—*Harm to None*.

"So, help me God, Arista! At two a.m. the neighbor's barking dog woke me up. I looked out the window and ..." Maddie's voice cracked, "what if they come back? Hopefully, Auntie can speak to the crystals or blend a concoction or whatever funky process she does."

"Okay, okay. Just give me a minute to think."

She rubbed her forehead, trying to ease some of the angst she had picked up from Maddie. But she did have a valid point. Dealing with two stalkers is never okay. While she could be dramatic, she was not usually this inconsolable.

"Alright, for sure. Can it wait just a little bit? I'm working at the shop today, and Auntie is away."

"When's she back?"

"Still another week. Sedona seems to draw her more and more lately. Her coven ... the vortex-thing, it's all a mystery to me."

Maddie groaned in frustration, then softened her demeanor. "Well, will you see little Zoelly today?"

She envisioned Analina's eight-year-old daughter, a definite perk to the job. "Yes. I can't wait to see her cute little face!"

"For sure. Hard to resist, huh?"

"Yes, indeed. Anyway, I don't like it when Auntie leaves either. But *c'est la vie*. Let's get together in the next couple of days. I'm working a couple shifts, and lately Shane and I have been talking on the phone a lot. It feels like we're, well, kind of getting to know each other ... even though we've known each other for years."

Maddie exhaled with a trill. "Finally!"

"Finally?"

"Oh, please, Arista. You guys were made for each other. Definitely better than the last jackass. Seriously, the rest of us have known this for years."

Thankfully, the distraction had eased Maddie's agitation, and what a distraction it was. It still perplexed her. All these years, she felt a transparent wall between her and Shane. Sure, he was a dear friend, and a lot of fun, but an unspoken rule was it would be nothing more. Luckily, the high school separation, perhaps a strategic move from his parents, seemed to have brought them even closer together. Whatever had created the divide had dissipated more so with each passing year.

"You really think so? His family is very Catholic, and I'm not sure his mom will approve."

"Oh gawd, Arista. He's a grown man now. He's only living at home to save money, like damn-near *all* our friends … and us too!"

The encouragement humored her. "Well … I'm going to take this one slowly. But …"

"But, what?"

"I drew *The Lovers* in tarot last month … at Yule!"

"No! Are you kidding me?"

She pictured Maddie's mouth agape and giggled briefly before she heard Uncle Pat bellowing from the background.

"That's sooo cool! Okay, anyway, I gotta get back to work. Thursday is fine." Maddie abruptly disconnected.

She had a job to get to as well. She threw on her cozy, faux-sherpa jacket. Obviously, Analina had left the day's start time up to her discretion. So, she took it upon herself to get there early.

After a long stroke down a loitering Royal's back she headed outside to her bike.

It made for an easy trek from her cottage to downtown Boulder Creek, the last of four hamlets in the Santa Cruz mountains. On this stretch of Highway 9, there were a variety of shops, restaurants, and even a veterinary clinic. Continuing on, you would meander deep into the redwood mountains, and eventually arrive in the bustling Bay Area.

In a short while, she arrived at the vibrantly painted shop of forest green with deep-blue trim. She secured her bike, carefully positioning it amongst a cluster of bright yellow pansies in the planter box and the bike that was already present.

A passerby grazed her elbow.

"Oh, sorry," she automatically said, before realizing who it was. "Oh, wow! Hey Michelle!" What a shock to see this old friend.

"Oh hey," Michelle replied nonchalantly. She kept pace.

Wow! No engagement at all.

She had long accepted Michelle was unreachable since their middle school years of girl talk and picking flowers. Further, she had drifted and by the later years of high school, Michelle had found more relatability in a gloomier crowd that felt derisive of her optimism.

"I'd love to get together if you ever have the chance." Only Michelle's back faced her. "Or come by the shop sometime, and I can get you my friends and family discount."

Michelle briefly turned and offered a pained smile before returning to her stride.

"Bye." Her cheerfulness trailed off in volume the further Michelle got from her. The disinterest was blatant, but she still wanted to show her kindness. The young woman had a difficult life.

She refocused on her bike and latched the lock.

The noisy engine announced the bulky truck before it growled into the space directly in front of her.

"Hey you," blurted the passenger.

She looked up, recognizing the voice. "Hey, guys!"

Shane was a welcome sight, as was his passenger Evan, though seeing the latter was also a bit of a shock. Now that his ailing grandmother lived with them, Evan's mother had returned to her old antics of devouring his time. In high school, it was keeping him safe from reckless peers. In the earlier years of college, it was over-managing his grades, and at twenty-three, it had become harping about his duty to family.

"We know you're headed to work, but just wanted to say *hi*," Shane said.

"Great! Evan, I'm shocked to see you out and about," she teased with a warm smile.

"It's not for long," Evan quipped. "Was that Michelle?"

"Yeah. I think she was in a hurry." Evan had liked Michelle throughout high school.

"Hmph." Evan's attention was now on something else as he stared into the distance.

She turned to see the source of his fascination. Margaret Troxel, a town elder, and a known target for Evan's mother's tirades, busily tottered into the crosswalk, halting the progress of traffic.

"My mom does not like that lady," Evan said. "She is downright rude about it, to the point of embarrassment. I just don't get it."

"She is quirky, but that's just her. She minds her own business."

"Is she homeless or something? She looks a bit ragged." He looked up at her with his eyebrows raised. "The homeless see everything I hear."

She broke off from Evan's intense gaze. "Oh, come on, Evan. No, she isn't homeless. She's a long-time friend of Auntie. I'll admit, she has an eclectic taste in clothing … and hair style. And I don't think she's ever said a word to me." She thought about her rare encounters with Margaret. "Anyway, like I said, she just keeps to herself."

Evan shrugged and looked at Shane, who was still eyeing the woman's awkward gait.

"Okay, well, we know you're busy." Shane snapped to attention and shifted his truck into gear.

"Yeah, thanks so much for stopping by you guys!"

"Call ya later." Shane winked at her, catching Evan's attention.

As the car pulled away, she heard Evan chuckling to himself, but it didn't matter what anyone thought. That guy, the one behind the wheel, diligently driving into the distance … he was going to be hers.

Arista walked through the door of Earth & Ocean. She settled into a tranquil state from the sounds of the softly gurgling, stone-adorned, and coin-endowed Fortuna fountain.

Zoelly disrupted the moment of serenity. "Arista!" Shrieking in a high pitch, she appeared in a yellow gingham dress, and adorned in two tiny necklaces—a silver pentacle and a dainty raw-Amethyst crystal.

"Wow! I see Mom was busy with your hair this morning. May I?" Her fashioned braid was as sturdy as the thickest rope and alluring to touch, but she always asked permission first. After all, respect is not just for adults.

Zoelly stilled to let her pick up her braid and admire the work. A small yellow rubber band, embellished with a strand of yellow ribbon, tamed what was usually a lion's mane of soft, dark auburn hair.

"You know you're my favorite reason for coming here." She set the braid down the back of her dress, appreciating the aesthetic.

Zoelly gave a flattered giggle. "I drew you a unicorn!"

"I can't wait to see it!"

The young girl ran toward the back, leaving her at the counter.

Ding-ding.

The bell rang as the door opened, making way for a very unusual couple.

"Good morning," she greeted, with a shopkeeper's friendly charm.

The male, clad in tight black leather pants and a white tee looked away from her. Upon his head sat a short-cropped top hat bearing a set of faux red eyes and horns peering from between its twisted black-leather wrapping. Maybe, his version of eyes-behind-his-back. His jet-black hair cascaded down his nape and swung with arrogance.

The female's outfit was similarly dark; her black lace dress with its low scooped neckline revealed a voluptuously swelled cleavage. The only break from the barrage of black material were the elegant, polished stones she wore set in sterling silver, on her fingers and around her porcelain-white neck. The pendant held a magnificent oval cabochon of Rainbow Obsidian that rested between her breasts, framed by two long wisps of black-and-magenta hair. Quite the contrast from her aloof friend, her eyes flickered, and a huge Cheshire Cat grin covered her face.

Used to and welcoming of colorful characters, she felt a slight twinge from their presence. Yes, the shop drew customers from all edges of the county, witches, and dabblers of many types. These two, however, brought something else. Something dark followed them.

A dropping sensation within her gut distracted her. It was a nauseating churn that prompted her to draw a breath. What was this feeling?

She whisked past Analina who had just emerged from the backroom. She entered the partitioned area of the store to set down her belongings and ready for work. Beyond her private space, she could hear her boss working her sales magick to entice the couple with the store's Rose Quartz Special.

Discreetly, she peeked out from behind the curtain adorned with a colorfully embroidered *Tree of Life* sigil. She watched the man's eyes study Analina, though he said nothing before looking at his companion as she talked.

"I'd love to look at a couple pieces. Thank you," the female said in a melodic voice from between full, magenta-painted lips.

Zoelly peeked through the partition beneath her, flapping the curtain. "She's really pretty," she blurted too loudly.

She backed away now that her fellow spy, devoid of adult stealth, had exposed their eavesdropping. "I don't think I've seen them before. I would have remembered her. And I agree, Zoelly, she is really pretty."

She motioned for Zoelly to follow her toward the backroom table, further away from the curtain, and the two perused the gaping boxes of new merchandise.

The uneasiness she felt from this couple nipped at her psyche, but first impressions can be wrong … right?

CHAPTER 3
A LOVELY ARRAY OF ROSEBUDS

"I just don't know why he has to stay over every night!" Michelle griped into the phone, then held it at arm's length to avoid the barrage of excuses.

Her mother's voice sent disharmony into the stillness of the night.

"Fine, whatever!" She finally conceded and disconnected the only lifeline she had left. "Every ... freaking ... time, they get worse."

She walked stiffly in the frigid winter night and emerged from the shrouded backstreets into the quaint downtown area of Felton. She found solace in the emptiness of the late hour—no obliged eye contact with strangers and no need to respond to a friendly *hello*. Anonymously blending with the nothingness around her, she felt at peace.

She tucked her cell into her pocket, crossed the empty mountain highway, and headed toward The Golden Lily. For weeks she had tried to get an appointment with one of the valley's tattoo shops, with no success. To get an appointment, you needed to call, and calling only led to unanswered voicemails.

Luckily, she began a relationship with a gothic couple she encountered outside of the Beach Boardwalk's arcade. Besides a secured tattoo appointment, the sexual spark she had with the couple instantly took. The guy, with his reckless rock star qualities and the woman, so full-bodied and sensual. They were engaging and provided her with a sense of protection, something she seldom felt in her own limited circle of friends, much less from strangers.

Yelena, the female of the two, boasted an ornate triple moon design on most of her back. An inked masterpiece recently recolored by Kane at The Golden Lily enabled the contact, and Yelena had texted him on her behalf.

She knocked on the glass door of the dimmed shop. A man quickly lumbered toward the door.

"Hey there," he greeted with a friendly smile. "I'm Kane."

"Hi, I'm Michelle," She added a half-smile out of courtesy.

"Yeah, okay, great. Do you know what you want? There's some designs over here." He walked her to the gallery of those who had come before her. A collage of biceps and chests, ankles and calves graced the wall, all adorned with Kane's artful work.

She promptly pointed. "Yes, this one."

"Aw, she knows what she wants."

The third-person reference irritated her. "Yeah, I already looked through your window a couple times this week, so I'd be ready."

"Good! All good." He ushered her to a vintage dental chair upholstered in teal pleather. "So, how long have you known Yelena?"

"Only a couple weeks." She settled into the chair and scrunched up the sleeve of her hoodie.

"Yeah, I just met them, too. They said they just moved here, but—" He stopped and lightened his tone. "I don't know. She just seems familiar. Like, I could swear I went to school with a chick that looked just like her. You know, same build, big smile, and all." He continued his busyness and returned his focus to the tray of readied inks and tissues. "Hmph. Maybe not. She seems pretty cool, though. Jaxon too, I guess."

After applying an outline to her arm, he grabbed his tattoo machine, already prepped for the session, and began his work.

Zzzzzzzzzz. Zzzzzzz. Zzz.

"They are a lot of fun to party with." She paused and gazed to the far side of the shop. Usually not a talker, it felt better than silently enduring the burning scratch of the needle. "They're kinda spiritual, ya know, understanding 'bout stuff. Just beautiful souls, and most of the people I've met through them are pretty cool, too." She felt her cheeks warm and knew she was blushing. What was it about sitting vulnerable in Kane's chair that induced her to express herself truthfully? "I mean, I don't know about you, but I can count on two hands the times the word *love* was said in my house."

"Man, that's brutal," he said with concern. "Sorry to hear."

Maybe Kane grew up with kind parents because the relatability just totally fell flat.

"Nah, my mom was the sss-motherly type," he said.

Knew it.

"Now, my pops would jump in and beat my ass on a regular basis, but she'd stop him if she saw it."

Zzzzzzzzz. Zzzzz. Zzzz.

"All I know is, it's good to meet new people in this boring Hoboken town. I'm tired of the same sunny sunshine *BS*." She thought of her run-in with Arista earlier that morning in downtown Boulder Creek. *Miss Everything-Is-Beautiful*'s abrasive optimism had always grated, especially during high school's eight a.m. English class, after a berating from her own drunken mother the previous night. "Oh, everything's so perfect," she mockingly cooed, before returning to her normal voice. "I'm just tired of *those* kind of people."

Kane didn't respond, too focused on his work now.

She sat watching segments of vivid images appear, and it brought a sense of accomplishment. First, the small candy skull. Next, a rose. Soon, however, the buzzing of the ink gun became only a dull whirr as her mind returned to the chance meeting with Arista. Even though she had scowled and tried to push by her, Arista had invited her to swing by the crystal shop. She even offered her the friends-and-family discount. While that would help with the budget, why would Arista think they had ever been real friends? And, no, middle school did not count.

"What do you think?" Kane's question snapped her back to the present. He wiped away the blood from the final sprigs of green that embellished the design.

"It's beautiful."

He completed his artwork with a few more finishing touches. Afterwards, he foamed her forearm with antiseptic, and took a video for the shop's website as he wiped away the froth. The tattoo looked cool with its array of blooms atop a floral skull. Coiling from the base, through the mouth and out of the eye socket, was a wispy coral snake, its skin black, red, and yellow. It covered a three-inch area on the inside of her medium-boned forearm.

"I love it. Thank you so much!" She grabbed her phone for a quick picture.

"You bet! And thanks for your patience. We don't always get to all our messages, so I'm glad we could connect."

Bandaged up and the transaction completed, she walked out of the shop and felt the warmth and safety of the interior vanish with the sound of the deadbolt locking behind her. As Kane's whistling faded toward the back of his shop, she braced herself against the cold bite of winter. But the pressure of her own hug uncomfortably pressed on her fresh wound. She lightened the grasp.

"Brrrrr." Shivering, an subtle eeriness swept over her. She walked alone in the quiet and sleepy town.

Where was she to go now? Home, and deal with mom's cologne-drenched, ogling boyfriend? Or a still-undetermined Plan B? Whatever she did, at least she had a wicked new tattoo.

She gathered her thoughts. Since no transit ran till morning, maybe the thing to do was hike it to the Jay's Timberline Lodge and see if Jaxon and Yelena were up for partying. They had taken her there twice before—the first time after the initial meeting at the Boardwalk, and again, just the past Friday. But she did not know if she qualified for the *just pop in* stage yet.

"Ugh!" Maybe the path of least resistance was the right one. Just go home, grab a bowl of cereal, and let music on her earpods drown out the exaggerated humping of dear-old mom and loser boyfriend.

Just as she decided, a familiar car pulled up to greet her. She happily acknowledged the driver, "Oh, hey! Looks like I'm going to the Timberlane after all."

"Yeah. Hop in."

The warm interior became a balm for her chilled body. Still, the extreme temperature change sent a brisk shiver up her spine as she situated into the seat.

"I'm so glad you came along. I was just talking about you guys to the tattoo artist."

"Really? What did you say?"

She noted the concerned tone. "Oh. Well, not a lot. I mean, I just said Yelena's real cool and stuff, and I like partying with you guys."

"Yeah?"

"Yeah. Thanks for the ride."

His expression looked more stern than usual. What was his problem? He seemed cool the other times she had seen him. Maybe they all got into a big fight or something?

"Sooooo," she said, piercing the uncomfortable silence, and hoping to lighten the mood, "what are you doing in Felton?"

"Not much."

As the car motored down the highway, he turned on a classic western station.

"I haven't heard this one in a while. I think my dad used to listen to this music. When he was around, anyway."

Still, he stared at the road.

"Are you okay? You seem bothered by something."

"Yeah, I'm fine," he responded curtly, with no eye contact.

The silence continued as they maneuvered through a deadman's curve, its history rich in deadly crashes if the driver's attention drifted. It also indicated the approach of their destination just beyond the threatening bend.

"Are you guys fighting or something?"

Finally, she found comfort as they approached the glowing yellow sign of Jay's Timberland Lodge. She thought of Yelena's friendly open arms and wide-smiling gothic image, and she could not wait to show her the new ink.

Meeting only his unyielding expression, she glanced back to the road right as they drove past the lodge entrance.

"Hey! You just passed it." She felt a surge of uneasiness. "Listen. I'll just walk back. If you could just—" Her voice trailed off as the car slowed to a pull-out.

"Oops, overshot. Hey, could you grab that duffel from the back?"

"Sure." She twisted and peered into the darkened backseat. "You're so pre-occupied tonight." She scanned the seats and floorboard. "I'm not seeing a duffel."

"No?"

A bustle of activity filled the cab. The driver who had rescued her from the wickedly cold night delivered a painful and violent blow upon her exposed head.

She had no time to cry out before a second strike sealed her fate.

CHAPTER 4
TO BRING A LOVED ONE HOME

Two men sit in uncomfortable silence—me, an old man, grizzled and worn, and Henry, my gallivanting son, still possessing remnants of his younger self.

Further, he eyed Henry, speechless.

This old guy in my ragged flannel robe and owner to a real man's haircut, the veteran's buzz. And my son, tidy in his buttoned-down shirt, and a premature, receding hairline pasted down by women's hair products. But he's all I got now.

"So, what … are you …" He hated the struggle his COPD and oxygen tank imposed on his true mental fluency and man's-man bravado. From the impatient look on Henry's face, it was a source of frustration for him, too.

"Fergus is searching for his niece," Henry said, bluntly interrupting the unfinished question.

"Fer … gus …"

"Yeah, Fergus. He's a friend, so that brings me here, Dad! You happy to see your only son?"

"Well … sure …" After all, maybe he could come by more often, and stick around a while longer. It was very lonely living so deep in the mountains and he could use the help.

"Look, I'm here for a while, but you won't see me too often. I need to be closer to town, so I'll be staying in Ben Lomond."

"You … look … good."

"Yeah, Pop? You think so?"

"Yes … son." It was much better than the holey jeans and the ripped-up denim vest he used to wear. Even his face had some color, not drugged out and pale. Finally, he was on the path of the righteous direction.

"Okay, well, I've got to make a quick phone call."

Henry went outside before he could respond.

Discouraged that his son would not be around much, he slowly got up, breathing apparatus pushcart at his side, and wondered if the phone call could reveal any more details. Carefully wheeling his oxygen over to the front door, he listened to Henry on the phone. He could only hear snippets of the conversation.

"Yeah, well, … important … feel your pain … nothing … don't see … similarities … Fergus, how do you even know?"

Henry's escalating impatience prompted a louder voice, which played so much easier on his ears.

"I've been here for months!"

He got the gist of Henry's purpose in Boulder Creek, and the call seem to verify his search. Though, it hurt to hear he had been there for months. Why hadn't he come by sooner?

Further, Henry's impatience worsened, and the old man watched him became combative.

"Look, I'm sick of hanging around this God-forsaken place. There's not shit to do!" He calmed his temper. "I'm all for helping a friend bring a loved one home, but this is for the birds, man. I've lived here, hate it, and want to get the hell out!"

Now the volume easily carried to his aged ears, as he inconspicuously listened behind his screen door.

"What makes you think she's here?"

He watched Henry gather in the information, inaudible to his own ears. It did not matter who he was talking to, because whoever this recruiter was, they had brought him to town, and had him dressing more presentable.

"Yeah, yeah! I got it. I'll give it some more time."

Henry disconnected from his call and looked into the wooded distance.

He grew was hopeful. Maybe his son appreciated nature again, like he did as a kid.

"I hate this fricken town."

Maybe he's the same loose cannon he's always been, just better dressed.

Henry stalked up the steps and startled at his lording presence. "What are you doing?" he asked as he yanked open the screen.

"Hen …"

Henry pushed past him, evidently miffed. "Pops, you should just stay on that couch of yours and not listen to other people's conversations. That's my best advice for you."

The tired old man had forgotten why he had gotten up. Tottering back to his perch, it hurt that Henry had such a poor impression of Boulder Creek, and still carried that nasty demeanor. He had liked the mountains on his occasional visits from Washington state as a teen, but it was no use believing that he would ever be the son he truly imagined.

Taking his seat, he looked up at Henry, and could see he was ready to leave. It disappointed him.

"Well, I need to get back to Ben Lomond." Henry gave him a firm goodbye pat on the back.

"I am … glad …"

"Bye, Pops."

He watched his son stalk out the door and soon heard the engine turn. The visit was too short, leaving him lonely and alone again.

He struggled with his out-breath, thinking of his only son. The welcomed change of Henry stopping by pleased him, and any visit was a good visit. It would also be nice to have him living in the vicinity, and hopefully, he would not find the missing person too soon.

CHAPTER 5
MY LOVELY BRIGID

As night settled, Arista situated herself in front of her altar with Royal observing from the comfort of her bed. She finished her day with a prayer for hope in troubled areas, followed by plenty of herbal offerings of homage and giving thanks for her blessings.

The finality of the day brought her relief after a hectic week at Earth & Ocean. Though, a fun craft project with Zoelly after her shift had yielded a fun adornment for her altar, and indulging in a post-work chat about customers with the boss proved quite informative. Analina reported the mysterious couple earlier in the week had spent money on sex-magick items and a pricey Rose Quartz obelisk. It had amounted to a helpful transaction, the truest benefit for the prosperity of the shop. Who knew the intense duo wanted nothing more than deepened love?

She lit her Abundance candle, which hosted a lovely essence—lavender, fir, and chamomile. She peered into its flame and grabbed her tapered four-inch Quartz-crystal wand and exerted a cleansing breath.

"*Amaris Chiltus. Amaris Felis.*" She softly chanted the words thrice.

Royal jumped upon her small wooden table beside the altar area and closely watched her every move.

"You're such an attentive spirit, Royal. I wonder if you're a *true* familiar?"

She refocused.

"*For the prosperity of Auntie and my friends and, most certainly,*
Royal.

For opportunity and protection.
And, for good health and love, honest and loyal love, that comes to
me and that I can give in return.
So may this be."

She picked up her brass snuffer and clamped it atop the anxious flame to stifle its last sip of oxygen. The fragrant evidence of its nightly use would linger for hours. Finally, she sprinkled dried rose petals and salts of rose and mint to finish her prayer time. These scatterings accumulated through the month until she thoroughly cleaned the area at each New Moon.

As the familiar routine ended, an interruption creeped into her psyche. Her throat felt scratchy, and she could not swallow. The odd new vision came upon her again—a grubby hand, and upon it, a lined design. Evidently, a repeat of her previous vision, but a little clearer this time.

Again, it vanished too quickly to decipher.

She gasped. This time, it had taken her breath. The recurrence of it dumbfounded her. She turned to her feline, who jumped down and walked away.

"Wow! What the heck is that?" She shook her head, giving further alarm to Royal, who picked up his pace out of the room.

"Fine, leave when I need you most." Catching the tail-end of his departure, she harassed him, blowing him a little raspberry.

But seriously, she should not ignore this, especially given the weird things beginning to add up around town.

Turning back to her altar, she closed her eyes. If only she could duplicate and hold the vision longer.

She inhaled, paused, then purposefully exhaled.

Nothing.

Again, a deep breath, the slow exhalation, and the thoughtful pause.

Only stillness.

It frustrated her. Why did the vision come so unexpectedly, with no time to focus?

"Whatever. Maybe next time."

With her attention refreshed from the novelty, she lifted a small cornhusk doll. Her after-hours workshop with Zoelly had resulted in a darling rendition of a Celtic Goddess, adorned with emerald-green ribbon ties and sprigs of fresh, deep-purple lavender jutting from the waist.

She placed the faceless doll beside the extinguished candle. With palms up, she reverently whispered a final loving prayer, then considered where to put the craft before wrapping up her night.

"And you, my lovely Brigid … an acclimation as you sit on my altar tonight, and tomorrow, we'll find you a nice home in my kitchen."

Time for bed. She removed her oblong Labradorite ring and put it on top of her beaded bracelets in her Moonstone-decorated jewel box. She slid the extinguished candle toward her shelf of crystals at the back of the altar. Turning toward her bed, she saw that her Siamese had stealthily snuck back into room and comfortably situated himself by her bed pillows.

"How do you do that? I swear you are pure magick, or at least part ninja."

Often, he came and went without detection, not even one click of a claw on the floor nor rustle from the jump onto the bed.

She got into bed and fumbled with her modern-day magic—a small remote.

Click.

And out went the lights of her room's dresser-top, faux-pine tree.

She smacked her lips and burrowed the side of her face into her fluffy pillow, sinking into its coziness. Royal, now beside her, readied for the long haul of the night, kneading the blanket before re-situating himself in the crook of her knees.

There silence permeated for a moment, followed by, and true to form, a creaking of her floorboards. It sounded like three long strides down her short hallway.

She slowly peeped open an eye and stared into sheer darkness.

"Sshhhh," she whispered to Royal.

She could hear something of a little substance hit the floor in the kitchen. The *tink* of it seemed of no consequence, so it would wait until morning. She was used to this by now.

"Good night, Ghost," she whispered, unafraid and humored by the habits of her supernatural roommate.

CRASH!

Shattered glass!

She grabbed her clicker and re-illuminated her pine tree.

Royal sprang up, his pleasant blue eyes of daylight presented as iridescent orange orbs in the dim-lit room. He jumped off the bed and peeked around the door jamb into the dark hallway.

"Well, I know that's not you knocking things over." After glancing at her curious feline, she returned to the uneasiness of what lingered *out there.*

She shoved her feet into a pair of furry slides and hesitantly scanned her hallway, and further toward the kitchen.

"Hel-lo?" She heard the rising inflection in her own voice.

She creeped to the kitchen, switched on the light and found a shattered jar and lavender buds scattered across the floor.

"Okay. This isn't good." She tried to calm herself amidst the abrupt paranormal activity. Ghost had never been so destructive.

Mew.

She jumped. "Oh Lord, Royal!"

She looked around the kitchen and found no other evidence of foul play. The windows and door remained sealed as she had left them.

"Hello?"

The air of the room held lighter, and she suspected the tension had passed.

"Well … plenty to do."

She turned to Royal and hissed him away. "No cut pawsies. Sorry, my love."

She dug into the chore, busying herself with the cleanup till she had swept up the last jagged shard. Unnerved by the late-night shenanigan, she put away her kitchen broom and grabbed her besom. In ceremony, she churned it. The scent of spicy, sweet cinnamon from its wispy oiled bristles filled the air, intending to banish any sort of negative energy.

"Widdershins for cleanliness.
Widdershins this space.
Widdershins, a blessed peace.
Send evil to its place."

She sang the words softly while circulating the broom counter-clockwise a few inches above the ground.

"There, that should take care of that. Ghost, I only say those words in case it's not you. And … if it is, can you *please* take it down a notch? Believe me, you have my attention."

But now what was Royal eyeing? His curiosity focused on something at the foot of her cumbersome table. She went over and knelt down by him.

"Whatcha got, sweetie?"

The glimmer of silver caught her eye, and she picked up a small charm that was once attached to the twine encircling the neck of her now-broken jar.

Pinched between her fingers, she brought it up to view. While any pentacle within her house was always single point upright with good intention, she had picked it up inverted.

"Oh." She sobered to a new understanding. The memory of her earlier vision, with its grubby hand and undetermined markings, struck her. The lined design it hosted, no longer held mystery. It was an inverted pentagram.

CHAPTER 6
STILL FRESH IN ONE'S MIND

The Timbermill was more than just a local favorite for food. The lively diner hosted a great ambiance for chatting with friends. The aroma of char-grilled beef drifted through the mountain streets and welcomed passersby to join the jovial party. Arista chose The Timbermill for budget reasons and proximity. It had become a habit since the guys turned twenty-one and called for any gatherings to be held at the location because of its ale selection.

Currently, one of the flat-screened TVs displayed the screeching of sneakers and cheering basketball fans. The other delivered the day's news.

Perusing the menu, she jumped when Maddie blurted out an alarming announcement.

"Hey, have you heard Michelle's missing?"

"No! That's terrible news. I just saw her ... like a week ago. Anyway, she looked great ... healthier." For the brief moment she had seen her, Michelle looked healthy, like the middle school days of innocent white witchery and flower magick.

"I know you held a special place in your heart for her, but she has not changed *that* much. She still walks the fringe."

"I hope she's okay. Maybe she's just off on her own. She does that sometimes, right? She always did."

"I don't know about that." Maddie raised her eyebrow.

Always prompt with customer service, the harried server strolled up, hitched her hip for stability, and readied her pad.

"Hey, guys, what can I get you?"

Maddie spoke first, quick to the punch. "I'll have a cheeseburger, well-done, and a tower of onion strings, please." She deliberated for a second regarding the beverage. "And a root beer. Not too much, right?"

"Of course not." Nice of Maddie to consider the cost, since it was not her turn to pay. "I'll have the apple-pecan fusion salad with just a little goat cheese on the side, please. And water."

"Okay, what's the recap?" Maddie's distractibility had her on to the next subject once the server had left.

"Well ..." Maddie loved to hear of the shop's juicy bits of gossip, most matters comprised of what the locals purchased in the way of occult merchandise. Older women requesting love spell ingredients and buying small Obsidian or Garnet phallic carved creations. Middled-aged men requesting vitality crystals and books on money magick. All meant in innocent fun, she promised discretion.

After all the fun talk, the time had come to readdress the darker topics.

"So, you just saw Michelle and now she's gone."

"Yes, I saw her right by the shop. Evan and Shane saw her too. The same day you called about the stalkers."

"Seriously? That's interesting. Well, I can't say that her and I ever got along. And, honestly, she was Miss Cute and all, except for her repeatedly flipping me off anytime I looked in her direction. But! I am worried about her and I would never wish anything bad upon her."

She winced at the unfortunate memories of Michelle's high school rudeness to Maddie, and the impression that it had left.

"Yeah, I'm sorry she acted that way to you. As for my very brief encounter with her, we didn't talk much, other than me saying *hi*. But she was in a rush, so I understood."

"You're too nice. You continually give her the benefit of the doubt."

She felt an emotional pang. "I just don't know how people you care about can become so lost. And I keep hoping that somehow I can brighten her day."

"I know. Well, did she say who she's been hanging with? I mean, maybe we can help find her."

"Not a clue. Seriously, it was not more than a minute, and she was gone."

Maddie harrumphed.

"Yeah, I don't know ... anyway, enough of that. What exactly happened at your uncle's store that has you wanting a protection spell?"

"Here you go," the server said, abruptly clanking the dishes and drinks down on the small, circular table. "Enjoy, ladies." She efficiently twirled around and left before a *thank-you* could leave either of their mouths.

She took a healthy-sized bite of the vibrant green lettuce while Maddie ignored her food and launched into her lamenting.

"Well, first ... we're walking out of the store, and it's dark, and two guys stroll up on us. That's creepy, considering they looked ... rough."

She widened her eyes, but her mouthful of apple sliver and leaves prevented a remark.

"I'm sent to the truck, and I hear them mumbling. So, I get there ... look back ... and Uncle Pat is tossing one of them to the ground in total take-down, Bruce Lee fashion!"

"Seriously?!" She wished she could have seen it.

"Then, I wake up around two a.m. from the neighbor's dog yapping. When she wouldn't shut up, I look out the window and there's two guys by the truck! And I'm almost a hundred percent sure it was them."

"Did you wake your uncle?" The story had her truly captivated.

"I was going to, but they took off. So, I stayed watching, and nothing. When I went back to bed, I figured if the barking started again, I would have woken him up. But the next thing I know, it's morning."

"You should have woken him up."

"But they left. I wasn't going to wake him up and have nothing to show. Anyway, I haven't seen them again ... but what if it's all related?"

Maddie paused, agitated and anxious at the retelling. "Plus, we think they keyed the truck. Anyway, between the shop episode, late-night stalkers and, now Michelle missing ... I just don't know ..."

"Hmmm. Well, we don't know that Michelle is missing yet. She's always been a wanderer and free spirit."

Maddie shook her head in adamant disagreement.

"Okay, *calmmm* Maddie," She drew out the directive. "Putting Michelle aside for just a minute, Goddess bless her ... I want you to take a breath."

Maddie relaxed her tensed-up shoulders, huffed, and took a healthy bite of burger.

"Let's focus on you. First ... Damn! Your uncle is kind of a bad ass with all his martial arts abilities. Wish I could have seen that. Anyway, he is going to protect you, no matter what."

"Maybe so. He tossed that guy to the ground with little effort. But what if that's why they came looking for us? Revenge!"

"Okay, maybe we need Auntie's magick for this situation. Especially since it's unresolved. And ... I gotta say things have even gotten a little chaotic at my place, too."

Maddie's eyes bulged, and it matched her cheeks filled with another bite of Black Angus beef. After a moment to clear the food, she punctuated her concern. "Like how?"

"It's not a super big deal, but my house spirit is acting a bit more ..." *What is the right word here?* "Bold."

"What do you mean, *bold*?" Maddie asked, devouring a crispy onion ring.

She held up her index finger while wiping the corners of her mouth. "Well, as you know, I'm used to little pings and creaks, but one of my mason jars smashed to the floor last night."

"What?!"

"And the little pentacle charm that was on it ... well, that reminded me of a vision I had."

"A vision?"

"Uggh, I'm not entirely sure yet. In fact, maybe too soon to bring it all up."

"Just tell me."

"Honestly, it's probably nothing. Let's just keep the focus on the very real encounter you had."

"Ugh! Why do you start stuff like that?"

"Seriously, I don't think it's anything yet. So, really … there's nothing more to tell."

"Are you sure?"

"Yes, absolutely. Without all this other chaos, it probably wouldn't even register. Anyway, what about the sheriff? Did you guys call him?"

"Yes, my uncle called first thing in the morning because of the keyed truck."

"Good! Well, I'd agree it's definitely time to go see Auntie."

A surge of brisk mountain air swept heavily through the diner's opening door, the seal of their pleasant environment now broken.

In walked a familiar sight.

"Oh, these two again," The same lurid couple from her shift at Earth & Ocean entered. "I saw them in the shop. You know I'm not one to judge … like ever … but they have a vibe. Don't look right now."

The server hurriedly attempted to seat the brooding pair, but they already made a steady pace toward the table next to her and Maddie.

The male trod boldly across the floor, causing the locals of fighting age to puff their chests and bristle. Luckily, the flirty glance of the female seemed to settle the issue.

When a chance arose, she nodded for Maddie to take a quick glance while the server's friendly greeting momentarily distracted them.

Maddie peered nonchalantly over her shoulder, as if glancing at the televised basketball game. When she turned back, her eyes widened. She mouthed very clearly, *'The guy, I think that's him!'*

This was a good time to exit.

She sprung out of her chair and gave Maddie the signal, before securing two twenties under her salad tureen. *So much for the half-eaten meal.*

Maddie promptly grabbed her remaining rings with an opened napkin while she motioned the money's presence to the server. They hurried out the door.

"I frickin' know it," Maddie said when they emerged on the strip. "That guy … I am pretty sure he was the one! Like almost a hundred percent."

"Yeah, there's something off, and they sure seem to get around. But, I mean, the friendliness is kind of there." She reconsidered, remembering the vivacious voice of the woman talking with Analina. "But, there's a definite heaviness, too. I don't know how to explain it. They have a darkened shadow … thing. I feel it." She turned to Maddie. "Are you sure enough that it's him to call the Sheriff? Like, right now? We can't bother him on my *darkened shadow* feeling, but if you think that's the creep who harassed you guys, we could turn him in."

"I want to say yes." Maddie said, biting her lip. "But what if it isn't them?"

"We can go get Uncle Pat. Is he in the shop?"

"Yes, I think. I really don't know …"

A suggestive whistle interrupted them. They halted their rising emotions. She tried to espy the inconspicuous figure within a large blue sedan, now pulling into the diner's parking lot.

"Ignore him," Maddie grumbled. "Another creep. I've seen the car a few times now. He rode by the hardware shop the other day too … when I was talking with you!"

"Oh great."

"I know. Another suspicious character in our little town. Where are they all coming from?"

They rounded the building to continue their conversation without an audience. With the bustle of the main street behind them, they lit into their concerns again.

"Good God, has the creep factor risen in this town or what?"

"I'm sorry you're so stressed. Uncle Pat is friends with the sheriff, right?"

"Yeah, they're good."

"Well, maybe instead of some formal report, tell Uncle Pat you may have seen the guy today. Maybe the two of them can talk as friends and see if anything comes of it."

They walked down a side street lined with wild blackberry bushes, and further on to Kings Creek Road. She found the idea of her homey sanctuary inviting. While she had her own worries, maybe she could help calm Maddie.

"Look, we're already halfway to my house. Why don't you just come over? We'll do one of my amateur protection spells."

"Arista, you are far more than an amateur, and getting better every day. But, yes, that sounds fun. It'll sure give me a chance to scoop up that lovin' fur ball of yours too!"

"For sure." She fawned at the mental picture of Royal and was glad Maddie held the same fondness for him.

Their destination neared. Only a short jaunt further down the road was her street, Hoot Owl Way.

CHAPTER 7
THE OGLE OF OLD GUYS

"15U15, come in, over."

"15U15, go ahead," Sheriff Michaels responded to his professional ID code called out from the radio dispatcher.

"We have a Code 10-54D, female, on the San Lorenzo River and Joyful Road, over," announced the dispatcher.

"10-4, on my way. Over and out."

He resigned himself to the grim scene awaiting him and shoved the remaining two bites of his streusel-blueberry muffin down his gullet, chasing it with a slurp of piping hot black coffee.

"Whelp, guess the day's begun." After dryly accepting the inevitable, another thought begged his attention. *I hope this isn't the Holmes girl.*

The county had been fairly quiet for the past few years, with most 911 calls being drunk and disorderly juveniles or potential DUI drivers. But a lifeless body affirmed a dreaded event, and he braced himself for the sad affair. Chances were it would either be a suicide, an accident from intoxication, or the beginning of a very unfortunate murder investigation.

With gravel grinding beneath the wheels of his cruiser, he pulled into the turnout nearest the river's edge. It would be a short hike to life's deathly reality. He swung open the door and threw his left leg outward.

"Oomph," he grunted, and swallowed the ache from his frequent reminder of a slowly degenerating hip, a side effect from years of strain under the weight of his utility belt. He had sought slightly lighter gear in the past year with the advice of his chiropractor. Still, he maintained a plethora of punishment—his pistol, mace and cuffs, radio, extendable baton, and flashlight, and one flashbang for shock-and-awe purposes—his necessities for ultimate protection.

He swaggered over to the awaiting men.

"Deputy," he acknowledged.

"Sheriff," Deputy Hendrickson responded in professional form.

He looked at the civilian standing with his deputy and noted his shiftiness. *Okay, what's this guy's story?*

"Sheriff, this is Paul Whitlock. He found the body and called it in."

Paul shifted nervously from right to left with his dog, a muscular, tan-pied Staffordshire Terrier, panting at his side.

"Mornin' Mr. Whitlock."

"Good mornin', Sheriff. God, I am so sorry for this, um …" the flustered man shook his head and gasped into his uprising hands, pulling the leash, and yanking his mongrel's head upward in the process. He caught his error, relaxed the leash, and released his pup back toward the ground.

"Can you tell me how you came upon the body?"

"Well, Tink and I go hiking every Tuesday and Thursday morning, and this morning, she was anxious and pulling right there toward the water. So, I humored my pup, and the closer we got … I could see the hand."

Paul pointed to the distant glimpse of stone-white, feminine fingers rising above the water's surface. They seemed to be purposefully beckoning for the attention of a passerby, as if in a fine restaurant.

He listened to Paul's story, and observed his nervousness—shifty eyes, rapid talking, and the visible thump of his carotid artery. Every few words, he glanced at the distant body.

He took another look at the hand as well, focusing on the index finger. A gut instinct arose at the sight of the motionless digit jutting above the water. *Damn, it might be her.*

After his spiel, Paul bent down to give Tink a quick, loving stroke before proceeding. "I always carry my cellphone, so I dialed 9-1-1 … waited here, and that was it."

"Mmm-hmph. What time did you first see the deceased?" he asked, bringing out his pen and pad.

"It's been about fifteen … twenty minutes ago. You guys got here real quick." Paul turned to Deputy Hendrickson, looking for confirmation.

"Yes, Sheriff. The initial call came in about six thirty a.m.."

"Did you see any other persons or vehicles leaving the area?"

"No sir. Quiet as usual. Not a soul out here this early."

"Okay, Mr. Whitlock. Is there anything else you would like to add?"

Paul shook his head, which prompted his bullish dog to jump up on his legs. He grabbed her loose jowls in his hands and gazed at her, as if wanting a dose of calm. The loving gesture seemed to work on Tink too, prompting her to close her eyes for a moment.

"Sheriff, I'm real sorry for this lady, whoever she is."

"Okay, Mr. Whitlock. I also have to ask—did you touch or disturb the body in any way?"

"Oh God, no!" Paul's face froze in shock, and he took a step backward.

"Alright, thank you for your statement. I understand you gave some information to Deputy Hendrickson here as well, so if we have questions, we'll be in touch." With his interview completed, he offered an appreciative nod.

"Thank you, Sheriff. Thank you, Deputy." After granting a humble acknowledgement to each officer, Paul turned back to his canine partner and rumpled her lovingly. "Okay Tink … you ready to go?"

He steadily observed Paul and his companion's departure and recollected parts of his history. Paul had lived in the mountains since the mid-nineties yet kept to himself. He always had the same Staffordshire breed by his side wherever he went, replacing them quickly, lest they get run over, run off or pass from natural causes. If he remembered correctly, Tink was number four. Further, no one knew much about his tastes, interests, or pastimes, other than he had retired around the age of forty after a huge corporate buyout of his former employer.

"I know the county hasn't seen something like this in quite some time, not since I started, that's for sure," Hendrickson said, breaking the silence. "And she's just a young girl … woman? Not at all what I was expecting."

"Young, huh?" *Yep, it's gonna be her.* He took one last look at the ambling departure of Paul. "It has been quite some—"

Unexpectedly, he caught sight of the deputy clutching his stomach and leaning over as if he were about to lose his shredded wheat and banana breakfast.

"You okay there, Hendrickson?"

The deputy held out his hand, requesting a moment. With breakfast preserved, he stood upright. "I'm good."

He offered his apprentice another moment of reprieve, prior to applying the dutiful pressure of a superior. "How long have you been working here now, Hendrickson?"

The deputy took in a huge serving of fresh mountain air. "About two years. I know I'm gonna see this stuff, but you know it's my first time … real time. I'm good though, sir! I'm good!"

"Mmm, well, Hendrickson—actually, Will. I hope you don't mind me calling you that at just this moment. Will, you may feel fine now, or you may be dazed. Perhaps the white of her skin …" He pointed toward the rigid fingers. "Well, perhaps it's a blinding white, whiter than the center of a laser. Or maybe you feel like time is standing still." He cleared his throat. "I just want you to know that's all normal, and if you need to talk to someone … well, that's normal, too. The department offers that service. So, you just take another big, deep breath and realize that you are here to help me perform the initial investigation. Maybe we can understand why this young lady is no longer with us. Okay, Will?"

He laid his hand on the deputy's shoulder as he delivered the speech he had given to many newer officers after seeing their first lifeless body.

The department could never adequately prepare them for the true grotesqueness of death—the smell of the rot, the rigidity of the pose and the body empty of a soul. Especially in this case, a young victim. And, deep down, he knew his own emotional saturation was one slip from being triggered.

"Thank you, Sheriff. I really appreciate your support. I'm good now."

Convinced, he turned toward the river and headed down to the body.

At the shore side, he reconfirmed the deputy's stability.

"You sure, Hendrickson?"

"Yes, sir!"

He gazed down at the form, transparently shrouded in the fluidity of water, but the obviousness grabbed him. *It's the Holmes girl. Son of a bitch!*

"Now, I can already see from here, this is a potential murder, as there is bruising about the neck." He pointedg. "Darkened thumbprints as clear as this morning is brisk ... you see that?" He locked eyes with the deputy. "And, therefore, I am guessing a strangulation." He moved past Hendrickson, repositioning himself. "Of course, the coroner will do all the detailed work. She's the expert, but I'm saying that is a strangulation by ... well, it may be presumptuous of me in today's climate ... but a male. She was bound at one time judging by the marks on her wrist on this arm propped up by the rocks. And I'm guessing the other one wedged under her body will bear resembling marks."

He squatted down for another vantage and looked up the river. "Someone dumped her up the highway. That, of course, judging by the flow of current, and ..."

Hendrickson stood wide-eyed, paying full attention, absorbed in the expertise of his commanding officer.

He stood up again. "She traveled awhile. That sprig in her hair, it's pretty rare ... yeah, can't remember the name, but it's only found further up by Big Basin. Learned that from my babysitter, Bethie Kelly, 'bout forty years ago. She taught me all about the plants in these mountains. Anyway, this young lady traveled downstream, and … here … this is where she settled."

He gave a final click of his tongue, satisfied with his theory, as a line of officials pulled into the area.

·   ·   ·

The inspectors gathered information and took samples for the investigation for quite some time. After a few hours, Sheriff Michaels and Josephine "Jo" Firpo, the coroner, remained at the scene and briefly summarized their findings.

He cut to the chase. "That's the Holmes girl. She's lived in this community for, probably, her whole life. I know she was at the elementary school when my brother's kids went there."

"I see it, Sheriff. And no missing persons filed from her mom?"

"Eventually, she went through the process. But not a peep at the get-go. She claimed Michelle would take off for days on end and just show back up. She thought she was off with friends."

"Hmph." Jo hunched down and disclosed her preliminary examination. "Bruising of the neck and crushed windpipe, without a doubt. This is all pre-lim, Sheriff, but I'm thinking, with all that I've seen over the years, cause of death was strangulation."

"Sure, looks that way."

"There is tissue damage on the side there … and I'm guessing the back of the head, from sustaining … got to be two or three significant blows. Maybe assault? Maybe the fall into the river? But the skull looks intact. Otherwise, no weapon wounds that I can see. Meaning bullets, knife, etc."

He listened to her details and added his own input. "That looks to be binding tears at the ankles and wrists. I'm thinking, tape. Rope would cause a burn. Why would he free her limbs before the drop?"

"That's the profilers call … if it comes to that. I will say the black, plastic-y bandaging there on her forearm is most likely a new tattoo.

That's the dressing they're using these days, and I mean new because it's usually removed within a day."

"Alright, I'll check the parlors around here and Santa Cruz."

Jo looked him directly in the eyes. "Sheriff, I gotta feeling she knew this guy. I mean, there doesn't seem to be a sign of a struggle that I can see from here. Look at her nails, no sign of fighting back. So, it's possible she was voluntarily with him before all hell broke loose."

"Unless he came up behind her."

Jo tightened her lips, shook her head, and looked down at the body. "True. Well, sorry Sheriff, looks like you've got a murder on your hands."

"Alright. Well, I'm sure the media is ready to eat this up."

"Oh, for sure. But it's good to let the citizens be aware. I really hope this is an isolated incident."

"Yep."

"Hey, I know I got here late, but is it true Paul Whitlock found her?"

"Has the deputy been gossiping again?" He raised his eyebrow in jest.

"Oh, no harm done. But that Paul … he's never been one of my favorites. Leery kind of guy … loner. I'm not telling you how to do your job, but I'd verify his story."

"Yep, I'll do that. He was shifty when I got here, but not many people have seen a dead body, and nerves can do that to you." He paused. "But … so can guilt."

"That's right! It sure does."

"Yep, but I'll reach out in town … see if any cameras caught the scene."

"Hah!" Jo abruptly scoffed. "You know we're behind in tech here in the mountains."

"Alright, Jo." Jo's boisterousness had worn thin.

"I'm not kidding on that Paul-fella. He has that ogle that some older guys get looking at young girls."

"Yeah, the ogle of old guys," he deadpanned, thinking of his own observations that could be misread as an *old-guy ogle*. "We'll look at all leads."

"I sure hope something comes up!"

"Thanks, Jo. You have a good day. You got some help coming for this?"

"Yep, on their way."

He gave her an acknowledging nod and left her standing by the stark, inanimate Michelle.

When he plopped back down into the seat of his cruiser, the shooting pain reminded him that a visit to the chiropractor was long overdue. But he would deal with that later because there was no time like the present to start investigating the local tattoo shops within his route. He strapped in for his journey through San Lorenzo Valley, intent upon checking in with the hamlets' tattoo shops that dotted the mountain top. Three, to be exact.

Upon his arrival to the first shop, he felt frustration when he saw it closed, despite the posted schedule's claim to the contrary. Beneath the erroneous times, another notice boldly demanded that appointments were a must.

"Well, how the hell do you get an appointment if no one's around?"

He peered through the window. But with its darkened interior, he needed to pursue this one later.

The second shop, seven minutes further out of the mountain, offered a little more to consider.

"Just wondering if you've seen this young woman?" He held up a picture of Michelle to the artist at the Ben Lomond shop.

"Oh, man! Yeah, it's been spreading around she's missing. No, she didn't come to my shop. But I got a buddy who said his neighbor did her tat a short while back."

"Mmm-hmm. And where does he ... she ... work?"

"The Golden Lily. In Felton."

"Oh yeah? You got a name for me?"

"Uh, that dude's name is … uh … Kane. Yeah, Kane. That's all I got though, man. But he's the owner. Probably only one Kane at the shop." The artist belted out a boisterous laugh.

Unaffected, he appreciated the tip. "Okay. Thank you for your help."

He got into his cruiser and headed to the Golden Lily. Set in Felton, the first hamlet nearest the city of Santa Cruz, it operated out of a small strip mall between his favorite Chinese takeout for lunches and his neighbor's dry-cleaning business.

Securing a parking space in front and center of the store, he rolled to a stop and thought of his approach with the owner.

At the door, he attempted the handle but, it too, was locked.

Suddenly, an abrupt unlocking maneuver revealed a burly man at the now opened door. "I'm thinking you aren't Dirk, and you aren't here for the ink," he joked.

"Sheriff Michaels. You mind if I ask you a couple questions?"

"Sure. I'm Kane, owner of the shop. What can I help you with?" He made way for him to step inside and promptly locked the door behind them.

"As you may have seen on the news, there's a young lady that went missing." Kane could find out about the gruesome discovery later on the news. "She had recently gotten a tattoo. Just wondering if you remember her in here … late January." He held out his arm and pointed. "The tattoo was about here, on the forearm."

"Yeah. I'm pretty damn sure it was her. I saw her picture on the news. It's a real sad thing! Hope she's okay. Small world too."

"Small world?"

"Oh! I just mean, I can't believe I'm the one who worked on her, and then the poor thing gets jacked."

"Mmm-hmm. Can you describe the tattoo?" He wanted to confirm they were talking about the same woman, and soon enough, Jo would have knowledge of the design Michelle had chosen.

"Yeah, she got a skull, some roses … a little snake. I took a shot of it. It's posted on our website." Kane fumbled with his phone to pull up the photo. "Kinda quiet and glum at first, but she talked a little." He held up his phone displaying Michelle's tattoo.

He realized he'd struck gold hitting the actual tattoo shop on only the third pass. "Did she come in or leave with anyone?"

"No, I know she headed that way," Kane pointed across the street to the small natural food store, "and I took off out back. My house is up the hill, so I didn't even see where she went."

"No mention of names or anything?"

Kane's eyes flashed. "You know, a lady by the name of Yelena set up her appointment. I'd just freshened her ink. Um, yeah, I don't remember the last name. But I think they were friends." Kane paused. "Wish I could offer more. She seemed to really like her, though. Said they were good friends. Yeah … but seriously, that's all I remember."

"Yelena, huh? Do you have any contact information?"

Kane led him to his desk and flipped through a file of consent forms. He pulled out Yelena's paperwork that hosted an illegible signature, then scrunched his face, and shook his head. "My girl keeps telling me I've gotta get a better system. But I just take referrals since the pandemic and don't ask too many questions once I get ID."

"You happen to have Michelle's form?"

Kane flipped through the stack, got to the end, and flipped through again.

While waiting, he scanned the shop.

Kane shifted uncomfortably. "Ugggh, I'm sorry. I don't seem to have it."

He peered at him and felt a tinge of suspicion.

"Oh, there's a similar tat over here." He led him to his wall of previous customers and pointed. "She said that she had seen it through the window."

"So, the tattoo, skull, and snake on a young girl? Pretty strong statement, huh?"

"Yeah, nothing shocks me. Ya know, she just came in, pointed to it, and I did it."

"Uh-huh." He stared at the barrage of tattoo snapshots—trophies of tagged arms, legs, backs, and every other body part.

Kane walked back over toward his reception area and tidied his paperwork.

BRUM! BRUM!

A motorcyclist easing into the space by his county vehicle interrupted the inspection. After eyeing the cycle, he looked over at Kane, whose eyes were set on his incoming client.

He got the hint. "Okay, well, I appreciate all the information. If I have questions, I'll be back in touch."

"Yeah, good luck!"

CHAPTER 8
FORFEITING USUAL SMUG

"Honk," Shane suggested as Kenny pulled up to Evan's house.

Kenny pressed the rambunctious horn of his father's brutish truck, announcing their arrival.

"Evan! Your friends are here," Rose Navarro, Evan's mother, screeched from the front porch into the house. Then, she exuberantly bellowed to them. "Hi guys, you be careful on the trails today."

"Hi Mrs. Navarro," Shane responded from the passenger window, "we will."

Evan bolted out the door, whisked past Rose, and hastily made his way to his friends.

"Oh, Ev, do you remember Michelle Holmes?" Rose asked.

"Nope." He jumped into the back seat, slamming the door shut behind him.

Shane witnessed the lie. Of course, Evan remembered Michelle Holmes. Too well, in fact. He had a crush on her. Obviously, he just did not want to get caught up in one of his mother's interrogations.

"Are you sure? She was your age. They just found her body. That poor girl."

Evan paused, obviously affected by the news, but still threw his mom a dismissive wave through the closed back window. "Go!" he said in a stern bark to Kenny, prompting all occupants within the truck to chuckle at his desperation.

"What is she doing?" Shane asked, watching her huffy busyness.

Evan peered back at the porch as the wheels rolled. "Hell, if I know."

He and Evan eyed Rose, distracted by something at her feet.

"It's probably an owl pellet. We find them all the time, and she doesn't like it." Evan snorted while inconspicuously looking back at her.

"Oh yeah? We dissected those little boneyards at summer camp." Shane said, remembering the mouse fur, skulls and femurs that comprised the pellet.

"Hey, we did that too," Jalen blurted, now watching Rose. "Those things were cool."

The guys watched as she grabbed a broom and gave the owl pellet a mighty fling toward the hedge, visibly irritated by its presence.

They chuckled at the sassiness of her effort as Evan shook his head in annoyance.

With Rose and her antics now behind them, the four settled in for the twenty-minute ride up to Big Basin.

"Yeah, so about Michelle?" Kenny looked into his rearview directly at Evan.

"That's awful," Shane said, and noticed Kenny eyeing Evan. "Knock it off, Kenny," he said in a low grumble. For him to look at Evan after talking of Michelle was a dig. He knew damn well that Evan liked her, and yet in high school, he moved right in on her and wanted nothing more than a quick tap.

"Yeah, she was cool and all," Kenny said with a suggestive tone in his voice.

"Kenny," he curtly reprimanded. How could he pull this crap with Evan now that Michelle had turned up dead?

"Shut up Kenny! It's effed up enough that she's dead." Evan barked out the objection, clearly affected.

"Hey, I said she was cool," he defended, forfeiting his usual smug. "Really, I honestly feel bad about it. But you know she wasn't the same after her stepdad left. It's not surprising she ended up … you know. I think she got mixed up in drugs, wrong friends. Her mom sure didn't give a rip." He shrugged. "Shit just happens to some people."

"She was murdered!" Evan cried out.

The silence returned, only awkward now.

"Well, anybody know what she's been up to? Who's she's been hanging with? Where she's been going?" Shane hoped to defuse the conflict between Evan and Kenny as well as help with the investigation. He looked back at Evan, who regretfully shook his head. "Ev, what's up? You okay?"

"It's just so bad," Evan responded woefully to him.

"I know, man."

"Dude, play some tunes," Jalen demanded from the backseat.

He turned up the volume of the radio.

"Nah, man. I'm burnt out on that stuff right now." Jalen said.

"Picky, picky." With Kenny busy at the wheel, he tinkered with the cable stations and set a different mood with a fluid electronic downbeat. The rhythm of the music paired well with a soft, melodic voice singing about a *far away place*. No one seemed to mind and hopefully it settled Evan's emotions.

On they rode. A whistling breeze came through the windows as they motored through the twists and turns of Highway 9. The drop from the roadway significantly descended to the depths below, offering glimpses of rooftops twenty to a hundred feet down the hillsides. Houses built on stilted legs like birdhouses within a towering tree, nothing to secure them but twigs.

With only a sliver of shoulder on the twisty road, many people had met their demise on a careening corner. An ill-timed walk home and an inattentive driver also transformed the ravine into a plunging pathway to Heaven. Equally impressive rose the incline of the mountain on the other side of the road. You could not see many of the houses that lorded over the highway, but they existed, offering only glimpses of painted wood and tiled rooftops through the dense forest of redwoods and pines.

The easy turning and familiarity of the route lulled the passengers until they came out to a short-distanced straightaway.

"Hmph," Shane snorted like the low woof of a sleepy, but alerted hound dog.

"What?" asked Kenny, before giving his best twanged impression of a redneck. "You ain't talkin' 'bout my drivin', right?"

All four gawked through the now-falling sprinkles on the window. Spatters turned into watery dust streaks as Kenny braked to almost a crawl and drove slowly beneath an owl perched atop a telephone pole. Its gaze stayed eerily unbroken upon them, its head tilted and peering downward, horn-like feathers blowing in the wind, and pupils in full dilation on huge yellow eyes.

"Hey!" Shane realized *all* eyes were on the owl. "Road!"

"Got it," Kenny dutifully corrected, attention now back on target.

Once past the novel encounter, Jalen and Evan swung their sights to the far back window.

Shane bobbed his head, trying to get a better look, but his friends' and their loaded bikes blocked his view. "What's it doing?" The day's owl activity—a pellet at Rose's feet and now the actual bird—brought amusement to his already-existing fascination with the predatory creature.

"And lift off," Jalen announced, "it's heading toward the trees. Man, look at the wings on that thing."

"I'm looking at the talons. They're crazy sharp." Evan marveled.

"Hmph, cool. Wish I could have seen it," he grumbled, then turned back toward the front.

Within moments, they reached the base of Big Basin Loop Bike Trail. The brutish, bicycle-laden truck pulled into the unpaved parking lot and narrowly missed a departing vehicle.

He glanced at the driver of the aged, big blue car, but quickly diverted them. There was no need to start any trouble.

They jumped out of the truck and readied the bikes before strapping on their aerodynamic helmets. They mounted their aluminum steeds and jetted off, ready for action and a little friendly competition. Navigating the forest roads, they dodged hanging branches and small muddy puddles. Further, they pedaled in teams of two, single file in the narrowest parts, their legs pumping them forward to an awaiting vista point. Without warning, Kenny raised the stakes and tore off sparking another friendly competition. The day felt ripe for shredding the hills. The air was cool and moist, and an occasional patch of warm sunshine in between the towering redwoods, firs and madrones created a welcomed sensation. Even the gentle sprinkling of spring rain posed no threat.

"Yeah-heh," whooped his fellow bicyclists from behind him in different volumes and styles before following suit.

They rode with intensity, with lung-clearing puffs of energized respiration snuffing out the serenity of their environment. Gears changing and pedals spinning, they pumped onward toward an imagined victory. Kenny kept the lead to the very moment of his equally abrupt sidled halt, then straddled his bike, feet to the ground, as he took a huge swig of filtered water. Refreshed, he smacked his lips as each rider arrived at his designated finish line.

"Too-Cool-Kenny," Shane harassed, coming in second. He stopped, appreciated the natural scene around him and took a swig of water.

"You guys realize that the trees here pre-date the Roman Empire?" Kenny spoke as if a distinguished history teacher.

"No way!" he said with a mocking interest, having taken the same classes.

Evan and Jalen laughed at the jab.

Kenny smirked, "Okay, wiseasses, let's go by foot."

These biking adventures were newer to the former athletic bunch who frequently commiserated about their bygone days of rigorous high school football trainings. What they used to endure year-round kept them supremely fit. Without that supervision, the discipline had to be self-motivated. Luckily, the forest yielded a great way to keep active.

"Hey, Kenny, you're not taking us out here to kill us, are you?" Jalen kidded.

"Yeah, this is kinda stupid. Where are we going? We should stick to the trail," Evan nervously said.

"It clears in a minute," Kenny affirmed.

Evan harrumphed as he abruptly snapped a twig and tossed it away.

Shane knew something ate at Evan. "Take it easy. It's all good," Most likely, his prissiness had carried over from the Michelle outburst earlier.

As Kenny said, they came to a clearing. Shrouded in shade, at least it freed them of the scrub brush that scraped their arms and shins from the narrow trail. With Kenny, Evan, and Jalen ahead of him, he took an appreciative pause.

"We should get back to the bikes." Evan griped. "I honestly don't have all day to be here, and I don't need my unattended bike stolen. Thing cost me a fortune! My money, not my parent's."

"Who's going to steal it? There's no one out here! And the bikes are just up the path. We'll hear if anyone comes." Kenny argued.

"Uh, that guy who we just passed going out of the parking lot was *out here*. Anybody could show up at any moment. And—"

Amidst Evan's rant, Shane noticed a cluster of foreign black objects at the base of a distant tree and interrupted. "What the heck is all that?"

"Human sacrifice altar," Kenny wisecracked, not invested in his debate with Evan.

Evan looked annoyed. "Shane, just leave it alone. You guys, let's go!"

He walked over to get a better look. Coming closer, he saw it was not just one black candle, but five. Aged by time, they were dusty and dinged with little clumps of hardened debris that littered the surrounding area. "What the eff?"

"Careful Shane! Don't get eaten," Kenny taunted, from behind him.

"Hey, you guys. Seriously. Come look at this." He felt a rising eeriness.

"This is just a bunch of *BS*." Evan huffed at the scene and turned back toward the trail from where they had just come.

But Kenny and Jalen strolled over toward the grove to join him.

He squatted down to continue his survey. With his two buds hovering over him, he spoke in a hushed tone. "This may be some kind of dark witchcraft stuff."

"Dude, it's ages old," Kenny said.

"Look, they burned something, too." He pointed to the blackened clumps and ashes. "Black feathers. Maybe a crow or raven? Those don't look aged at all!"

Kenny remained silent. No usual wisecrack.

"I don't like it. What if we came upon this when the freaks were still here?" His anxiety rose. He looked to the trail and saw Evan waiting with an annoyed look on his face. "Yeah, I'm with Evan. Let's get back to the main trail."

Kenny reached down and grabbed a candle for each hand. "Oh, mighty Satan," he mocked, shaking his head, contorting his face, and wagging his tongue. He burst into incredulous laughter. "Dude, I'm serious! This shit has been here for years. My dad and I hiked this trail in high school. That's when we first saw it."

"This is stupid. Let's go!" Evan impatiently bellowed, disappearing into the brushy trail.

Jalen walked toward Evan at the trailhead. "I'm out."

"You sure, Kenny?"

"Yes!" Kenny looked at Evan in the distance, then back to him. He lowered his voice. "It could have even been Michelle and her friends. They used to burn black candles in circles back in the day. I'm sure Arista has a few as well. It's not that big of a deal."

It was true that Arista had black candles. "Well, what about all the burnt stuff? Has that been here the whole time, too?"

"Most of it. By the way, Arista says that they use black for banishing, and even good witches banish." Kenny tossed the candles to the earth, unaffected by the scene. "I would have thought your little crush would have told you that by now."

He eyed Kenny as he rose to standing.

"Yeah, I see it. You guys are finally getting together," Kenny said in a jibing tone.

He grinned, distracted by his mental picture of her long silky hair, and purposefully dropped the ritual remnant back to the ground.

"I gotta admit …" Kenny paused, "the feathers are new."

He stopped. "Are you kidding me?"

"Dude, birds get eaten. It was something's dinner. But Evan and Jalen are being bitches, so let's just get back to the bikes."

Kenny assumed his lead toward the trail.

"You really think this has something to do with Michelle?"

"It could. You never know."

. . .

With the last sight of the young bikers disappearing into the thicketed trail, a rustle high above released a small, intricate pinecone spiraling down toward the earth. Instead of landing on the cushioned forest floor, it ricocheted off the steel toe of a solid black leather boot.

The owner of the sturdy footwear reached down to pick up nature's small offering. He passed the trinket along to his girl, her hands alabaster white with nails of dark red allure.

They looked up toward the origin of its fall and could see an owl take flight further into the darkened canopy.

"Mack's gonna be back soon. We should start walking."

CHAPTER 9
LITTLE WITCHY FRIENDS

Arista looked up from her letter to Michelle, a handwritten ritual for celebrating a friend who had passed. She dabbed her tears and put a finishing touch on the lengthy tribute of good times from years ago. Then, she kissed the letter and folded it into a tight square. She reached for her small iron cauldron, placed it inside, then grabbed some matches, and went outside to complete the ritual.

It was dreadful news. The morbid and heart-breaking announcement of Michelle's death devastated her, especially after seeing her for the first time in years, only a few weeks prior.

She set her cauldron down, struck a match, and lifted the letter. She set ablaze the lower corner, held it up while it established a healthy flame, and placed it back into its fireproof container.

Maddie's ringtone resonated from within her cottage.

She regretted the loss of her old friend to such a violent ending and waited for the last ember to die out. When the smoke diminished, she exhaled the grief and left the heated iron vessel to cool in the air.

As she went to her phone, Maddie's ringtone announced a second call.

"Hey! Auntie's back," she blurted, all sadness aside for the sake of a positive front to Maddie. "I'll meet you at Earth & Ocean. I gotta pick up my check. After that, we can go see her?"

"Okay. Hey, you heard they found Michelle, right?"

"Yes, I processed it … had my tears, and wrote her a letter. What about you? Are you okay?"

"Yes, I am really sad for her. She didn't deserve that. I hope they catch the piece of crap who did it, and I'm here to listen if you need me. I know you wanted the best for her, and I remember you guys spent a lot of time together when we were younger."

"Thank you Maddie. It will be sore for a while. I just hope they catch the killer."

Maddie hummed an agreement.

"Okay. About Auntie, how about we meet in an hour?"

"Got it!"

She disconnected and turned to the silky black face and crystal blue eyes, awaiting her next move. "That girl was a Goddess-send to me, Royal! We've been friends ever since I was just a little girl, not much older than Miss Zoelly."

Mew.

Pained by memories of Michelle, she drew gratitude remembering the first day she had met Maddie. Dropped into third grade mid-year proved a daunting challenge. Scanning the busy schoolyard, Maddie stood as the only individual devoid of a friend group. She approached her and complimented her hairstyle selection of a French braid.

"I hate this stupid braid," Maddie responded with a pout.

"Why? It's really cute. And it's not just a braid. It's a French *braid."* *She exaggerated with a young girl's inaccurate accent.*

"Hmph. My aunt did this stupid … French braid."

"Why do you keep calling it stupid? It's a braid. Hair is not smart or stupid. It's just hair, and I think it is really pretty!"

"Embarrassing."

"I think it's pretty."

"Thank you."

They had been friends ever since, bonding over what turned out to be a similar history. They both lived with relatives other than their parents, found forest-living perfect for their tastes, and had strong opinions that they kept discreet amongst themselves. Plus, when they were younger, the light-haired Arista was an outgoing, vibrant Yang to dark-haired Maddie's introverted, settled Yin. Though these days, Maddie had come out of her shy little shell.

"It was before your time, Royal, but Auntie allowed Maddie and me to have sleep-overs at her house. She'd show us all her crystals, and tell us about the properties, and of course, all the powers associated with them."

Mew.

"Oh! And the lavender, rose petals and salted-milk baths. Auntie said it would help us grow into beautiful young women someday." She looked at her arm. "I mean, I don't look too bad, so I think it did wonders for my skin. And you know what the funniest thing was about all that? It was through me and Auntie that Maddie realized that not all witches were ugly, nor evil."

She brushed her strawberry-blond locks and watched Royal stroll toward the door, her point well taken.

"And dear Aunt Peggy, long before she left, she'd take us to the beach or the Boardwalk for amusement rides and all the junk food that Auntie would never allow. Ugh, my stomach churns just thinking about it, but it was all meant in good fun!"

She looked around her room. "Hey, where'd you go? I wasn't finished with my story yet."

She grabbed her phone and money pouch. Time to go.

"And you know what, Royal," she said, bellowing from her front door through the cottage, hoping her words would find him, "I love you!"

The walk from home to the small downtown felt pleasantly brisk with birds chirping and squirrels posed as frizzy-tailed figurines dotting the fences of the surrounding neighborhoods.

Arriving at Earth & Ocean, she kept to a brief chat while picking up her check and placed a small Green Aventurine offering to the Fortuna fountain, before saying goodbye to Analina.

"I'll see you two in a couple days."

"Bye, Arista. Blessings!" Zoelly said.

"Blessings to you, Zoelly."

Analina smiled and lovingly pulled Zoelly into her embrace. "Take care of yourself, Arista."

"You, as well!" The care in Analina's voice must be alluding to Michelle, but she could not get caught up in a discussion about the sadness at the moment. She and Maddie were headed to Auntie's and instead of just talking about Michelle, perhaps there was something they could actually do to help bring her killer to justice.

Neatly folding her paycheck envelope, she deliberately jammed it into her back pocket, and exited the shop to find Maddie gazing into the distance. "Okay, let's hit it."

"Yep!" Maddie snapped to attention, and the two began their trek back to Hoot Owl Way. "I can't believe it took so long for her to get back."

"Yeah, she loves the heat in Sedona. Maybe old bones? Or maybe she shapeshifts into an iguana?" She flitted her tongue like a lizard.

"Oh gawd, Arista!" Maddie cupped her mouth and laughed, obviously surprised at the uncharacteristic outburst.

"I'm kidding! It just irks me sometimes, but I let it go. Her friends are there and when you're part of a close-knit coven, you feed off of the others' energies … or so I'm told. I would not know so much about that, because I'm a solitary witch."

"Understood."

"But you know how much I love her. I just get a little miffed at her extended absences."

The duo ventured past the berry bushes with green sprigs of spring growth and onward toward her and Auntie's street. She took a breath, intending to review Michelle, strangers, and broken mason jars as topics to discuss with Auntie.

But in a shocking moment, someone grabbed her from behind, jarring her from her senses.

Her and Maddie's high-pitched screams rang out through the neighborhood. So loud that Kenny and Jalen each clenched the girls' arms even harder from fright, and involuntarily echoed the yell.

"What the hell, Kenny!" Maddie ranted with a furrowed brow, yanking her arm from his grasp.

She copied the reaction with a swift, but gentle hit to Jalen's arm.

Shane barged forward now that the damage was done. "Hey, I told them not to do it." Wrapping his six-foot frame around both the petite girls, he cuddled them in like a mother hen, for good humor.

Maddie politely stepped away, leaving the two of them side-by-side.

"Aw, like you're the innocent one?" She razzed him, looking up into those beautiful caramel-colored eyes.

"I am."

"What are you guys even doing here?" Maddie asked.

"We just got off the trail and we're parched," Kenny said, pointing over to the truck prominently displaying their bikes.

"Hi Evan." She waved at him and noticed he was hesitant about getting out of the truck.

"Hi Evan!" Maddie waved, then turned back to the group. "You guys wouldn't have gotten that reaction if there weren't so many weird things happening around us. Of course, Michelle. Stranger danger at our store. Things are getting creepy as F! So yeah, thanks for another scare!"

"Sounds like Shane with his black candles on the trail." Kenny laughed, causing Evan, now amongst them, to cast a glare in his direction.

She looked at Shane. "Black candles?"

Before Shane could respond, Kenny dismissed the subject. "Yeah, but I know you and your little witchy friends do that stuff, too. So, I don't think it was that big of a deal."

Maddie grunted and looked at Kenny with an impatient side eye.

"True, I use black for protection." She gathered herself before launching into sermon-mode. "But good witches don't light candles in the fragile forest, lest they start a forest fire and hurt all the innocent creatures. It doesn't matter what time of year it is. And anyone from around here, including *my little witchy friends*, knows that. Whoever did that knew nothing about what they were doing. Or they didn't care, and that's just as bad."

"Okay, Arista, I get it. They weren't mine," Kenny said, surrendering with open palms.

"That feeling I got in the grove …" Shane paused before looking at her. "It wasn't like innocent … *you* stuff. You could tell it was shady."

"Hmph, well, Auntie just got back from Sedona, and we're headed her way. You guys want to join us?"

"I gotta get home. I'll just catch you guys later." Evan walked off in a huff back toward the bed of the truck.

"Bye, Ev," Maddie said, looking disappointed at his retreat.

It was an unusual vibe from him, and she watched him retrieve his bike from the truck. "What's wrong with Evan?"

"He just needs his diaper changed," Kenny quipped.

"Dude, stop talking about him like that," Shane said, shaking his head in frustration.

"It's just a joke. People gotta relax." Kenny responded, defending his humor, before promptly taking the lead toward Auntie's house.

CHAPTER 10
AN ELDER'S TALE

"Well, I'll be!" Bethie Dandelion Spiritbrite impatiently sassed while peering out her window from her beadwork at the kitchen table. "Darn jays keep stealing from my little birds!" She rapped squarely on the windowpane. "Don't ignore me." Insulted, she rapped again knowing if she did not, the entire feeder would be scattered to the ground by day's end.

Outside, the Scrub-jay delighted in the succulent little seeds not meant for his pleasure.

She unlatched and forcefully pushed up the aged wooden pane.

"Hey!" She hissed and *Raaoowww!* like a rabid alley cat.

The bold, blue bird launched itself into a limb a few feet above in wait.

"Go on! I see you and I'm not going away. SSSsssst."

She tasted victory from the intense stare down as the jay set out for other territories to pillage.

"That's right!" The outcome satisfied her.

She left the window open to let in the early-April, fresh morning air and readied to string another elegant set of witch beads. Currently, she created a sample for Arista, who helped her assemble the inventory for her summer trip to Sedona. There, she would sell them at a tourist marketplace for double what she would get in their small town.

As much as the beads brought income, they also fed her artistic side. The set she held before her comprised irregular Larimar beads, aka

Atlantis Stones, aka *Dolphin Stones*. Pleasing to the eye, the marbled sea greens and light blues blended well. Some pieces also merged the colors into white, dark teal, and even tinges of a deeper blue. Together, they created a gorgeous trinket to behold, especially with the addition of petite Labradorite rounds as spacers.

Near completion, she added four small elemental glass beads—green for earth, opalescent for air, blue for water and a matte copper for fire. Finally, she capped the project with a narrowed, silver filigree on one end and a Celtic-inspired *Tree of Life* medallion on the other.

While crafting on this temperate late-morning, she sipped hot ginger and peach green tea and listened to the birds sing their harmonious songs, competing against one another as to which could carry the longest tune or the highest pitch.

Her mind briefly wandered to her recent trip to Sedona. Aside from her crystal fair earnings, Sedona attracted her for more important purposes. There, with her coven, she regularly performed protection ceremonies for Arista's continued safety. Gathering their intentions into a vortex of energy, she found assurance in her group's unity. To date, it had shielded Arista from her soulless uncle, the beast from her past, keeping her safe and undetected in the mountain for well over a decade. However, with her childhood friend now dead, what if there was substance to her concerns of Fergus still searching? Something did not feel right.

After taking a sip of tea, she picked up the beads again and mindlessly eyed them. The other matter existed as well. The benefits of the desert region that lay in wait for Arista to discover. While not entirely aware of where her nephew and his wife lived, the proximity to their supposed Arizona location provided a way for her to be in the same state without having to actually draw the parents back into Arista's world. The consequences of doing so prematurely could prove dire.

"Well, there you have it." She held the carefully constructed string up, gently coiling her fingers around the length as if it were a baby garter snake. "Whoever gets this lovely ensemble will experience peace, unspoken confidence, and clear communication. And a bit of magick and manifestation to boot! Sounds like goddess qualities to me. Hah!" Finding her own companionship compatible, she often talked to herself, something her grandniece had picked up over the years, though she shared her conversations with Royal.

She placed the newly-crafted beads on her table and rubbed her achy neck. With the outdoors calling to her, she packed up all her supplies—wire, extra beads and charms, end caps and pliers—into a small chest and pushed it to the far side of the kitchen table for later use. She sipped her last drop of tea and set the ceramic cup, adorned in various-colored hummingbirds, by her sink. Then, out the kitchen door she went.

She eased down onto her porch to pull on her heavily used khaki-green rubber boots, caked with crusted, red mud before entering her garden area.

Even though clay made up the primary element in the mountain's 'soil', her garden already showed signs of an oncoming lush Shangri-La, full of tight early-spring buds, baby green leaves and earthy natural scents. All, attributed to her green witchery and earthen efforts. Most of her daylight hours, she spent in this refuge. She watered, tended to, and fed the new growth. She pruned, spritzed, and dead-headed any unsightly sprigs when the flowers were in full bloom. And, once their life cycle completed, she fully cut back the stems and stalks.

The still-dormant rose bushes were the most notable, not to mention plentiful when in full bloom—red roses, white roses, and white roses with red edges—the latter of which she referred to as *Fire & Ice*.

The abundant wisteria vines intertwined into a braided mass, still naked of their fragrant and cascading clusters of lilac and white blooms. Years of their maturing occurred within the lattice canopy that protected her small patio area from the mid-summer sun.

Currently, she watched a random honeybee search for the prospect of nectar, before buzzing away to return another day.

Relaxed within the beauty of her garden, the sudden presence of five invading humanoids startled her peaceful existence.

"Hi, Auntie! Sorry we didn't call first, but we really need to talk to you."

"My dears! You scared the bejeebers out of me!" She let out a shrill hoot and patted at her pounding heart. "Come on over!" She gave them a welcoming wave to enter her garden.

Arista got right to the point. "Auntie, there are a lot of strange things beginning to happen around us. First, someone killed my friend from middle school. It's so sad! She was just thrown in the icy river!" Her voice drew into a pitch, prompting Maddie to compassionately touch her arm.

Arista took a breath to calm herself. "It's so tragic, you know? There were also some creepers at Maddie's house, and her Uncle Pat had to fend some guy off at the store a few weeks back!"

"Oh dear! Well, this all sounds real concerning!" She eyed Arista to make sure she was okay. She was, so the duty of hospitality came first. "Please, can I get any of you something to drink?" She motioned over to the pitcher of amber sun tea steeping by her aged, gray-shingled wall. When each guest politely declined, she nodded for Arista to continue.

"Well, it seems like a darkness is upon us. Michelle's death is the most obvious and terrible. But there's also a new couple in town. We've seen them a few times now, and Maddie thinks the guy might be the one who harassed her uncle." She looked at Maddie, who nodded in agreement. "They crammed right up next to us at The Timbermill ... just staring ..."

"And the candles," Shane added.

Arista looked at Shane, then back to her again. "And the guys were concerned after seeing black-candle remnants in a grove at Big Basin."

She knew she must have added this detail to appease her crush.

"It's just too much to be unrelated, don't you think?"

"Well, that is an awful lot. And yes, I heard that they finally found Michelle ... that poor girl. She was a sweet friend of yours. I remember." She pursed her lips. "Hmph! This appears very troubling." She sat back and closed her eyes, pondering. "I had hoped that it wouldn't come to this. I swear sometimes I wish I could just hide my head in the sand and deny the presence of evil, but when it threatens the people around me …" She paused considering the seriousness. "Something must be done!"

"Is there anything we can do?" Arista asked.

As she nodded, she noticed Kenny shifting impatiently. Behind him, she became distracted herself by a ruby-throated hummingbird whizzing past her kitchen window.

"My totem animal!" she blurted out, smiling at Arista. Perhaps she was on the right track with all of this.

Arista grinned.

"Anyway, magick is all around us. Sometimes it is good and presents us with the notion that we are on the right track … and sometimes it's not magick at all, but pure malevolence meant to disrupt the beauty of magick."

Kenny cleared his throat and nudged Shane, who ignored him.

She knew what this behavior meant. Arista was young, cute, and harmless with her magickal tendencies. But this Kenny-fellow seemed uncomfortable seeing an aged crone ponder a right-and-proper approach. The ideal response to this situation? Make the young man squirm a little longer!

"Hmm." She closed her eyes and pretended to linger in thought. "Hmmm." She took another mighty breath with eyes squeezed shut, bounced her eyebrows, pursed her lips, and inhaled deeply through her nose. "Hmmmmmm."

Shane politely cleared his throat. "Uh, ma'am, if you don't mind, I think we will take some of that tea."

Her eyes popped open. "Oh, yes! By all means, please do!"

"Thank you," Jalen asserted with a friendly smile.

Shane led the guys over to the little daisy Dixie cups for a shot of the sun-soaked, black tea.

There are freshly-picked Meyer lemons there as well."

Shane nodded and gave her a thumbs-up.

Patiently, she waited while they filled their cups and walked over to her far hedge.

She turned back to Arista. "I need to focus on this for some time, but you are very right to be concerned. I feel it. There is danger. Especially for beautiful young women."

"I thought so." Arista bit at her lip. "Also, I didn't want to draw alarm to it, but my presence at the cottage … it's more active, too."

"Really? Is it aggressive?"

"Well, yes, and no." She released a nervous chuckle. "It's never made a huge mess like it recently did, but no one got hurt or anything like that."

"Mess?"

"A broken jar and a big mess to clean up."

"Hmph, that is quite rude. Well, as I've said, that spirit is thought to be good. Don't worry, it's not your fetch or anything of that nature." She cocked her head and second-guessed her flippant reassurance. "You're not seeing your double, right? Doppelgänger sightings?" If that were the case, it would be a terrible omen.

"No, not at all."

"Oh, thank goodness!"

"It's just the same knocks and creaks in the night. It's just … it's never broken anything before, so it creeped me out a bit. But I cleaned it up … with both brooms."

She gave an acknowledging nod. "Bristles up?"

"Bristles up," Arista reassured, regarding the post-positioning of her besom against the wall. "And I re-coated it with cinnamon and orange oils for good measure."

"Well, that's good," she chirped, relieved Arista had retained her instruction. "Anyway, that spirit has been there for ages. We felt it soon after your great-great grandpop passed. You know, in those olden days, people died at home all the time."

Arista raised her eyebrows and looked worriedly at Maddie.

"Oh, come on, dear. I've told you that many times over the years."

"I know. It just feels different when you put it like that."

"What? You mean all the dead people in your cottage?" She deadpanned, winked at Maddie, and chuckled at her own harassing nature. "I'm just playing with you, dear. Only your Great-Great that passed in that cottage."

Arista smiled, though with a bit of trepidation. "Anyway, it still seems friendly enough … I guess."

"Of course. But keep an eye peeled and let me know. Be sure to burn some sage too. That way if it is a new, random presence, you'll be rid of it."

"Okay. As always, thank you for your wisdom."

"Thank you Auntie," Maddie lovingly added.

The young women stood up and hugged her before walking toward her outer hedge where the guys were quietly talking.

"Oh, Arista!"

Her grandniece flung around in response.

"I just finished another string of witch beads for you to use as a template. Would you like to take them now?"

"Can I pick them up later? I'm not going straight home. We're going to walk the guys back to their truck. I don't want them to get damaged."

"Okay, I need to come by the house sometime this week, anyway. I want to show you something. Oh, and dear … are you okay?"

"Yes, I'm good! I have my friends, Royal, and you! How could I not be?"

"Good to hear."

Waving until the very last sight of her, she immediately dropped her guard. "Oh dear!"

She hastened up her porch, through the door and down the hallway, past the rosy ambience of her sunlit kitchen. Her far-back bedroom contained her *work* area. With the home's least natural lighting, it housed a fine-looking altar laden with dazzling crystals in all colors and forms accumulated throughout the years. Extravagance at its finest, it construction was that of a rich, dark Cherrywood, a carved scrolled floral design at its crown, and a poster-sized arched mirror. Nestled into its crook stood a cushy, red, brocade-upholstered bench upon which she sat her wide rumpus.

Beyond the usual array of stones, candles, and herbs, one piece stood out with the highest regard—her ornate athame. The base of its grip boasted a large, milky-white, iridescent Blue Moonstone. The Celtic-inspired braided handle twisted further up to a sturdy steel cross-guard. All beneath a poetically curved dual-edge blade of fine steel, of which she sharpened and oiled regularly.

She reverently clutched it, preparing for candle magick, and slid a small black chime candle toward herself. She stopped. "Nope! I think we're going to need a bigger boat."

Giggling at her own *Jaws* reference, she selected the larger, thick black pillar candle.

"With Fergus ... and I believe this *is* him ... I mean business!"

She readied for a banishing spell to neutralize this sense of oncoming dark magick. Reverently, she took the athame in hand and carved an inverted pentagram, encircled it, and crossed it out with a deep gouged line. Next, she etched her own self-created rune upon the candle, giving her authority over this emerging, ominous situation.

She rubbed a smidgeon of juniper oil around the pillar, before pinching a dash of birch bark and dandelion root from their individual jars. Sprinkling the herbs atop her work surface, and onto her oiled candle, it developed into a unique scent of magick.

A lesson learned the hard way, she knew to light the candle last. For if she were to do the opposite, the herbs would instantly burn up in the flame and shoot glowing embers throughout her heavily wooded room. This proved especially hazardous to the tight curls upon her own head.

She adorned her bony index finger with a raw, bulky Black Tourmaline ring for ultimate protection. Finally, she pinched the cold black wick to remove excess length, and then picked up her long-nosed lighter. Lighting the candle, she took a few deep breaths and gained a presence about her.

She appreciated her previous, similar efforts had been effective for so long. Now, as she watched the melting and the dripping of wax over her carvings, she hoped it would bring clarity to the shadow upon their community. And for this pentagram, drawn upside down and crossed out, it represented the one aspect of Arista's past that she had not revealed to her.

"Was Michelle's death just an unfortunate act of violence? I think not. I think that uncle is up to no good again."

She worked quite some time on her protection spell—using her magickal tools, holding the proper vision and meditating on a positive outcome.

Coming to a close, she picked up her miniature mallet and thrice rang a cylindrical aluminum chime that reverberated through her room. As she absorbed the lingering hum of its resonance, her thoughts turned to a time over a decade prior. She had wondered what might come of sheltering her nephew's gifted child, taken into her care at the age of eight. Now this child had become a woman, well into her twenties, and prophecy indicated that she would hold the greatest power of their entire family.

It all started with that first moment her intuition pricked at her. She followed through with a late-night phone call to Ian.

"Ian, Arista is in danger," she told her nephew. *"I am afraid it could be dire."*

Less than appreciatively, Ian responded, "Well, that's certainly going to keep me awake at night. And how am I supposed to tell Keira? It's going to worry her to death."

"I'm sorry. I wish it was better news. How is she doing?"

"She's great. She's a chatterbox. Friendly at school, good with the teachers and her subjects. Sometimes a teacher's note about the talking too much." He stretched to find the flaw. "We drop her off at school, and if neither one of us can pick her up, Fergus does. No babysitters. No strangers. No unsupervised, long walks home."

"Fergus is Keira's brother?"

"Yes, family. They're working at rebuilding the closeness they had when they were younger, before he left. And he's great with Arista. He reads to her when she asks him to, plays games and she climbs all over him like a jungle gym … he seems to go with the flow of it all."

"Okay, just be aware. That's all we can do for now."

Of course, Ian discovered Fergus had diabolical intentions, and after a violent showdown, the family fled the big city of Los Angeles for the small mountain community of Boulder Creek.

She had done her best the night of their arrival to keep her opinions to herself as Ian and Keira argued about the safety of their little girl.

"*Bethie has always been in tune with Arista! She is what prompted this whole thing. Whereas he stalks you!*" Ian had blocked his brother-in-law's name from his vocabulary and swore to never utter it again.

"*Yes, I know she has. She was right about Arista being born two months premature …*"

Ian nodded in agreement.

"*And she knew she would have strawberry blond hair, though neither of us do … and that she would have 'the gift.' It was all correct, I know this. But how can that help now?*"

An unusual gathering marked the second night of the Kellys' arrival in Boulder Creek. Several 'relatives' Arista had never met donated miscellaneous home furnishings, toys, and groceries. They gathered in the cottage's small front room.

She watched the converging of family and friends, a meeting that began with laughter and hugs that transitioned to a more serious tone.

After sending Arista to bed, the women comforted a tearfully angry Keira, while Ian talked with the men.

"*What will come of taking the law into your own hands?*" *her friend asked Ian.* "*I don't believe Fergus will let this lie.*"

"*I should have just killed the bastard,*" *Ian muttered.*

She watched Ian motion for the men to follow him out to the front yard. A moment later, she placed herself between the two unfolding scenes—the women inside encouraging Keira, and the men outside strategizing the next move.

"*Ian, I gotta tell you … you guys shouldn't stay here,*" *said another friend.* "*Fergus might not know about Boulder Creek now, but if they are truly attuned to one another, he soon will. As long as Keira is with her, Arista will never be safe. He will come looking, and what if you're not there to save them?*"

She knew her friend was right.

"I know," Ian admitted, staring into the distance. "I just don't know if she'll have the strength to leave her here. Not after what Arista's been through. It's going to be hard enough for me." He clenched his jaw. "Arista can't know."

From the door, she thought it time she asserted her two cents. "Ian, it needs to be done."

· · ·

On the morning following the emergency meeting, Bethie watched from the door as Ian awakened a young Arista.

"Where's Mom?" she sleepily asked, wiping her eyes, and holding her stuffed Siamese cat.

"Mom and I have to take a trip. We wanted you to meet your ... well, she's my aunt, but you can call her Auntie too. She is a really, really special lady. She's going to take care of you for just a while and teach you lots of cool stuff!" He grabbed his daughter's hand. "You can trust her. I promise, with all of my heart, that this is true."

"Yes, but where's Mom?"

She crawled out of bed and followed Ian. The two of them passed by her on the way to the kitchen, with Arista wearily looking up into her eyes.

"She loves you, Riss," Ian reassured, as he grabbed his awaiting duffle.

"But why can't I go too?"

Ian did not answer.

Arista started crying, her freckled face streaking with tears. "Where's Mom?"

She walked over to her sad grandniece and smiled. "Sweet child, all will be well."

Arista ran over to Ian, her crying becoming more intense. She clutched at his waist. "Please! Don't go, Dad! Please!"

Visibly destroyed, Ian squatted down to her eye level. "One day, this will all make sense to you. Until then, just trust me. Can you do that?"

She watched as Arista nodded to her father, not comprehending the magnitude of the departure, nor what it truly meant.

Ian stroked her bangs away from her eyes. "I just wanted to raise you like a normal, most blessed child. I am so sorry." He wiped her tears and pulled her in for a mighty hug. Then, releasing her, he wiped away his own sadness. "Just know, we'll be back … we will! And we dearly love you."

He squeezed his crying child once more. Then, he placed his hand lovingly on her stomach, knowing beneath her bright yellow sunflower pajamas was a wound still healing. He gently nudged her toward the wide-open arms of her new Auntie and left.

She held tight to Arista so that the car could safely depart, while the young girl inconsolably wailed. Every second elicited another decibel of her suffering, a heartbreaking exodus that changed all of their lives forever.

CHAPTER 11
A CLIFFSIDE FALSE START

Walking West Cliff Drive made for the best location Arista could imagine for Shane and her first formal date. The scenic coastal trail meandered for miles, and ended at a habitat of tidepools, rich with lively crabs and a seasonal Monarch butterfly garden. Along the way, they might see a humpback whale or even a pod of dolphins if they were lucky.

But today, she would first take Shane for a quick peek inside the surfing museum at the lighthouse. They could refresh their knowledge of how Hawaiian royalty introduced the sport to the small ocean side city.

Shane peered through the plexiglass, studying the damaged surfboard with an arced imprint of shark teeth marks from an attack in 1991.

"Damn! That would hurt," he said, grimacing at the damage.

"No doubt," she said, mirroring his expression.

They perused the vintage photos of timeless men in swim trunks with their boards erect in the sand behind them. On the ceiling above the photos was a surplus of the same surfing implements suspended and secured by ropes and sturdy metal clasps.

"They always looked a little like ironing boards to me."

Shane looked around them. "Careful what you say. I think that's blasphemous around here."

They shared the laugh.

Their walk back outside the museum met with a boisterous ocean wave crashing against the cliffside. The natural commotion inspired her wilder side. What if she were to strip naked, run to the edge and jump into the water? She had seen the surfers do it, regardless of the posted signs insinuating death and dismemberment. But the notion was short-lived knowing of the water's freezing temperature. Plus, Shane would think she had lost her mind. She pictured the look on his face and giggled.

"What?" Shane asked, an amused smile crossing his lips.

It was apt. On this brisk spring morning, the area brimmed with pleasurable sights and joyful sounds. In addition to people's comments on the beautiful scene, the effects of non-humans begged attention.

"Let's check out the dog beach." Giddily, she pulled his sleeve further along so they could peer down to the sandy beach at the base of the cliff. "You'll love this!"

"It's true. I do."

The two of them looked down onto the sizeable cove known as *Its Beach*, alive with happy canines. There were many moving bodies to keep them amused—large, long-haired shaggy mongrels and tiny, short-haired yapping pipsqueaks, and everything in between the two. The animated chaos of chasing and yapping, fetching, and panting brought forth their laughter.

"And any unaccompanied humans will be turned away," Shane quipped, uniting their laughs again as they started the trek along the coast.

She felt sheer bliss. For so long, their friendship remained solid, but taking it to the next level was an exciting next step.

The farther they got from the lighthouse, she noticed a change in conversation. Usually more talkative, his comments became fewer, and he stopped initiating topics.

"So, whatcha doin' this weekend?" she asked playfully, before noticing a large blue sedan driving past them. "Oh, wow."

"Oh wow, what?"

"I think that was the weird guy we've been seeing around town."

"What guy?" Shane scanned the passing traffic beside them.

"Remember the couple we told you about from The Timbermill? I swear, the guy was in that car just now. Same one who Maddie's uncle had to fight ... supposedly." She discreetly nodded at the car as it signaled to turn right. "That blue one."

"Really?" He turned to look, just as it disappeared from view.

"You missed it."

"Hmph."

The silence returned.

She decided not to dwell on the possibility of trouble. After all, there's a lot of long-haired guys in the area. He may not have been Maddie's bad guy. "Anyway ... weekend?"

Still distracted, Shane peered down the street as they neared the right turn escape route.

"They're gone," she declared, also staring down the side street. She swung her head to face him. "Weekend?"

"Yes. The weekend. Well, I go to an orientation for my new job. Kenny hooked me up with a lead on a Phys Ed position at the elementary. It's a part-time assistant for now, but a good start."

"No way!" She hit his arm with a playful tap. "That's so cool! So, you're doing the Phys Ed and he's assistant coaching. That's familiar territory for both of you!"

"Yep."

The quiet returned, and onward they ambled in silence.

It had to be addressed. "You're quiet today."

"Well, I have to be honest. It creeped me out finding that stuff at Basin the other day."

Oh boy. Here comes his old fears again. "Shane, if it was only candles, it could've been an innocent ritual. I stand by the *noob* remark. I hate to think of flame and forest, but seriously, probably nothing to worry about."

He shook his head in disagreement throughout her explanation.

"You guys said it was old, right? Like ages old. Kenny said it had been there since high school."

"It's creepy that witchcraft is in our mountains. I don't like it."

Oh damn! He just went there. Just … maintain.

"And I know you play with this white-witchcraft stuff, and I guess I'm fine with that. But for the most part, it's just too creepy for me."

She kept quiet, but inside her opinion of his outburst was not so accepting. *Creepy? I'm not into 'witchcraft stuff', I'm a witch! He 'guesses' he's fine with it?* She took a deep breath and looked at the horizon to steady herself.

Along they walked in silence. From there forward, they only uttered snippets of appreciation for the surrounding nature or grimaced at rude bicyclists whizzing past their exposed bodies, too close for comfort. In no time, two blocks became twenty-two, and the tidepools neared.

The view to the below beach captivated her from the upper parking lot. The ocean glistened from the sun's glare as if it were a vast cauldron of molten gold. She lost herself in its magnitude and tempered her annoyance with Shane.

The playful squeals of two females running down the beach caught her attention. "Oh wow! I think that's Vivi's friend, Tiffani. Hmm, and with her … that might be … maybe Hailee?"

Shane peered down at the young women dancing around like little girls. "You want to go say *hi*?"

Had you asked me a few minutes ago, I would have said yes. "No, it's okay. I'm here with you today." She smiled, forgiving the internal spat with him only moments earlier. "But I do need to use the restroom."

They followed the walkway, keeping to the right of the beach's rim. It curved beneath a massive sprawling eucalyptus tree, its gray peeling branches reaching over and beyond them as if a giant octopus pulling itself to safety.

She inhaled the scent, appreciating the fresh mint-like and earthen smell of nature.

"I think I remember Vivi. Has she been at a couple of your birthdays?"

"Yes! They're all a couple years behind us. Still at UCSC … her, Hailee and Tiffani." *Looks like someone is finally taking part in conversation.*

"Got it," He affirmed with a nod. "Okay, see ya in a sec."

He disappeared behind the red-bricked wall leading into the men's restroom. But as she headed toward the ladies' room, the blue sedan appeared, cruising down the small roadway from the above parking area.

The passenger caught her eye. It was him. The same guy she saw earlier at the lighthouse … at Earth & Ocean … and The Timbermill.

The car slowed.

"S'up?" he said from the open window. Obviously, he recognized her too, and he seemed nice enough.

The driver, barely visible from the darkened interior, bobbed his head forward and sideways trying to eye her while also keeping his car on the road.

She froze, and for a split second, thought of her recurrent vision. Just as quickly, she snuffed its ominous warning. This guy was just a new local, and customer of Analina's. Maybe a little *hi* would not hurt.

Shane emerged from the restroom, interrupting her thought process.

The passenger, noticing his arrival, motioned for the driver to move on, but he did not.

Shane's eyes locked on him, and his posture became rigid as he glared at both occupants.

Again, the passenger motioned for his driver to proceed, and this time, he did.

Shane clench his jaws, and his chest broadened. He kept an unwavering focus on the car until it rounded the bend, then shot a glare down at her. "Is that the car you were talking about earlier?"

She stared back at him, feeling an edge of defensiveness arise within her. Now it was she who stood stuck in silence.

"Well? Did they say anything to you?" he asked, full of impatience.

She shied from his irritation.

"Do I really need to remind you of the peril in this county right now?"

"No, of course not! But I honestly think he's just a newcomer. The driver, I don't know, I still haven't gotten a good look at him."

"Are you kidding me?! Those guys are creeps, pure and simple. And I swear I've seen that car before." After a moment of thought, he pressed his lips tightly and looked away. He shook his head in disappointment, gazing into the distance, before looking back at her. "I think we should call it a day. You want to just head back to the car?"

"Yes, that's fine."

Mainly hurt, she also felt annoyance with his lack of understanding. Not only did her witchcraft still bother him, now he condescended her common sense. Of course, she knew the peril at hand! But what's wrong with getting to know your customers? After all, it would give her a better take on his character.

Rejoined with silence, they climbed the windy walkway, retracing their steps beneath the eucalyptus octopus, passing the scene of two friends enjoying a day at the beach and back to the four-mile trail. With the mood dampened again, the walk would last an eternity.

CHAPTER 12
VOICES, VISIONS, AND A LEOPARD THROW

Arista heaved a pitiful sigh, remembering the spiral at the cliffs earlier in the day. Relaxed for the quiet evening, she headed for the Zen corner of her bedroom that contained the cat post, fur, and lots of purring.

"Hi, Royal-kitter-do. How was your day?" she asked, dejected from her boyfriend woes.

After rubbing Royal's cotton-like belly and giving a nice long stroke to his jet-black tail, she dropped onto her bed.

"Something is changing, Royal."

The failed date depressed her. Everything seemed so promising this time. Then … Flop! Had she been crazy to believe it would ever be anything else?

On the other hand, thank goodness Auntie had returned, especially with all the other chaos building.

"You can't always have everything. Anyway, I can't."

Mew.

Taking one last soak in her pity bath, the time had come to find something to distract herself.

But her pensive mood disappeared at the sound of a knock on her door, followed by the jingling of keys, and subsequently Auntie's surprise appearance.

"Hey Auntie." She came to attention and dropped all uncomfortable heaviness at the sight of her honored mentor. She had forgotten that Auntie mentioned she would stop by this week to show her something. Now, here she stood … but empty-handed.

"Hi dear! Okay, let's get to this!" Auntie motioned her toward the kitchen table. "This may be premature, but I think I've held the information long enough. I think you are ready. Good Goddess knows that there's trouble brewing around us." She lowered her voice and threw a piercing stare her way. "I fear there is an unyielding presence. Your dear Michelle … she was only the first."

She listened intently.

"So, under the circumstances of your independence and readiness, I am here to share with you a very important family relic."

Auntie put her hand under the tabletop and fiddled with something until the table made a clacking sound. Next, she vigorously pulled the bottom of the table out toward her, and it clanked. Finally, she flipped it up and over the top, to reveal a grand-scale Ouija board. *Yes, No,* numbers and letters were all charred into the reclaimed wood next to a century's worth of dings, cigarette burns, and notations scratched in indigo ink.

She gaped at the glorious sight to behold. "Oh, wow! It amazing! All these years, I thought it was just a cumbersome monstrosity."

Auntie tapped her shoulder. "My dear, it is time for you to come into your own so that we can work together. I don't know if this presence is here for you or here to simply cause us all a lot of pain. But we *must* act on it!"

"Do you really think there's more to come? Like … more than just Michelle?"

"Oh yes, child."

She froze at the declaration, a sudden sense of fear beyond what she had expected. What did this mean for her?

Auntie clapped her hands, and her demeanor became that of an enthusiastic teacher. "So, let's get started." She pointed to a few of the written numbers on the table, now noted as dates. "Your grandfather, that was Ian's dad—and my brother, mind you—was very concerned for your grandmother when they first lived here. This county saw an increase in the amount of murders in the '70s. Knowing of its history, your grandfather used this board to help him determine certain facts to the murders." She paused and became giddy. "Oh, Arista dear, I'm so happy to *finally* show you this part of our history!"

"*You're* happy!? This is amazing. What an honor!" Such an authentic artifact dazzled her. She anxiously anticipated Auntie's coming explanation.

Auntie regained her poise and began the education.

"Our Ouija is rich with a past of providing details about serial killers—which is coming, my dear, you watch!"

She pointed to the first set of initials on the board notated from the 40s. "These were the original two from your great-great-grandfather … aka my grandfather. Our lore has it that this F.A. killed a few of his hunting dogs!"

As an animal lover, she squirmed while eliciting a regretful groan.

"He was a hound trader. You can imagine the hills here, alive with the barking of dogs. Well, it must have been too much noise for this fella. Every few days, another dog dead! But when the killer struck the third time, they took his favorite! A blue-ticked hound dog. You may have seen him in one of my albums. He loved that dog almost as much as his old, grey porch-cat. Well, that was it! He and your great-great-grandmother sat down and gave the Ouija its first test run, and be damned if it wasn't his own neighbor. Now … way back in those days, that may have been two miles away! Nevertheless, he confessed when approached and promptly got beaten senseless."

Auntie cackled, leaving her uneasy by the violence of it all.

"And this set …" Auntie pointed to another set of initials. "These represent tragedy within our own family. A great-great-uncle three times removed … or something like that … it was a big controversy when a brother killed a brother. Sometime later, the father disappeared in a supposed hunting accident. Those were the rumors anyway. They were not our immediate family. Anyway, I can't even imagine how that went down, but I'm guessing it was an inheritance or something similar. I mean, you would not want to think that simple family dysfunctions could end so brutally."

"Wouldn't know." Not with her an only child and Auntie her only familiar relative.

"Hah! Good point! Anyway, your grandfather! We're talking about your grandfather now and the '70s. Such a violent time. He had hoped that they could anonymously help the police and get the killers off the streets." Auntie ran her fingers down the itemized characters. "As you can see, the board replied with initials and a date. Here you see the first set your grandfather received—they arrested the murderer within days of him killing a wealthy family. Now, he had not given the info to the police, but it matched that of the news. This is when he realized he was on to something big."

Wealthy family? She flashed a pained look as it sounded like children could have been involved. She interrupted any chance of hearing heart-wrenching details. "So, to clarify, the table gave accurate information all these times?"

"Yes, dear. They found it to be the killer's initials and his birthday. As are the other five." She gestured towards the dates on the table. "The murderers all spanned the decade between the '70s and '80s. Five serial killers ravaging this county, all eventually caught!"

Please, no detail.

"This E.K., what a horrible, horrible monster, killing so many beautiful women and his own mother." Auntie took a thin crystal wand from her colorfully-quilted jacket pocket and used it as a pointer, moving further down the list. "T.C., Yuck! Another nasty villain ... as was H.M., who was as clinically crazy as they get." She huffed in exasperation. "But aren't they all? Anyway, don't know why they didn't already have this one in jail or the looney bin."

She appreciated that Auntie skipped the gory murder details, especially after the hound dog story.

Auntie tapped on the last set. "Even this D.C., he wasn't a local, but still stalked our beautiful trails. The Ouija picked up his vibration, for lack of better words, and the details matched the eventual news story."

The tale astounded her. "So, did they go to the sheriff with that kind of information? And did the sheriff believe them?"

"Well, they didn't drop everything they were doing to run with it. But your grandfather was acquainted with the sheriff who happened to be our very own Sheriff Michaels' father."

"No way!"

"Now, even the most Christian folk here are respectful of the mountain's energy. The mystical element may not be their thing, but they recognize those of us who do. And I believe with the proper introduction and knowledge of our history, it wouldn't be taken for granted even now."

"Wow, this is all so unbelievable! All this time, right here."

"Well, dear, now you know. Now we put it to good use. I believe it's imperative to have four participants, one for each direction, and ideally one for each element." Auntie paused. "And because there are four sides to the board."

She smirked as Auntie cackled at the obviousness. "Okay, I'm game."

"The choice remains of whom will join us. You, Maddie, and I could have a go, but who's the fourth? It is something to ponder, for sure. They must be serious about it ... and a bit gifted is a plus."

"I'll work on it!"

"Please do and let's be snappy. I believe this is important for everyone's safety."

Excusing herself, Auntie gently pushed her out of the way as she reestablished the table to its practical use. "We don't need it exposed unless we are using it."

"Got it."

In a whirlwind, Auntie had come, delivered incredibly electrifying news, and exited just as quickly.

Royal came over and twirled his tail about her legs as she stared at the nondescript tabletop. She bent over and swooped him up into her arms. "Yes, my love. I will try to make you part of the session." Though she doubted Auntie would go for that kind of distraction during a ritual.

She carried her lump of fur to the bedroom and released him to the floor. While early in the night, much had happened that day—a disappointing date, a strange encounter, and now, an old piece of furniture made entirely new.

"Wild day," she said, watching Royal assault his catnip ball. "Look at you go."

She sat down on her bed and scooched up toward the pillow. Too early for sleep, she did not want to get too comfortable lest she ease into an early slumber. Instead, she thought of all the things that Auntie had taught her through the years. Tonight, yet another lesson of their rich history. Perhaps this new information even beat out her favorite session of *Harm to None*—the most ingrained ethic of their devotion. She remembered that day in vivid fashion, taking place within a month of her coming to live with Auntie.

"Arista, our ability is to be used for good. There is a cosmic karma that we must abide by, and this is how I will teach it to you—Harm to None. For what you put out into the world will surely come back. If you must protect yourself, you must do it without harm to the offensive. For instance ..."

Auntie led her over to the hedge that hummed with bees. The two stood beside a plump, black hard-shelled, bumbling bee busy at buzz pollination on the tall potato tree shrub.

"This little fella is just busy living his life. And I know it will sting me if I put myself in harm's way. Some would kill this creature to be rid of the risk. But that is taking power away from another. This represents black magick ... taking power from something else, affecting another, for the benefit of self. This is not divine. Even worse, in this case, we would kill another living creature." Auntie shook her head before leading the two of them back toward the house. "White, light or high magick is empowering yourself to endure and overcome or simply avoid the harm altogether. The action simply affects you. For instance, we walked away

from the bee and left the potential for a sting behind us. We can choose to go to the potato tree after the bee has finished its work."

Her thoughts of past lessons faded, and she felt contentment thinking about her life rich with Auntie's lessons.

She looked at Royal on the floor. He also looked content. Now relaxed from his lively slaying of another neon-pink, feather-tailed mouse, catnip residue covering his whisker pads.

She snickered, sighed, then sunk into her oh … so … soft pillow.

She startled awake at the sound of a man's voice, firm and authoritative. "Arista."

A flash of a vision came forth—the inverted pentagram upon the thick heel of a grubby hand, a line at its base.

"Royal!" She automatically called out, now jarred fully awake in pitch black.

With her eyes adjusting to the night's darkness, she wondered if the voice in her room was real or just a dream. Sleepy and incoherent, she blearily blinked to sharpen her sight. The room and her surroundings slowly materialized. There in front of her, where she laid, and just above her knees, hung her snow-lynx leopard blanket, vertically suspended in the air.

She screeched, and swung her leg out from under the covers, hooked the hovering throw with her ankle and flung it to the floor. Swiftly, she brought her leg back to safety, her heart racing with fright.

She tightly closed her eyes shielded beneath soft, cotton armor and curled into a tight ball.

Why, Ghost?! Why the sudden creative antics?

"I don't want to be afraid of you," she said with a snappy demeanor to the stillness of her room.

After a moment, she peeked out from beneath the covers. She saw nothing but moonlit steaming in through the window.

Working to settle her nerves, she took a deep breath. At the foot of her bed, Royal's silhouette approached her, bringing further calm. She invited him to come nearer.

"This is a bit too much."

After gathering her nerve, she sat up, looking over the side of her bed, and peered down at her inanimate snow lynx throw in a heap on the floor.

"You know what, Royal?" She fell back into her pillow, and stroked the beastie settling on her chest, intently eyeing her.. "You and me … we're gonna *Go Ouija!*"

Mew.

Now, who of her friends could fill that fourth role?

CHAPTER 13
AN ISOLATED INCIDENT

Still appreciating the relief from his morning chiropractic adjustment, Sheriff Michaels continued his usual route through the mountains. With no achy hip pain in his prolonged sitting, he weaved his way through the back roads and neared the area where they had found Michelle's body, almost two months earlier. After rounding the bend, he came upon a familiar figure. He pulled into the graveled turnout and rolled down his window.

"Mornin', Mr. Whitlock."

Paul had already startled at the cruiser's sudden appearance and offered the sheriff a forced smile as Tink barked out a friendly warning. "Heya, Sheriff."

"It's a shame that this beautiful area holds such a horrible secret."

"It sure is, Sheriff. I tell ya, I just keep seeing her." Paul reached down and patted his mongrel. "Such a sad fate."

"It is."

"Why did I have to find her? It eats at me day and night. You know, I'm just an older guy. I've worked a good, long time, paid my bills, and followed society's rules. I don't want this to be what I remember the most."

"Well, there's help for that, Mr. Whitlock. I can have the office call you with a resource if you'd like."

"I would, Sheriff. Thank you. That would be real nice."

"You got it."

He waited briefly, an ear for a troubled man, if needed. But Paul offered no more conversation. "Alright, you try and have a nice day."

"Yeah, Sheriff. Thanks. You too."

He merged onto the road and gave one last wave. On his way, he glanced at Paul in his rearview mirror, his intent gaze fixed on the riverbed.

"Today's your lucky day, Paul." While not uncommon for a killer to return to his crime scene, Paul's alibi had checked out. A couple days earlier, the office received confirmation that he had secured a temporary work visa for Canada from early-November to the very week of the discovery. He had spent his days in literal darkness helpfully consulting in his field of expertise. The return to Boulder Creek had been a dreadful homecoming for the weary traveler, and his despondence was no act.

And this day continued to be a cruel reminder of the unsolved murder of Michelle since, next on the agenda, marked an appointment to follow up on an accusation. An anonymous tip had come in that her mother's boyfriend had acted inappropriately toward her, and at this point, every tip merited pursuing.

He arrived in Felton and pulled into a sliver of a driveway wedged between two small homes that lead him to a dilapidated white house further to the back.

A small, bony chihuahua announced his arrival, barking incessantly from behind its screen door until a petite, haggard woman appeared.

In his friendliest tone, he reminded Ms. Holmes of his business with her. "Good morning. I hope the office informed you of my visit ... just need a little more of your time."

She responded by opening the screen door.

"I appreciate it, ma'am."

"You haven't found my baby's killer yet?" She lit a cigarette, then clenched one arm tightly into her body.

"No ma'am. But we're definitely working on it."

The pained woman led him over to her rusted aluminum rimmed kitchen table, a small pine candle lit at its center beside an ashtray full of butts.

"So, the last time we spoke, you had a house guest named Dennis—"

"Denny." She took a drag of her cigarette and promptly released it.

"Okay, is Denny here today?"

"Not at all, and never again. I tolerated his business for too long. Why do you want to talk with him?"

"Any idea where he might be?"

"Last bit of news on him, is he went back to Ohio to his mother's house. Why?"

He looked down at the small, fawn-colored guard dog sniffing at his pant leg, and briefly considered acknowledging the boney mutt with a pat. But he changed his mind when it gave a low grumble, and quivered its lip to reveal little, sharp, white teeth.

"Well, this may be uncomfortable to hear, but an acquaintance of Michelle's mentioned that Denny acted inappropriately around her at one time. Do you know anything about this?"

"I think I do, and it wasn't anything crazy. But she went cold, hard, livid on him over it."

"Can you tell me a little more about that?"

"Well, he smacked her butt with a pillow once, and God knows how much I love my baby, and I miss her with my whole heart, but Denny didn't mean nothing by it." She paused and took a drag, then slowly released the smoke. "I saw him do it. I'd ask her to get the phone, and she was being slow about it. So, Denny tried to get past her and do it for me. And she was resistin' him … kinda daring him to get by her. So, he grabbed one of the couch pillows and whacked her butt. You know … just to get her movin'. I gave a little laugh cause I thought it was funny." Ms. Holmes' short-lived smile drew to regret. "She was always a stubborn child."

He gave her an understanding nod.

"Anyway, I thought it was harmless, but she came unglued. Yellin', he's a pervert and swearing at him. I'm telling you right now, he didn't mean nothing sexual by that. Not at all."

"Were there any other similar incidents?"

"No, and I was here anytime the two of them were together. I was protective of my daughter with any of my guy friends. You don't give too much rope lest someone hang themselves. That's the old saying I live by. And believe me, if she had a real problem with him, she wouldn't have hesitated to get him thrown out." Her eyes filled with tears. "I miss my baby, Sheriff. I miss her with all my heart."

He bowed his head and let the grieving mother shed a few tears before proceeding. "Would you mind giving me his phone number?"

"Of course, Sheriff. I gotta tell you though, Denny's as lazy as they come for holdin' a job and all, but I surely don't think he'd ever hurt her. He actually thought a lot of my baby."

"Alright ma'am. Are you aware he may have given her a ride the night she is thought to have vanished?"

"Yes, and I was right there beside him. She was gonna get that tattoo, and we wanted a late-night snack from the diner in Scotts Valley. We offered to drive her, but halfway there, she got all huffy. So, we dropped her just before the main road. She said she'd walk the rest of the way."

Her desperate look for reassurance begged a response. "Yep."

"She said she'd see us later, but she immediately called me ... all mad I was still with him ... that she'd had enough of him and wanted me to find someone better. So, when she didn't come home, I just figured she'd gotten mad at me again and went to stay with friends."

"Mmm-hmph," He relentlessly scribbled the details into his pad.

"That was just her way. And she wasn't no kid or nothing. So, I let her do her thing. But after a couple weeks ..." Her voice trailed off and her face grew somber. She flicked the long ash of her cigarette.

He detected the guilt and headed it off with his trained efficiency. "Well, ma'am, most often the survivors experience undue guilt because of tragedy, especially when it involves their children. As is your case. Truly, I'm sorry for your loss."

She grabbed a tissue and dabbed at her falling tears. "Thank you Sheriff. It's just so hard."

"Yes ma'am. Well, that's all I need. You take care of yourself and call us if anything else comes to mind. We promise to keep looking until we find 'em."

With another part of the investigative process complete, he walked to his cruiser. The yapping of the tiny, bubble-eyed creature faded behind him.

He would follow up with Denny, but her story seemed pretty convincing. Most often, a grieving parent will fine-tooth comb everyone, possibly even their own actions, in the event of such a tragedy. No stone is left unturned. While a parent does everything in their power to find the perpetrator, Ms. Holmes had just given Denny a full pardon, despite sending him packing.

As he backed out of the narrow driveway, easing his steering wheel left, a tick right and peering intently into his side view, he felt a sliver of chance he could accidentally scrape his cruiser. Or worse, knock off a mirror. However, as he neared the open space behind him, he realized the chance was similar to this lead's substance, very slim.

Thank God, Michelle's murder remained an isolated incident.

CHAPTER 14
FRESH BUTTERY CROISSANTS

Auntie had made it look so easy. Now, two weeks later she had departed for an impromptu trip to Sedona and Arista's curiosity had her wanting another look-see.

"What … the … heck?" She struggled to find the assembly combination for the puzzling table. She blindly grasped at the underside metal latch. If she remembered correctly, once it clacked, it would easily transform the unassuming dining slab into its alternate identity.

CLACK!

"Ouch!" The latch snapped, smashing her fingers, and shattering any ounce of enjoyment from the mechanical victory.

In her pain, she swept inward to a vision—an intrusive sight of a grubby palm, its hand glistening with sweat. An upside-down pentagram sat at its heel, and the bottom tip of it sank into an inked slit.

The mystical trip became short-lived as the throb of her knuckles brought her present with the task at hand. She caught her breath from the experience. No longer a flash, the vision had become clearer. And the after effect of her beating heart more rapid.

"Hopefully Auntie checks in soon. Maybe I should call her."

Knock. Knock.

"Hold on," she bellowed, going to the door.

"Hey, Riss."

Shane casually strolled in with a small black-and-white checkered bag, its scrumptious meaning immediately clear by, not only the container, but the wafting aroma.

Her troubling thoughts disappeared at the sight of him. He had worked hard at getting back on her good side since the disastrous date. Yes, it had set them back on romance, but at least they were talking again. Even better, while their progress had slowed, he still made sure his visits were solo.

"Your treats, my lady," he said, setting the bag on her counter.

"Aww, you didn't have to do that."

"No big. I was already in that area, anyway." Peering down at her bloody knuckles, his eyes widened. "What happened?"

"Ugh. My table is being a real pain."

"Really? Let's see." He abandoned the aromatic bag, full of fresh, buttery croissants, and headed toward the table.

Oh, no! It was too soon for him to see this family relic, especially after his tirade on witchiness She rustled the bag's paper exterior, hoping to distract him. "It's okay, Shane. You don't have to do that. My goodness, these croissants smell soooo delicious."

He focused on his mission, squatting down, fumbling beneath the table, and pulling firmly. The table clacked, without poor consequences, and he pulled and flipped the wooden slab. Within seconds, he revealed the oversized Ouija.

"Damn!" Taking a step back, he looked at her. "I'm betting you knew that was there."

"Um … yeah," she sheepishly admitted. Without missing a beat, she nonchalantly pursued a notion. "Hey! Have you done a Ouija before? It's very mainstream. Very! They sell them at a bunch of stores. Definitely not just a *witchy* thing."

"Uh, no," he said firmly.

"Do you want to?" She grinned at him, already knowing the answer.

"Riss, you know that's not my thing. I'm a Catholic guy … sports … and way leery of the occult." He walked back to the treats.

"But I really, really think we could do some investigative work if we tried, and it wouldn't be today, nor would we be alone. Auntie and Maddie would do it with us."

"Sorry." He picked up the bag of flaky goodness and held it up with an exaggerated smile. "But I can bring you treats."

She returned the smile and sighed. "Okay. But, at least, consider it. We really need a fourth participant."

"Okay, I'll consider it." His eyed widened. "Hey, not to bring up a sensitive topic, but did you hear Michelle had gotten a tattoo before her—"

"No! Was it a pentagram?" Of course, the grubby hand in her vision wasn't Michelle's, but what if it had something to do with her murder?

"I don't know. I just overheard a couple of her old friends talking about it at the gas station. They said she was all hot on getting it and had booked The Lily."

"What if it's a clue? What if we can help?"

"Yeah, that'd be cool."

It was time to wrap up the conversation. "Okay, I know you have to get to work. Thank you so much for the croissants!"

"Of course. There's one sprinkled butterstar in there, too. Have to admit, I ate the other one." His confession came with a guilty smirk.

She giggled.

"Anyway, enjoy."

He turned to leave.

"Hey," she said, coming up from behind him.

He turned around, and she draped a big, appreciative hug over him. "Thank you."

They held onto each other a little longer than usual.

She watched his departure and gave a final wave. How could she be disappointed with him? After all, he came to deliver pastries, not get roped into a séance. At least, he did not seem too bothered by the table's secret identity.

But still, the absence of the required fourth participant persisted.

CHAPTER 15
VACANCY IN HER EYES

Yelena and Jaxon strolled along the Pacific Garden Mall, Santa Cruz's downtown hot spot of shops, eateries, and clubs. While the daytime had numerous families and couples shopping and dining, the night catered more to their taste.

They found amusement in the crowd lined up for the month's only midnight showing of *The Rocky Horror Picture Show*. The scene abounded in extravagance, and they became part of it, strutting alongside the partitioned line of theater goers. Abundant pizzazz drew color to the dark night—neon pink wigs, black corsets and fishnet stockings barely covering the plentiful exposed flesh. Adults of all ages wore vibrant pearlescent-white eye shadow, heavy black eyeliner and false, sweeping eyelashes. It truly blurred the lines of biological identity. Could any of these lovely beauties fill their need?

Jaxon eyed the many attractive possibilities. But Yelena's disinterested demeanor moved them further down past the theater. Finally, they came to the end of the well-lit street mall and into its peripheral. The shadows grew longer as the streetlights became fewer, and the liveliness faded.

That is when they saw her, alone, with no vibrance nor fanfare. Attracted to the isolated litheness of her silhouette, they savored the wait to meet her. She looked diminutive in the limited illumination, sitting atop a stacked mound of layered stone, as if she were being offered at a sacrificial altar. The peculiar piece of earth she sat upon abutted the left side of the city's popular metaphysical store. In the daylight hours, you could purchase crystals, medallions, books, and candles meant to bring you well within a world of magick, be it white or black.

"An apt location for a young miss." Yelena ruminated on the young woman's potential, then grinned at him while they waited for the traffic light to turn.

He snickered, then returned to his stoic expression.

They approached the building where she sat, its walls colorizing into a putrid yellow that was more pleasant to the eye when drenched in sunlight.

Yelena admired the overhang's appearance in a raised voice, announcing their oncoming presence to the young woman. "In fact, Jaxon, I have been meaning to point out to you that a green witch must have had a hand in this remarkably lush corner. I mean, you can just feel the spirit within this glorious ivy." She fawned audibly and rubbed one of the ivy's leaves. "It must have flourished for decades now."

He peered at the foliage.

Yelena continued to eye the female now within a short distance of them. Usually, her voice and friendly conversation with him captured the intended's attention. This time, it did not.

"Just look at these sss-snaking, cascading vines ... so lovely. And the buds. You can tell the flowers are vibrant red when in full bloom." Her words flowed until the moment they stood directly in front of the young woman.

"Hey, beautiful girl," Yelena said.

There came no response or eye contact as the young woman's head hung low.

In sharp contrast to the lush foliage, she was colorless, clad in a white crop tee, a silver stomach chain, faded jeans and dingy sneakers. Her skin looked pale, perhaps cold from the night's air or simply a reflection of her near malnutrition. While her youthful sexuality appealed to them, her hollowed expression told of forlorn tales.

Unhappily, she stared at the ground. Yes, they found her a perfect fit, an inconsolable and self-destructive street urchin.

"Hello?" Yelena attempted conversation again, drawing her lips up into her friendliest smile.

Still, the young woman sat silently.

Yelena giggled. "Aren't you cold, sweetheart?"

When she finally lifted her head, they saw the vacancy in her eyes—drugs or alcohol.

That was Yelena's cue. She sat down on a level of stone below the girl, fluffing her full, black lace-adorned skirt, and gazed up at the waif. "We won't bite," she said coyly. Then, in bouncy, sing-song words, asked again, "What's … your … name?"

"Lil-ith," the young woman slurred, surprising them both with the sudden engagement.

"Oh, that's just a beautiful name, my love. Jaxon, isn't that just a beautiful name? Lil-ith," she repeated in a sensual tone of voice. "Mankind's first wife and the truest primordial she-demon. Are you a she-demon, Lil-ith?"

Lilith smirked. "Haaa! She-deem-on. That's fun-ny." Just as quickly, she dropped her lips back into their previously frowning stupor.

"You up for a little fun tonight, Lilith?" Yelena held up a small packet of green buds. "We have goodies." She waved the weed like a doggie treat.

Again, Lilith's frown transformed into a smirk, holding a little steadier this time. "Oh, I see," she said, a little more animated.

Observing the successful engagement, he took a seat on the other side of the young miss, but at Yelena's lower level.

"S'up, beautiful girl," he said, peering into Lilith's eyes.

Lilith gave a nervous titter to his attention, while also engaging more coherently in the encounter. "So, who … are you guyzz?"

They shifted up to her level, framing her petite body between the two of them with an appropriate space.

"This is Jaxon and I'm Yelena, and you are a beautiful girl, Lilith."

"Awww, that is real-ly nice."

"So, beautiful Lilith, would you like to come party with us?"

Lilith's head dropped downward as if it were too heavy for her neck, but she brought it back to the right posture. "Oh, uhhhh ... I don't know. Maybe. You're cooool ... right?"

"Oh yeah, for sure, sweetie." Yelena separated Lilith's bangs and stroked a wisp of the young women's hair down behind her ear. "We are filled with love, darlin'."

As Lilith zoned out, Yelena scooted in closer and lovingly put her arm around the waif, a fraction of her own buxom size. "Oh, sweetie, your skin is so cold. No, you have nothing to worry about from us. We just like to have a little fun with beautiful girls, and you are soooo beautiful, but ..." She took Lilith's chin between her thumb and index finger. Controlling her head like a puppet, she added, "... only, and I repeat, only, if you want to." She smiled and released her chin.

The corners of Lilith's chapped lips turned upward into a crooked smile. "Well, it is ... hel-la cold out here. And your hug ... it feelzz ... sooo warm."

"Oh, sweetie, our place is cozy, and warm, too. I promise you that."

"And ... my frienzz ... aren't com-ing back. Not to-night."

Yelena flashed her an assuring smile.

Slowly, Lilith stood up and swayed a little before she found her balance.

"Jaxon," Yelena said, as cue.

He hopped up and courteously offered Lilith his hand.

"Oh," she paused at the chivalrous gesture. "Thank you."

He helped her climb down from the throne of stone, and once secured on the sidewalk, returned for Yelena's hand. Giving a mighty tug to hoist his dark angel from the stone platform, the two joined Lilith on the sidewalk.

Yelena winked at him, and the new acquaintances made small talk while they walked in unity toward the parking garage.

CHAPTER 16
A PLOY TO SABOTAGE

Taking a quick break for lunch from the hardware store, Maddie barged into the small house she shared with her uncle. She found him with a turkey sandwich, cheese puffs, and a soda sitting at the dining room table.

"Hey Uncle Pat!"

"Hey Maddie. How's the shop this morning?" Uncle Pat was brief, but efficient with formalities.

"Same ole, same ole." So was she.

However, this perfect timing became a lucky find. After bottling up her curiosity about the violence at the hardware store months ago, the time had come for answers. Usually, a real crank with details, especially those rife with adrenaline, it had to be old news by now, right?

"So, can I ask you some questions? I mean … you don't have to answer them. But I just really want to ask you about … that night." She paused, hoping for approval and encouragement to continue.

Uncle Pat let out an incoherent grumble without taking his eyes from the daily news on his tablet.

Nonchalantly, she rummaged through the cupboard and grabbed the box of oaten honey-nut cereal. She sat the box down, hummed a little tune and grabbed a bowl and spoon.

Gulk-Gulk-Gulk.

While she poured her milk, her uncle cleared his throat and finally offered the formal encouragement to continue.

"Before we go into that, do you know anyone named Lilith Grainger?"

"No." She paused to reconsider her answer. "Nope, no Liliths. Why?"

"She's been missing a few weeks." Pat looked up from his screen and directly at her. "She reminds me of Michelle ..."

As she munched her cereal, she realized his insinuation. *If she looks like Michelle—*

"And you. Look, I know you're an adult, but I think you should be in by dark until this madness stops."

She walked over to see Lilith's image on his screen.

"Oh, wow! I didn't know her personally, but I have totally seen her. I mean, she's really out there though ... just like Michelle was. Total partier since high school. Hanging out with rowdy groups and scummy guys. Harvey West Park in the late hours ... clock tower, too."

"Maddie ..."

"Lotta drugs there, and I know that—"

"Maddie, this young woman is missing. I want you home earlier."

"Yeah, for sure. But I don't really—"

"Madison Patrice Hilgard ... home early, period."

She relented. It had been a while since he used her full name in reprimanding form. Little did he know, it would be easy because she enjoyed being a homebody, anyway. Still, she appreciated his concern for her safety.

"Let Arista know too and stress the stay-at-home aspect. I know Bethie goes away a lot, so she's welcome here anytime."

"That's cool. She'll appreciate that you said that."

She had to get this info to Arista, and not just her uncle's invitation. The uncanny similarities of Lilith to Michelle were alarming. The demographic vibed too close for comfort. What if a serial killer had come to their county?

First, there was that other matter.

"So, that guy you mashed at the store that night ... he wanted drugs?" She awaited a reaction through crunches of her cereal and milk.

"That's what he said. But I think he was going for my wallet, and I didn't wait around to find out. Plus, I didn't like the way he was looking at you. I'm telling you, I *knew* …" he stopped his rant and looked directly into her eyes, "… there were no good intentions on that face. Druggie, thief, I don't know what the heck that guy was about, but when it's dark outside, there's two of them and one of me, and I'm responsible for keeping you safe, someone's gonna get cracked." His face tensed up with hostility.

Luckily, she had learned how to neutralize his temper long ago. She smiled with a mouth full of crunching and held up her spoon, heaped with cereal and dripping milk, as if offering him a bite.

He relaxed a fraction and started again, calmer. "Look, I hope you remember what I told you that night. I love our town, but these freaks come and go in between. I want you safe. And this," he pointed to his screen of Lilith's photo, "is a perfect case in point."

"Okay, I get it." Time to lighten the subject. "So, that was a real tough guy move you pulled on him. You got some training there, Uncle Pat?" Seeing her uncle's awkwardness, she added, "Nah, we don't have to talk about it. I was just curious."

"You were, huh?" he commented with a wry smirk.

"Yeah. Ya know, I think me and Arista saw that guy again."

"Oh yeah? Where?"

"Timbermill."

"And?"

"Nothing much. He actually has a pretty wicked lookin' girlfriend. Real witchy, but not in an Arista-way … bit more gothic. But we didn't give it any time and bolted." *Perfect opportunity.* "Which should show you how *careful* we are."

"Good."

She thought her discussion about the parking lot melee would be much more involved. Whether a ploy to sabotage further discussion or a true distraction, Uncle Pat had skated free of her list of questions.

With her last bite of cereal eaten, she gave her uncle a firm pat on the back. Now, she had only one thing on her mind—telling a media-free Arista about this recent development of Lilith missing and getting her butt back to work.

.　.　.

He chose a suitable time for the drop, noted after watching the late-night flow of traffic ever since the initial abduction.

He exited the car, his footsteps crunching into patches of dislodged asphalt, and grunted from the deadweight of the body as he lifted it from the trunk. Plodding over toward the small bridge, he exerted a mighty heave and released her.

The stranger in the night whistled a soft tune as he returned to shut the trunk before taking to the driver's seat. He ignited his departure. Slowly rolling onto the road, he headed back toward Highway 9.

.　.　.

Gracefully flowing downstream on the swelled river, Lilith Grainger gently wedged into a crevice of three boulders. Settled at last, there was solace in her shelter, the water brushing over her animated, dark brown hair as if it existed without her.

The dawn would soon break, and still, she would gaze to the heavens.

CHAPTER 17
FESTIVE GARLAND AND VARIOUS SUITS

"Authorities search for a missing kangaroo from the Alabama Zoo."
Sheriff Michaels raised his eyebrow while reading his national morning news aloud. "How whimsical," he dryly said to himself.

He exited his news screen and sipped his last bit of coffee. For the second time that morning, he stretched out his chest to loosen the solid grip of stiff morning muscles. Then he released a grunt of relief for his upper back while readjusting his hips in the seat.

A static arose on his police radio, and a familiar call beckoned him to attention.

"15U15, go ahead," he responded into the radio.

"Report of a Code 10-54b. Deceased female ..."

It felt like a punch to the gut. Immediately, he thought of another female similar in stature to Michelle, reported missing out of Santa Cruz a couple weeks prior. Similar to Michelle's case, her family delayed filing the missing persons report.

How could this criminal activity be happening in this day and age? Cameras and cellphones were everywhere, yet no clues available. Still, the possibility that the body he had been called to investigate could be the missing woman, weighed heavily on him. The implications would be devastating.

He quelled his beleaguered mind after having the dispatcher repeat the location and uttered a calm response.

"Copy that. On my way, over and out." He mentally preparing himself for what he would find. "If only it were a kangaroo."

Traveling down the steep grade of Graham Hill Road, he found himself stuck in an untimely traffic snarl from a felled tree. While the cleanup crew diligently worked on nature's mess, he called in his delay and waited patiently while they finished the job.

With every elapsing minute, he grew more anxious. What if a serial killer had come to his county? Months later, and they still had no solid leads on Michelle's killer. He ticked off the usual suspects. Tattoo artist—cleared by his wife and his own home security camera. Paul—cleared by the timely consulting job. Even Denny dropped from the list after insufficient evidence to pursue the weak lead.

Finally, the roadway cleared, and his cruiser proceeded in a slow crawl behind the backed-up line of cars. The setback had caused a twenty-minute delay, and he had an additional twenty minutes to get to the upper mountain. Disappointed, he knew the delay had cost him his usual 'first-come' posture.

When he arrived at the scene, many service cars, marked and unmarked, lined the country road. They had strung yellow police tape like a horror movie's festive garland, and various suits and badges dotted the area.

As he exited his cruiser, he saw the body in the distant creek bed.

Deputy Hendrickson interrupted his study. "Good mornin', Sheriff. Probably should brace yourself for this guy." He gestured to the FBI agent loitering by the river's edge.

He fixed his attention on the investigative official. Directing his team, he appeared to be taking full control of the scene. He stood as a stiff, upright replica and epitome of the stereo-typical G-man, tall with boxy shoulders and a rigid jawline. His attire also stood out, a grey silk-sheen suit. It cast a preposterous contrast to the casual nature of his own simplistic, earth-toned uniform. This guy was definitely an outsider, and by his approaching march, and the undertones of Hendrickson's warning, he knew he would not like him.

"Sheriff Michaels, I've heard some good things about you," the agent said mechanically, while offering a rigid and controlling handshake.

Dutifully, he shook the vise grip, holding his own with equal pressure.

"Things seem to be out of control here in the mountains. We see similarities, not only to the Holmes' murder but also to a case out of San Mateo late last year. I don't know if you recognize it, but I find we have a situation here."

"Well, Agent …" He briefly waited for the agent's name, but none came, so he continued. "I am sure, working together, we can catch this piece of shit." He loved to add a zing when dealing with demeaning big-city suits, and he had dealt with many *new sheriffs in town* over the years so he would not be swayed by this guy.

"Sure, that would be great," the agent agreed patronizingly. "But we'll be involved from here on out."

"Yeah, of course. We need all hands-on deck." He calmed his agitation, realizing the priority was to stop the carnage, not succumb to his ego.

One of his team pulled away the agent, leaving him to ease the simmer of his irritation. He shook it off, seeing his deputy hurrying over to him.

Gesturing toward a disheveled and withered man on the perimeter of the scene, the deputy had news. "Sheriff, we have a witness over there who claims to have seen the victim with," he looked at his notes, "a tall, black-haired, jerky guy and a chubby girl with purple hair." He regained eye contact. "His words, not mine. Anyway, he said he's also seen them at The Timberlane and thinks they may lodge there."

CHAPTER 18
THE MURDER OF LILITH GRAINGER

The wearing cries of Evan's cousin filled the mauve and smoky-blue wallpapered rooms of their fastidious and floral-scented home.

"But I don't wanna watch this show, Aunt Rose."

"You will watch this show, young man. We can't keep starting and stopping movies after only five minutes. You've done that to me twice now."

"But this one's for babies. I'm not a baby!"

"Well, you're sure acting like a baby. Let's finish this, then find something better."

"Nooooooo," he wailed, albeit slightly less dramatically after the *baby* comment.

Fed up with the obnoxious scene, Evan left the dining table for his bedroom to finish his psychopathology homework. With the door ajar, he sat down at his desk, opened his notebook and the textbook, and lifted his pencil. His previous train of thought forgotten, he scanned his notes.

Outside his private space, the fussiness turned into an obnoxious wailing.

He fought to ignore the cries. An exercise of mental control, he focused on the various brain illustrations and read aloud to drown out the noise. "The four Ds of psychopathology are deviance, distress—"

"It's not fair!" The angry outburst traveled past his door as the bratty tyke ran down the hall.

He raised his voice. "Deviance, distress, dysfunction—"

"You come right back here, young man!"

He got up and gave his door a mighty slam, hoping his message struck and the dissonance ceased. After all, this imp-imposed racket was ridiculous! And his mom did nothing about it anytime the child-members of his extended family came to visit. Why did he have to grow up walking a narrow, well-behaved line, but these brats could run rampant and throw fits with no consequences?

It was not just him, a resentful son, and his wailing cousin who held discord toward his mother. He could tell many bristled when she walked into a room. She was a sassy and mean-spirited office manager for the county's least favorite dental office, a title given because of its unfriendly staff, and she the lead. She walked like an indignant and hangry bulldog and probed the shops of their small town, mostly looking for a worthy topic to gossip about later.

She had kept him, her eldest of two, on a short leash his whole life. And the *First-Born Syndrome,* with its correlative controlling parent, had never been a good-enough excuse. Even now, in young adulthood, it was early-to-rise and, usually, early-to-bed, since the nagging of being too noisy too late for his ailing grandmother's health, would excessively wear on him. She gave even less leeway during the week since they fully supported him during his part-time master's degree program. Still, shards of her motherly kindness appeared once in a while … usually a Saturday night … if the night was clear … and no crickets chirping. Overbearing was an understatement!

Conversely, his good grades and academic proficiency in psychology reflected his parental-inflicted discipline, and his professors praised his studious efforts and predicted a job for him in the industry. His mother's ambitions for him would eventually pay off, and it would be at that time when all of her badgering would finally make sense. Anyway, that is what she told him.

But for now, it sucked.

Grabbing his hoodie, he pulled it over his head and adjusted the fit as he bolted through the house. He exited out the back, bypassing his mother's probable interrogation of his intended destination.

Further, he walked out of his neighborhood feeling the exhilarating distance between him and his house, releasing his pent-up tension into the accepting mountain air.

A couple miles down the road, he stopped to relax and absorbed the solace of his freedom at the unoccupied Boulder Creek Scout Reservation. He took a seat on a handcrafted redwood bench and reached for his phone.

'*So sad about Lilith!*' read one post, a picture of her pixie-like face as she held a glass of blushed wine.

'*Hope they find her killer!*' read another, showing Lilith in the arms of a guy friend by the Clock Tower.

He saw the resemblance to Michelle, and even Arista and Maddie— young, cute, petite, and all had few familial ties.

Everyone was abuzz about the murder of Lilith Grainger.

"Enough." He scrolled to find other news. Perhaps something funny, like a pet macaw cussing out its owner, a chipmunk struggling with a corncob or people slipping on icy surfaces. Further, he perused with each glimpse of comic relief, followed by another published reminder of the cold reality of Lilith's death.

He clicked off his screen and set down his phone.

"I'm sorry."

He clenched his jaw and felt the rise of his shame. When his eyes welled, he tightly shut them. "I'm so sorry. " He dropped his face into his open palms. The stress bubbled up from within him and he released an intense holler of anguish into the trees.

How could he make this mess go away? He could not bear the guilt of betraying his friends and community and had to answer for it.

CHAPTER 19
THE MEANEST APRIL FOOLS

Kenny strolled through the bustling school corridor as the youngsters hurried past him along to their next class. Further he hustled, out of the common area, and through the parking lot until he reached the field.

"Heya Kenny!" The head coach greeted him as he neared the baseball diamond.

"Hey Coach!"

"You're bright today!"

He looked down at his bright red sweatshirt and shrugged his shoulders. "What can I say?"

"Hah! I'm just playin'! Anyway, I really appreciate ya doing this. I'm running crazy, but ya got the rake over there for grooming the sand and use the broom to sweep the bases. It looks like it's going to rain ... not sure of practice or tomorrow's game, but let's do it just in case. Real easy stuff, but time consuming."

"Yeah, no problem."

The coach firmly patted his back. "You got any questions?"

"Nah, I'm good!"

"Thanks Kenny!"

An easy job, it also killed time, since he had to wait for Shane to dismiss his class before they could drive home together.

Diligently, he groomed the area and upon completion collected the maintenance supplies. He would run them to the equipment shed to save the coach even more time. Maybe *going the extra mile* could land him in better standing.

He started his walk from the diamond, but an unusual sound coming from the surrounding woods caught his attention. He eyed the backstop but kept walking.

The effect repeated, a soft hiss and a sporadic giggle that resembled a little girl … but not quite. Perhaps it *was* just kids, and they should be in class.

"Hello?" He approached the thicket behind the cage with an authoritative walk and firm voice. "Hello."

The sound became a buzzing hum around him. Definitely, not kids. Unsure of its source, he looked at the distant campus. There were no faces to see with all in their classrooms. He cautiously stepped off the sandy turf onto the rim of the forest floor.

Suddenly, all became still.

"Hello?" He called once more into the thicket that hugged the baseball diamond from third base to the backstop. But with all buzzing and humming now gone, realized it moot.

He turned to leave.

Ssssssss-Ch-Ch-Ch-Ch!

The punishment swiftly came. He felt the excruciating strike to his ankle. His knee drew upward, and he grabbed his foot. Shock and agony from a second, solid strike to his wrist. He flung with all his might, trying to get the snake to release its hold. But a trip on uneven ground caused him to lose his footing. Hobbling backward toward the cage, he fell to the ground, smashing his head at the base of a backstop pole.

·　·　·

Shane stepped out of the gymnasium, answering simple questions from his new class of cheerful little beings, half his height.

"I really like dodgeball. Can we play dodgeball sometime? Our other teacher never let us."

"Dodgeball is a possibility," he confirmed.

"What about flag football?" another squeaky voice inquired. "He never let us do that, either."

"We'll find stuff to keep you guys busy. Don't worry."

"Are you Arista's boyfriend?" the little girl with a lion mane's head of hair inquired.

Catching him off guard, he sought a politically correct and age-appropriate answer. "I have a good friend named Arista. Please remind me of your name."

"I'm Zoelly."

"Zoelly! Your mom owns the crystal shop. It's nice to have you in my class. I have heard many good things about you."

"She's just weird," mocked a young boy, loitering with his friends.

"Okay, guys. Let's keep this all friendly. No need to throw shade."

Zoelly gave an insecure smile and took her leave.

He watched her tailed by the critical young man in his baseball jersey and noticed he and his co-ed friends began to harass her with incessant schoolyard remarks.

"Weirdo. Weirdo," he chanted, eliciting giggles from his girl fans. "Hey Zoelly, why are you such a weirdo?"

Zoelly stopped and slowly turned to face him. "Be careful, Eric. Wouldn't want anything to happen in softball today." With a defiant glare set upon him, she slowly turned and started walking again.

"I said friendly … all of you!" He could not play favorites. Thankfully, she had enough confidence to stand her ground.

Eric's group looked at him, quieted and proceeded to the buses.

"You're still a weirdo," Eric mumbled as Zoelly veered off into a direction different from his pack.

Seeing them conform, he went back into his gym office to grab his belongings, turned off the lights, and headed for the parking lot.

Though May was around the corner, this day still held a chilly bite to its breeze. Shivering on his way to the car, he realized his choice of a short-sleeved polo had missed the mark on warmth. While it had reflected his expectation of the usual mild spring weather, the sunny day now filled with un-forecasted dark clouds, hovering over him. A rumble from high above announced a coming rain.

Arriving at his car, he caught an unusual sight at the edge of the baseball field, a red heap on the ground. He strained to focus. It looked like a person.

He set his effects on a convenient bench and took to a small jog toward the diamond. As he neared, he could see it was not just a person, it was Kenny in his signature red hoodie.

"Kenny!" he yelled and broke into a run.

The sky further darkened and wrung its heavens, its drizzle quickly becoming rain.

He came upon Kenny in an unconscious heap and dialed 9-1-1. As his call ended, he experienced the effect from a terrifying sound that only his gut could biologically process. His legs sprung him backward in retreat before his awareness even realized what had happened. In the overgrown grass rested a triangular head atop a coil of scaled tan and brown diamonds.

He looked at Kenny, then at the instigator, coiled and ready.

Strike!

He jumped further back, dropping his phone, and slipping to the ground as the rain steadily fell.

First Aid training, he had it! But what to do? With his friend unconscious on the ground and this snake the likely culprit he had to get him to the hospital. He had to push forth.

With plentiful branches of many sizes at the perimeter, he spotted one large enough that could work. If successful, he could fling the viper away from both of them. He had watched similar instances on internet videos.

The distant ring of the school bell momentarily interrupted his thought process. The ensuing rush of rambunctious students bolting out into the corridors worried him.

He slowly backed away from his problem and edged over toward the branch. He picked it up, keeping his eye on the serpent, and circled around behind it, trying to draw its attention away from Kenny.

In the distance, curious faces from the parking area began to gather and proceed to the field. The falling rain did nothing to hinder their eagerness.

His problem filled him with the conflicting logistics. If he were to grab Kenny, the snake would surely strike again. If he did not get Kenny, he could wake up and also trigger the snake to strike again.

The voices grew louder as their bodies neared. He could not yell because it could also trigger a strike. But so could their thundering approach. Any which way, Kenny would bear the brunt of it all. He had to do something fast!

A roll of thunder grumbled from the raining heavens, and the drops became a soaking shower.

He carefully reached the branch toward the snake.

Strike!

The viper sprang to an enormous length. This time, connecting with his hand.

He retracted and clutched at the pain. Retreating backward from the danger, he shouted a stern warning. "Stop!" It was all he could offer at this moment.

The crowd slowed but still neared.

"It's a snake!" Now at a safe distance from another bite, he buckled to the ground in pain, clutching his hand. He released the hold and shot a quick glance at the damage—two tiny, blood-specked dots with a tinge of yellowish venom on one. He winced and, again, clenched his hand with a mighty grip.

Without warning, the chaos heightened. A screech rang out, followed by a flapping blur, and a whoosh of confusion as the bird dove from the height of a tree, enchanting the crowd.

"Ooooh!"

The voices rang as a choir, the assorted vocal ranges creating resonance.

He could barely grasp the commotion through his searing pain, and only his peripheral vision was privy to the spectacle. In a flurry of speed and precision, and before all eyes that were present, all became still again.

With the sound of their amusement, he struggled with the effort to warn the gawkers again. "Stop! Snake."

"It's gone," announced one voice.

"Dude, that owl was so dope!" marveled one of the older youths.

"Oh no! That shouldn't have happened!" Zoelly said in a worried voice.

He heard all the comments, but the pain overshadowed any response.

Several teachers came upon the scene and ushered the kids back toward campus. Two of them offered helping hands, assisting him to stand and walk toward the parking lot, while another stayed with Kenny. After all the activity, he could only focus on enduring the throb of venom in his bloodstream.

Finally, a tide of relief washed over him from the shrill sirens of the approaching ambulances.

· · ·

"Evan, will you please come here?" Rose bellowed from her main hangout within the Navarro household.

As soon as he appeared, she ushered his little brother out of the kitchen with a napkin and two fresh-baked cookies.

"Evan, Dad, and I've been thinking, and we would like to give you the car to use on a more permanent basis. Would you like to go out with your friends this weekend?"

"Sure?" He suspected a provisional downside to her sudden generosity.

"I've given this a lot of thought since you got so upset the other day. I know I have always been very demanding of you, but it was necessary in your younger years. Still, I know you're an adult now, even if Gran-Gran needs us all. Maybe I … well, you needed to be kept … just like every teenager should be …"

He felt like a deer in the headlights as his mother stammered and rephrased herself.

She stopped mid-sentence and grabbed one of her freshly baked chocolate-chip, sour cherry, and pecan cookies. She held it hostage while she completed her announcement. "You are an adult now, Evan. I realize that. Now, you *do* still live under my roof, and we are putting you through college and paying all your expenses, and God knows everything else!"

What on earth was this charade all about?

"So, it's important that you follow the house rules. But you have been a good and respectful son, and I think it's time that you get a little more liberty." She stopped and nodded, looking quite pleased with herself.

"Okay. And?" He hinged on the anticipation, speculating her definition of *liberty*?

"And Dad and I have decided you can take the car … whenever you want!" She smiled. "But, like I said, our rules."

With her speech completed, she released the cookie to him on a crisp, folded paper towel.

Still feeling wrecked with his own problems, he remained leery of the offer. However, the heavenly scent of her baking had been wafting through the hallway for the last thirty minutes. He took the offering, thanked her, and turned back toward the hallway.

"Well, Evan, aren't you happy? I thought you would be happier. If it's no big deal, why did I bother?"

"It's fine, Mom. Yes, I am thrilled. Thank you." The effort toward sincere appreciation felt painful, but he needed to pacify her needs. Still, he resented the timing, years too late.

"Just be leery of that weird one. We all know the rumors of her family being a bunch of devil worshipers."

And there's the dig. "She's not a devil worshipper." And back to his room he went.

His mother's distaste for Arista had been present since middle school, confusing her Celtic ways for something far more sinister. She insisted Arista worshipped the devil, her and all her relatives. And there was just no use trying to educate a stubbornly, ignorant woman.

Shutting the door, he set the cookie on his dresser and flopped himself down on his barracks-tidy bed. He had secretly adored Arista since elementary school—her friendliness, her joyful smile and warm personality. Still, it was always him left out, and at home with his overbearing mother while the rest of the friend group got together. As children, it may have been playing freeze tag in the park, and as older teens, the sporadic and sneaky underage kegger, wherever possible.

The rumors of her liking Shane had always made things even worse. Now, as a twenty-three-year-old man, while he had long accepted Shane and Arista as a good couple, he felt ill at the audacity of his mother's sudden gesture of freedom.

And it made his current problem worse. It came after the authorities had found Michelle's body. And now Lilith. No, he did not personally know her, but a friend of a friend did! He felt awful about his actions and misdeeds.

Now mired in an anxiety attack, he decided to take his mother up on her severing of the umbilical cord. To escape the suffocation bearing down upon him, he had to get out of the house … now! In what was becoming a habit, he jumped up from his bed, grabbed his hoodie and his phone, and aimed to leave.

Catching sight of his energized departure, his mother startled, "Where are you going?"

"Out," he snapped.

"Hang on just one minute! I don't like that tone, Evan Navarro! You're not taking my car with that attitude."

The phone rang, and she motioned for him to standby.

"Oh, hi Magda," she cheerfully said.

He eyed her friendly façade as it turned into worry.

"Oh No! Oh, that's awful!" She shook her head and squinted her eyes as she received the info. "Well, God Bless and keep us posted."

The anger toward his mother dissipated as he awaited her recount of Magda's worrisome news.

"That was Shane's mom. There's been a terrible accident on the campus. It's the guys. It's Shane and Kenny!"

"WHAT?! What did she say?"

"I think she said snakebite. She just sounded so upset! They're on the way to the hospital now."

CHAPTER 20
QUITE A FEISTY DEITY

"Blessings, Iris." Arista said, with a little wave from the counter. This particular customer lit up the room, not only with her twinkling voice, and sparkling light blue eyes, but also her own, handmade, vibrant fashion—a pumpkin-orange and fuschia-pink, crocheted shawl and bucket hat.

"Blessings to you, Arista," she responded in an aged and raspy voice.

She watched as the petite woman strolled toward the door, impulsively browsing all within reach to the very moment she exited.

The absence of customers made it a good time to broach the topic with Analina.

"Hey. You know … I'm wondering if you would be interested in doing a Ouija session with me. I am putting together a small group, and so far, number four has been a hard one to peg."

Analina paused with an odd look on her face. "Arista, I would. I truly would …"

And here comes the rejection.

"Truth is, a couple of years back, I had an unpleasant experience in a Ouija session. It can be quite insidious, you know."

"Sure, everything turn out okay?" Since she had never done one herself, she hoped to encourage further explanation.

"Eventually. And I know it could be totally unrelated, but I suffered a sharp pain shot straight through the center of my head. And for a month thereafter, I had a terrible bout of vertigo."

"Oh wow! I remember that! That was from a Ouija?" She remembered her paychecks being double during that time, as she filled in for Analina several hours a week.

"That, my dear, was indeed, Ouija. I think. Who knows? In all fairness, my client had asked me to help her contact the Norse goddess, Hel. I thought it would be a challenge for my abilities. And even though I knew she could be quite a feisty deity …" Analina grit her teeth. "Yeah, anyway, it could have been unrelated to the session, but it has definitely lowered my confidence in that ritual."

"Of course, I totally understand." *Wow, I didn't think Ouija could stir up that kind of trouble.*

"It's conceivable that I'll try it again someday, but it won't be for a while."

"Of course! No worries! Thank you for that insight too. Makes me think twice." But really, it did not. With her family's history, she would just need to keep searching for the right person.

Analina donned her shop owner's smile as her front door chimed, alerting the ladies to another customer.

At the same time, Maddie's ringtone grabbed Arista's attention from the backroom.

"Hey, what's up?"

"Shane and Kenny are at the hospital!" True to her usual punch, Maddie belted out the disturbing news with no filter nor warning.

"What? Why?!" Her heart raced.

"Not sure, but Evan is on the way to pick me up. Can you come, or do you need to work?"

"Yes, of course, pick me up! I'm almost certain Analina will understand."

"Okay, we'll be there."

Arista dialed Shane's cell. It went directly to voicemail. Again, she tried … and again, resulting in the same dead end. She began to worry.

What could have merited the hospital? Wouldn't Shane have just texted or called her if it was just something like a broken arm? But then again, highly improbable that both had broken their arms. It had to be something worse.

"Oh, dear-oh dear-oh dear!" She fretted aloud while gathering her items.

Analina poked her head into the backroom. "Are you okay?"

"I am so sorry, but I have to go to the hospital. My friends are in … something happened, but I don't know what yet."

"Yes, of course. Do you need a ride?"

"No, they're coming to get me."

"Of course. Let me know if you need anything from me."

"Thank you!"

Analina hugged her, and out the front door she went. Waiting for Evan and Maddie, she prayed for *her* Shane. She ached for him and felt utterly helpless. She envisioned his smile, his beautiful, rich brown eyes, and comforting hug. This feeling, this ache, felt awful, and more than distress for a buddy. It went much deeper. More than ever, it became clear. True love had reached her heart, and now he was in trouble.

CHAPTER 21
THERE'S YOUR DILEMMA

Sheriff Michaels finished his bank transaction in downtown Santa Cruz. Just finished from his lunch with a retired fellow officer, he decided to run his errands in the salty ocean air instead of the redwoods.

Like any other day, he observed the town clock area teeming with individuals uninterested in a life filled with menial work and suffocating rules.

Two young men passed by him as he pecked in his ATM information.

"Dude, for real. I saw her leave with a goth couple," said the rattier of the two.

"No way. You sure it was her, cause that chick is D-E-A-D," said the scrawnier friend, before toking on his vape pen.

The overheard statement piqued his interest, and he watched them cross the small side street. They took a seat on the ground in front of a bronze sculpture that, at first glance, could be mistaken for sensual embrace. Upon noticing the baby's head comes another inaccuracy of familial love. In truth, the artist had created it to hold reverence for those lost to war, the pedestal upon which it sat filled with guns exchanged for bouquets of flowers and sealed with a Tibetan ceremonial singing bowl.

Dwarfed by the town clock tower, they settled into their lowly spot where they shared the vape pen and bouts of amusement.

Inconspicuous in his plain clothes, he strolled over to them.

"Yeah, I'm sure it was her. She was sitting right over there." The ratty young man pointed to the Viper's Kiss, before taking his hit from their community pen.

"What if ... they're like ... the ones ... who killed her?" He strained, attempting to hold in his toke, prior to exhaling a huge steam cloud.

"No shit, man!"

He had heard enough. He walked directly up to the street rats dressed as humans and towered above them.

"Hey guys!" He peered down at them, smiling.

The abrupt greeting from an older, put-together father-figure startled them. They gawked, stunned by the interruption.

"I heard you mention that you may have seen Lilith Grainger leave with a gothic couple."

After a brief pause, and glances to one another, the rattier man spoke. "Dude, mind your own business. Nobody's talking to you."

The stoned friend spewed out a snicker.

He opened his jacket, exposing the badge on his belt. "I know you'd want to help find those who hurt Lilith. Wouldn't you?"

Lowering their heads and looking at each other, the attitude adjusted.

"So, you're a real cop?"

"Santa Cruz County Sheriff. Officer Michaels." After his curt introduction, he stood taller awaiting the story.

The ratty young man hesitated and looked at his friend before continuing. "Yeah, I think I saw her leave with a couple. It's been a while back now."

"When you say *couple*, you mean a man and a woman?"

"Yeah."

"Mmm-hmph. Could I get your name, please?"

"Trevor, uh ... Trevor Hite." Trevor glanced at his friend, unsure of the encounter.

"Okay, thanks Trevor. Can you describe the man and woman?"

"I guess." Trevor quietly relayed the information while looking around at who might be watching. "The guy was all in leather and had long hair. Think that dude in The Lost Boys. The '80s version."

"I'm not familiar with that movie. Can you be more specific?" *Actually, that was a great movie.*

"Well ... kinda tall."

"Are you talking six feet, or taller?"

"Yeah, yeah, probably 'bout six feet. I think a little taller than you."

He looked Trevor in the eyes, inviting more information.

"Yeah, and kind of a rocker guy. Wait, hold on." Trevor grabbed his friend's phone, leaving the scrawny young man miffed. He tapped in his inquiry and awaited the result. "There. Seriously, he looked a lot like this guy."

He jotted the information while Trevor held the phone. "So, shoulder length hair—black or dark brown. Looks like he's late-twenties to mid-thirties. Fairly fit, and there's the dark clothing you mentioned." He pointed to the image. "And who is this?"

"Umm, looks like he's ..." Trevor enlarged the text and held the phone to him. "Here ya go. Yeah, he was one of the vampires in that flick. And ..."

He scribbled in as much detail as he could. This looked to be a good lead.

"Ironically, the 80s *Lost Boys* was filmed right here in Santa Cruz!" Trevor laughed aloud at his realized irony.

"Whoa! Dude, that *is* wild," his scrawny friend agreed, and added a nervous laugh at his own sudden outburst.

"But, I mean, it wouldn't really be him, 'cause that dude's gotta be hella old now."

"And the female? What did she look like?"

Trevor described the woman's colorful hair, weight, and black wardrobe. And from what he could tell, the two descriptions were similar to those from the tip received at Lilith's crime scene. However, the homeless young men of downtown fell short on their own contact information. They could only offer the friend's phone number and their names.

"But we're around here most of the time."

"Thank you Trevor. So, are you aware that Miss Grainger had been missing for a while? Is there any reason you didn't come forward sooner?"

"Yeah, I'm not into the news, and people are always coming and going here."

"Mmm-hmph. One more question. Do you recall what she was wearing when she left with them?"

"White half-shirt, jeans … and yeah, that's all I remember."

This young man's drug use could have compromised his recollection, but he nailed her clothing. "Alright. Thank you." He cocked his head. "So … you two aren't under the influence of anything, are you?"

"Aw c'mon, du—, er, Officer. Weed is totally legal in Cali."

"Well, Mr. Hite, you are correct about that, but you must not be aware that you cannot consume, smoke, eat, or *vape* cannabis in a public place." He let the fact sink into their hazy mental capacity. "And for your future reference, even though it is legal under California law, you also cannot consume or possess cannabis on federal lands, like national parks. It seems like you two aren't fully aware of the law."

Trevor slumped his shoulders and cocked his head conceding his guilt, while his scrawny friend sat motionless.

But he had to get going, so the time had come to stop toying with drug abusers. "Anyway, now that you two know the law, I'm going to let you go back to your business. So, no fines this time, but you need to smoke that stuff in the privacy of your own home."

"What if we don't have a home?"

Already walking toward the bank, he turned back toward them. "There's your dilemma."

CHAPTER 22
UNSETTLING AT FIRST

Arista nervously looked out her kitchen window and relayed what little details she had to Maddie through the phone.

"No, still nothing, and the hospital won't give me any information, either. No one's answering phones. It's just awful! But I don't want to be a pest."

"Just hang in there."

"Magda and Kenny's mom's Insta has requests for prayers. But that's it ... for a week now!" The lack of information had turned maddening.

"We'll hear when there's news worth hearing," Maddie reassured. "I really don't think you need to worry. People get bitten by snakes all the time and they're fine. Shane will be too, especially since he went straight to the hospital. Kenny ... well, that's a disaster. But we can pray. Why not do a protective spell for them to make yourself feel better?"

"I've done one for each of them daily. Though Saturdays are the best for a Protection Spell, so tonight is big! I just really wish I could talk to him."

"You mean Shane?"

"Yes. I think ... I love him." Never had it been clearer. Kenny lay in a coma from his head injury, but it was Shane that she just could not stop worrying about. "I just know he's hurting, not only from the bite, but the whole ordeal!"

"Well, I'll keep checking in with Evan. It's possible his mom will hear something from Magda. Don't worry, Arista, he'll be okay."

She heavily sighed. "Alright. Thank you for listening."

"Of course. This is what we do for each other."

After ending the call, she knew she had to keep busy. All week she found herself dwelling on him in moments of slowness at work and home. So, she jumped into Auntie's beading project and knocked out two dozen sets. When the colors of a lilac dusk softened the evening sky, she set the borrowed supplies aside and declared it time to start a formal protection spell.

She stood in front of her altar and scooped her loose hair into a tight, messy bun. Intent upon sending good vibes toward her stricken beau, she selected a small Hematite obelisk based on his sun sign and a splendid, seven-point Smoky Quartz cluster. The latter she would give to him after much ceremonial blessing upon it.

She centered both crystals in front of her while contemplating a few magickal approaches. Remembering *The Apple Spell*, in her purchased book of spells, she decided to improvise with the ingredients she had on hand.

Under the darkening sky, she went out to her garden and snipped several sprigs of lavender buds. On her way back in, she stopped at her window planter and clipped a handful of pert green peppermint. She set the botanical variety on her kitchen counter and grabbed her onyx mortar and pestle, then macerated the mint leaves with a few drops of almond oil until they formed into a natural paste. The invigorating scent filled her kitchen. She would omit the usual process of it sitting overnight in the moonlight because of the urgency.

Now she only needed one last item—the apple.

From her fridge's crisper drawer, she grabbed the biggest, roundest, and most beautiful red apple of the bunch. She carefully eyed it and found it free of imperfections and firm to the touch. This satisfaction must have been how the wicked queen felt with her brilliantly toxic creation. But instead of bringing chaos and heartache, her use of this plump *Garden of Eden* original aimed for true love and healing.

With supplies in hand, she went back to her altar and chose chamomile and eucalyptus oils from her vials. She smooshed the old ash within her cauldron up its sides and proceeded with her process.

Over the next hour, the room went from a sundown of natural light to a soft, candlelit glow amidst darkness. She diligently wrote, prayed, concocted, and focused. She chanted, poured, burned, and meditated. This spell work had to have been the most energy and intention she had ever put into her craft. Finally, after covering the apple in herbs and oils, she gave the Smoky Quartz a final pinch of rosemary salt and a sprinkle of crushed, dried rose petals. With the enchanting process complete, she had fully dedicated it to Shane's recovery.

"Who knows, maybe he will even love me back … but it's always his choice."

And then she felt it. The slight and subtle sensation of a fingertip stroking up the back of her bared neck.

A torrential chill shot up her spine. She released a brusque shiver as her forearm hair stood on end. As the chill bumps burst through her skin, she whirled around to see the source behind her.

Nothing.

"Royal!" She released another spirited shiver and felt the thickness of the air around her.

Always unsettling at first, her ghost seemed to only want recognition, then it would be gone. Since Auntie showed no sign of concern and, in fact, touted the presence as family, she dealt with the encounters one episode at a time.

"Hello?" She calmly took a breath.

But it had never touched her as it just did. Nor had it broken a glass jar of lavender buds. Nor had it ever led her to a vision … which seemed to be missing this time, but still!

"Hello? I acknowledge you. Friends? Actually, I think we may be family." Nervously, she searched for the right words trying to control her angst. "You seem to be quite social this year."

Momentarily, she held her breath to better observe the silence.

She heard nothing. She turned back toward her altar and nonchalantly proceeded to tidy up her spell work scatterings.

A whoosh of a strong breeze brushed behind her.

Her witch bells jingled.

"Royal!" Adamantly, she called for her guard cat to get his furry butt by her side.

With her heart racing again, she went over to her bed and turned on her small lamp, instantly illuminating the room in a soft, warm glow. She looked over at her half-settled altar, then into the darkened hallway.

"I really wish you would not scare me like this." She could still feel the presence in her room.

In her darkened hallway, two glowing red eyes appeared.

Her heart jolted.

It was Royal.

"Get in here," she said, in a whispered staccato tone.

As Royal reached her feet, she anxiously bent over to pick him up, but became distracted by a tiny crystal pebble by her door. The stray Peridot stone sparkled against the aged wooden floor. Also, her birthstone, the crystal represented good fortune.

Huffing out her tension, she grabbed it and intended to pick up Royal. But her eyesight blurred, and her knees buckled beneath her, sending her to the floor.

The haunting vision of the inverted pentagram consumed her consciousness. Its bottom point sunk into an inked red slit at the base of the owner's thumb. The vision persisted, bringing a new urgency. She felt a dark and threatening presence pursuing her. Her heart raced as the scene became her very own Hoot Owl Way.

Thud.

She snapped out of the chaotic vision when her bewitched apple hit the floor.

"And there's the vision." It had become routine, but no less exhausting.

Catching her breath, she felt the bruising effect on her hip from the fall, while picking herself off the floor.

Royal peered at her, now perched on the tallest rung of his cat post from the far side of her room.

"I understand. I'd look for high ground if I were you, too. It's just not a normal cat's life for you, is it?"

She felt the buoyancy of the air around her, and relief that the supernatural wave had passed.

Her eyes darted over to the small mess of apple, herb paste, and stray rose dust on her floor. However, with senses heightened, she waited for the next move. Anything else coming?

Mew.

She took a deep breath to reset her thoughts. "I declare right now that telling Auntie is a priority ... and *someone* is going to do that Ouija with us!"

She went over to pick up the dressed apple. She held it at arm's length and inspected the damage. Deeming it acceptable, she dropped it into a red velvet bag that would bask in the moonlight. "It's still of merit. After all, I don't give it to him."

Her recipients seldom knew of her white-magick spells for their benefit. It was nothing but good vibes she actually *gave* them.

Setting the pouch aside, she grabbed a pen and paper and wrote down all she could remember. She would not miss a detail when relaying the night's episode to Auntie.

Upon completion, she ran down the list. "The heightening of encounters with my dear ghost ... recurring vision ... tattooed, gross hand, and now, our street." As she read it aloud, it became more obvious. "Great! This is just getting way too scary!"

Rattled and anxious again, she headed to her dining table, in its practical form, to work on more bead sets for Auntie. She turned her music on in a low volume and hummed along focusing on melody, lyrics, and the activity at hand. After this brazen episode, she needed the distraction.

CHAPTER 23
AN UNATTAINABLE CASTLE

After a week of enduring the family-requested privacy for Shane's healing, Arista felt relieved to finally get the approval for a social call. In fact, the friend group decided to participate together, and all piled into Evan's borrowed SUV to make the visit.

She had always found it unnerving to go to Shane's house. The plush furnishings, marbled floors, and high ceilings were so unlike her own cozy dwelling. His parents were also a far cry from Auntie's bohemian groundedness. Shane's father spent long hours at his biotech company in Redwood City and frequently traveled on business. Magda, his mother, could be controlling at times, especially, when it came to her healing son. But she usually came across as quite friendly and approachable, and performed many community services for the county. Perhaps influenced by her own upbringing in the southern countryside, she chose a practical SUV, low-key clothing, and minimal makeup. But when she had an event to attend, her glamor could rival the ritziest celebrity.

They pulled into the circular driveway, and followed the path around the eight-foot, three-tiered fountain full of glossy black birds with red-notched wings taking turns at vigorous baths.

The landscaped, lush green grass lay amidst a burst of spring glory—large, royal-blue hydrangeas, stalks of white fox glove and deep purple lobelia ground cover. Two large terracotta pots on the front porch hosted orange pansies with chocolate brown faces, and bright pink petunias. Cascading pearl-like succulents that looked like green peas on string lined their rims.

Jalen grabbed the iron ring within the mounted lion's mouth and knocked. Her friends chattered anticipating the visit, but she stood near the back of their group, her stomach full of butterflies.

The behemoth door slowly opened to reveal a pint-sized human, Shane's little sister. Then Magda appeared and widened the entry. "Hey y'all! Come in. Come in." Her slight southern twang ushered them into the spacious foyer. "He's in his room. He'll be so thrilled to see y'all. Shaaaane," she bellowed up the stairs, "we're comin' up."

She looked at Maddie. How nerve-wracking to see Shane's mother, especially after she had kept her at bay for the past week. For that matter, she had long-thought that his parents did not like her, even though she had been told the opposite by him many times. This, mixed with the anticipation of seeing him for the first time since the accident caused her flutters to heighten.

Atop the stairs, she could see his room streaming with sunlight. As they neared, she saw the team photos and season trophies from years of high school championships and college accomplishments.

But her heart sank when they entered his room. His expression looked sullen and destroyed. He showed none of the joy his mother had conveyed. His bandaged hand rested on a stack of pillows, and a light fleece blanket covered his body while he reclined against his headboard.

"Okay, Shane …" Magda flashed a toothy, encouraging smile to her woeful son, and took a quick exit.

She intensely gazed at him but kept a subtle presence just behind the guys. When the group spaced out so all could see their bed-bound friend, it exposed her again.

After a moment of awkward silence, Shane mumbled, "Thanks for coming." He made no eye contact with anyone.

"Hey, of course, we're here for you," Jalen asserted. "How are you doing?"

"I'm fine. It's Kenny, though," Shane's voice cracked, "he's still in the coma from the way he hit his head. Don't know what happens next."

Arista gasped at the news. No wonder there had been little said. Kenny's parents must be heartbroken.

Jalen offered reassurance. "We just gotta pray for him. I've read a bunch of stories that people survive these things. And you know he wouldn't want the pity. It would just irritate him."

"Yep," Shane said, heaving out a sigh. He glanced at her but diverted his attention back to Jalen without formally acknowledging her.

Maddie caught the moment and offered her a supportive smile.

Should she even be here? It might have been better to let the guys come alone. But Evan did not talk much either. While she knew he felt supportive of Shane, he seemed anxious, swaying side to side, and biting his lip. He could have been upset seeing Shane in this state, but really, he had been very uptight for weeks now.

"You look like your old self." Evan added in a cheery voice, as if he caught on to her observation of him.

"Thanks."

For a few minutes, the friends caught up, but they could see Shane was not up for it.

Jalen called the meeting. "Okay, we know you're still beat up from this fiasco. You need your rest. We just wanted to come by and say *hi*, and let you know … we love ya. Okay?"

With all heads bobbling in agreement like plastic desktop dolls, it pleased them to get a small, accepting snicker out of their wounded friend.

Thus began the procession of hugs, after which the bearers trailed out the door.

With the blessed Smoky Quartz in her pocket, she second-guessed her gift. He obviously disliked all the witchcraft stuff, and now, he barely looked at her the entire visit. The last thing she wanted to do was irritate him while he struggled, mentally and physically.

But she encouraged herself and held back to be his last goodbye. She *would* give him the enchanted crystal for protection and healing. And maybe her chances were greater that he would accept it without an audience. And if not, she would be less embarrassed without witnesses to the rejection.

Now alone with Shane, she gave him a lengthy hug. Seeing him in such a state of physical and emotional distress, troubled her. After a moment, she pulled away and noticed a spark of attentiveness in his expression. She took it as encouragement, and proceeded in the magick she knew so well.

"Shane, I am giving you Smoky Quartz." She could not look him in the eye in case of disappointment so, she looked at his hand as it took the stone.

He ran his finger along the smooth surface of the points.

His observation of the cluster encouraged her. She looked at his face. "It's a cluster of healing, and it's going to absorb and transmute all the negative energy swirling in your body. All the pain and negativity from this entire ordeal. And it could promote a more encouraging outlook."

"Hmph. This is really pretty." He continued to rub the translucent brown crystal in genuine appreciation.

She mentally ran down her list, seeing if she missed anything, and noticed him studying her—her face, then, hair. With his gaze stopping at her lips, another thought popped into mind. "Oh, and any sadness for Kenny—may he heal soon—for that, it will help you too … like, if you're feeling depressed." Of course, he felt depressed, but it was his call to own it.

"Thank you, Riss." A smile softened his face. "I really appreciate it."

"I'm so sorry you're going through all of this." She hugged him again out of compassion, but also in happiness, that he had graciously accepted her gift.

She felt his embrace tighten around her, and they floated in a moment of bliss. When she backed away, his eyes were bright and alive, holding the gaze.

Contented with her interaction, she backed away from him. She did not want the awaiting crowd in the foyer to sense the intimacy, especially Shane's mom. A breathless, beaming smile radiated from her, and she casually strolled out of his room. "Bye, Shane!"

She bounded down the stairs, feeling afloat from her natural high, and no intimidation from the grandeur of the home nor she who waited at the door. She fell in line with the departing procession.

Magda used each of their first names to express her sincere appreciation for visiting her gloomy son. As she approached Magda, the mama bear draped a friendly hug upon her. She followed up with a light touch to her arm. "Arista, honey, you have always meant so much to Shane." Her eyes shone clear and direct. "I wanted you to know that, and I hope you weren't too hurt by us wanting privacy while he recuperated. I let him know you were inquirin' about him."

"Of course!" So nice her to say, but it did not matter. She had no displeasure toward her anymore. Gaining Shane's receptiveness in his room was all she needed to brighten her day and give her hope.

In a jiffy, they loaded up and drove toward the exit. She considered the beauty and health of the picturesque front yard with its humongous hydrangeas—now occupied with a fluttering swallowtail butterfly—and the fountain with its bathing flock of happy, black birds. She, too, felt the renewal and bliss of the blooming spring season.

"That went well," Jalen declared. "Shane looks good. He'll be fine. Good idea, guys!"

They agreed in unison, except for Evan. Not engaging in the conversation, he focused on driving. This same preoccupation had held him for too long now. Shane was doing as well as could be expected, and Evan and Kenny were never close. Something ate at him.

Her answer came soon enough.

"I think I've done something horrible!" Evan's emotional declaration came as soon as Maddie and Jalen were out of the car. He pulled into an empty parking lot and turned off the engine and looked nervously over his shoulder and in his mirrors.

She felt the paranoia as if it were her own. "Jeez, Evan, what is it? I've been worried about you."

"It was me, Arista! I think I've caused all this horrible shit that keeps happening."

"What are you talking about?" His confession alarmed her. He was always so contained and careful, a book-smart nerd yet good with sports, funny and easy-going, and a master's program student. Why would he fall apart now?

"It's all my fault everybody's hurt … dying … dead!" He clutched his thighs as he confessed to, so far, nothing.

"Okay, just slow down. What do you mean you caused it?" Her eyes welled with tears as she took on his anguish.

"Michelle, Kenny, maybe even that girl out of Santa Cruz! Who knows?" He hunched over the wheel and sorrowfully shook his head. "I gotta make it right."

"It's okay, Evan." She reached over to give him a supportive hug. She doubted him guilty of actually killing someone, but he felt distraught over something. "Let's figure it out, okay? I mean, you didn't take a weapon and actually kill someone. Right?"

"No, it's just I think I may have …"

"You may have what?"

"I don't know. I think I called these things."

"Like you called someone?"

"No, I called upon them."

"What on earth do you mean?" His vagueness was exasperating.

"Well, I called … I called them in a magick ceremony."

"Are you serious? Like my kind of magick?" *No freaking way.*

"Yes."

For a second, her concern transformed to shock. "Wow, since when do you practice magick?"

He shook his head in regret when she verbalized his deed.

"Come on, we can figure this out. Talk to me."

Evan exhaled the weight of his confession. "God, this is all … just … so stupid!"

"You know what? No need to hash it out here. Let's go to my house and I want you to tell me everything."

. . .

Arista handed Evan a glass of her blueberry green iced tea and two lemon-and-lavender shortbread cookies she had baked to keep her mind off of Shane. She sat across from him, waiting to learn more about his mysterious admission.

He bit into a cookie, swigged the tea, and began his story.

"I think I summoned all this pain on us. I sat in a circle of black salt and asked that the guys go away. And they mostly did ... to private school."

"When was this?"

Evan sat hunched in his shoulders, and his head hung in shame. "In eighth grade. Because while I was homebound, everyone else was always out having fun." He looked sheepishly to her. "And I'm sorry you have to hear this."

"Are you saying you wished ill on ... like ...," she hesitated to verify and pursued it carefully, "Shane and Kenny?"

He sat in silence.

"Is that what you mean?"

"Not just them. All the jocks that—"

"Evan, you were a jock, too."

"I know I technically was, but I could never do jack because of my mother." He looked at her with a shameful cast. "I swear I didn't mean for any harm to come to them."

She considered the confession for a moment, annoyed at the animosity toward Shane, but she also felt for his distress. "Hmmm. Let me think about this." Evan had always been her most avid Catholic friend, the one who wore a St. Christopher pendant during the school field trips, attended the most church, and frequently told friends to *trust in God's plan.* "I think you may be feeling unnecessary guilt."

"And Michelle too. I really liked her since middle school. And with Shane and Jalen gone, I thought I'd have a chance. But then Kenny slides in Junior year." He shook his head as if trying to erase unhappy memories. "It was just too much! At that point, I was done, and I sat in that black-salted circle again. And I prayed to something powerful … wishing them all gone! And now they're fucked up. All of them. Except Jalen, thank God! But Michelle is dead, Kenny is … maybe dead! Even Shane got hurt!"

"So, you sat in the circle twice, then?"

"Yes, in eighth grade and junior year. And it sure looks like something came of it. Well, eventually, anyway."

"Where did you do all of this?" It couldn't have been in the house under Rose's nose.

"Okay, don't be mad at me, but in junior year, it was me at Big Basin. Those were my remnants we saw on our bike ride. I'm the witch noob you were angry about."

"Oh wow, Evan." Stunned by his use of black magick as well as the reckless endangerment of her friendly forest, she sat in silence and analyzed the facts. Mostly, it looked coincidental. After all, it had been by choice of a better football experience that Jalen and Shane eagerly accepted their parents' invitation for them to attend the prep school. And truly, it would have been one hell of a delayed reaction had it been Evan's magick circle-sitting that caused the community's current chaos.

"I know, it sucks. I feel horrible about it!"

"Well, I think it's healthy that you own the results of your actions. Luckily, I don't think this would send you to jail." She tapped at her mouth, letting the story take shape in her mind. "Magick and incantations rarely work out of the blue like that … a onetime shot from … no offense … a disgruntled, inexperienced individual. Or maybe they do?" She shrugged.

"I feel awful! I really do."

"I do not do black magick … like never! So, I'm not sure … the timing is significantly delayed." Tilting her head, she pondered the possibility. "I have to admit, it's very intriguing that both times you sat, the wanted result eventually materialized."

Evan groaned.

"Though not the way you had imagined." She peered at him. "What did you say in the circle?"

"I don't remember exactly. I just googled some chant about undue competition and banishment." He grit his teeth. "I think I said I wanted them gone." His face crinkled in anguish. "I swear I just wanted them to move or something. Like, going to another school was perfect! Then Kenny went with Michelle to junior prom, while I'm freakin stuck at home … it was just too much! I just wanted them all to disappear."

She watched him continue to reason with himself, suspecting he was trying to find an escape from his guilt.

"I did not mean for anybody to die."

"Hang on just a minute. Let me think." She peered out her window, trying to find the right words. "First off, I'm really sorry you felt so left out. That sucks. I wish I would have known how lonely you were." She placed her palm on his arm and studied his face.

"Thanks." He lowered his head.

"You know I'm the first to grab a crystal, mix up herbs or wave a wand, but I really think you can forgive yourself for this." While she felt confident something was in motion, Evan's novice prayer to big, bad juju could not have been the driver. "I don't believe our trouble is because of you at all. However, if you want to help rectify the predicament, there is something you can do."

A giddiness bubbled in her belly as she walked him to the awaiting mystical table. Displayed in all its glory, she had perfected the assembly process while ruing over Shane. "I really want to use this, but I cannot do it alone."

"Wow!" Evan studied the Ouija's charred, intricate detailing.

"Me, Auntie, and Maddie are three, but we need a fourth."

"I'll help anyway I can. But it seems like anything I do causes trouble. Are you sure you want me a part of it?"

"Yes. I do. In fact, how about you and I try a little test run right now?"

His eyes widened, and he took a nervous breath. "Okay."

Finally, a Ouija rehearsal!

"Yes!" she squealed, her brimming excitement bringing an amused smile to his face.

She hustled to her room and rustled through the closet, looking for a substitute for the triangular piece. *What is that thing called?*

Resting on his cat post, Royal lifted a sleepy eye, but her search did not hold his interest.

"Evan, I don't have that little triangular thingy." From her room, she rushed to the kitchen. "What else could we use?" she rhetorically asked, opening, and closing each kitchen drawer. With the participant finally found, she stood ill-prepared.

"Oh, the piece you put your fingers on?"

"Yes."

Shuffling through the pantry, she found a small triangular box, the original wrapping for a piece of jewelry. "This may work!"

Walking over to her junk drawer, she pulled out three stick pins, and poked one in each corner of the box's lid, tossing the base of it back to the counter. "Okay! Let's do this."

The pair approached the table and stood on opposite sides.

"Okay, we can lightly touch the lid and it will answer our questions by sliding to the answer, or by spelling it out. Full disclosure. I have never done this."

"Yeah, okay."

Evan followed her lead, standing like she stood, touching the makeshift triangle piece lightly, like she did.

"Spirit, are you with us?" she asked.

With their breath held, they both peered at the triangular box that sat inanimate.

"Spirit, are you with us?"

Nothing.

She took a deep breath and tried to calm her thumping heart.

"Spirit, I invoke you. Please help us."

The widget made a sudden movement, causing them to jump. But no movement followed.

"Spirit, I invoke you. Please help us. We want to know, uh … the date! Can you tell us the date?"

The widget moved again. This time, it attempted a journey to the numbers with a jerky scuffle, however, just short of the charred numeral -1-, a peg leg gave way and disappeared up into the lid. The makeshift vessel tilted beneath their fingers.

She picked up the box and poked the stick pin leg back out of the bottom. She quickly put it back in place.

"Spirit, it looks like you were going to point to number one. Is this correct?"

No movement.

"Spirit, was it number one?"

Still no movement.

Evan waited patiently while she tried to coerce the board to divulge more information. But the box lid fell short of the Ouija's true and sturdy component.

Evan looked at her. "So, what now?"

"Ugh, Evan. I'm sorry. It's the triangle thing." She abruptly grabbed her cellphone and pecked for data. "The planchette! Auntie must know where it is. Also, I think Ouija is best done at night." She grabbed his forearm. "But please promise me you will help! When Auntie gets back, I know she'll make it work."

"Sure. Just let me know when."

"Okay, wait here for a minute." She walked to her bedroom, while bellowing at him. "Actually, it's like the tenth or eleventh today, so that it was going to the number one is promising."

In her room, she grabbed a couple of crystals from her plentiful collection and brought them out to him. "In the meantime, put out your right palm … wait, you're right-handed?"

"Yes."

"Okay, here—this is Lepidolite." She spritzed the crystal. "I'm spraying this with a sage blend, and taking all my energy off of it, so you receive it free and clear."

"I don't mind your energy being on it. In fact, it's probably better than my own."

She smiled but insisted. "Knock it off, Evan. You're not the bad guy you thought you were. Just rub in the oil."

He followed the command.

"I want you to meditate with it once … no, twice a day until your guilt is gone. This crystal will help you heal the emotional toll that you've inflicted on yourself. Look at its designs and colorings and meditate on the beauty. Hold it in your palm and absorb the energy, letting it radiate through your arm and up into your brilliant mind. It'll have you back to your studious, rational self in no time."

He eyed the purple and white dappled stone appreciatively, rotating it to see all the angles.

"Now this is Blue Aventurine." She held up the milky, medium-blue, polished cube. "This is also going to be of great help to you." She rotated the stone for his perusal, placed it in his palm, and performed her cleansing ritual. "This is a really nice blend. It's Quartz with various inclusions, including Mica and Dumortierite."

He rubbed in the oil, and rotated the crystal in various directions, admiring its charm.

"The shape is grounding … stable, and reconnects you to earth, while the crystal itself is good for self-discipline and inner strength. It will also attune you to higher spiritual guidance, and possibly psychic ability."

Her voice changed from educator to friend. "Evan, I'm so excited that you have like-minded tendencies. What if we can work together with the Ouija and stop the killer before he hurts anyone else?"

"Does it do that kind of stuff?"

"Long story short, yes!"

"Then, yes! Count me in." He vigorously nodded. "Jeez, you've helped me lift a mountain of worry off my back."

"Glad to help! So, when Auntie returns from this impromptu trip of hers, I know she'll help us get things straightened out. We'll hold a real, true-blue Ouija session."

"Okay, any idea when that will be?"

"Not yet, but she left me a voicemail that it won't be much longer. My guess is that means a week … maybe two. I honestly don't know, and it's a real trick to get her on the phone."

"Okay, just let me know."

She walked her new comrade-in-magick to the door.

A grand startle awaited them as the aged door creaked open. Instead of the usual serenity of her yard, a wide span of wings took flight from atop her small shed.

"Hey!" Evan blurted as he involuntarily threw both fists up in front of his chest, guarding himself against an attack.

She giggled, used to the many jump scares of her home, including this majestic raptor.

"Damn!" he said with wonder, catching the last glimpse of the great horned owl as it flew into the depths of the trees. "This is the second daylight owl sighting I've seen this year."

She giggled. "He really likes it here. I've seen him more and more over the past few months."

"How do you know it's a *he*?"

She paused, looking for the answer, and laughed. "Good question."

CHAPTER 24
A CONSENSUALLY GOOD TIME

Jaxon anxiously chewed his last semblance of a thumbnail. The activity relieved his impending stress of uncomfortably sitting on a rigid metal chair in a stuffy, windowless room. The two-way mirror taunted him by reflecting his own nervousness. He regained his composure, sat up straight, and arrogantly stroked his jaw.

The door opened, and the sheriff walked in, emitting a potent scent of woodsy pine cologne. He cleared his throat and took a seat. "I'm Sheriff Pete Michaels. Do you know why you're here, Mr. Jaxon ..." He looked at his notepad. "Anoki?"

"No idea." They could not pin shit on him, so he answered with a smug, chin-up gesture.

"We have a couple of witnesses who reported seeing you with a young woman, Lilith Grainger, a few weeks ago. You and Yelena Summer. Do you remember that encounter?"

He felt a guiltiness creep into his facial expression and shifted in his chair. He had thought Lilith might be too young for their purpose, and now flinched to think that age could lead to their downfall. "Yeah, we met a chick named Lilith. Not much to talk about. Why? Is something wrong with meeting new people?"

The sheriff sat stoic and silent.

"Look, I swear to God, man ... we picked her up ... and I know that sounds bad, but we picked her up and took her to our place. You know, to keep her safe from any bad people out there. She was really messed up. So, we just let her sleep it off. 'Cause you know we don't take advantage of that kind of situation." He paused and looked to the sheriff for acknowledgement regarding the thoughtfulness.

"Mmm-hmph. What else?"

"In the morning, we woke up and hung out for a while."

"What do you mean by hung out?" He scribbled into his note pad with each posed question.

"We smoked a little. I know that's legal here. And we … um …" He wanted to be as truthful as possible because he did not know the witnesses, nor how much information they had given the sheriff. Weighing the consequences of lying, he went half-truth. "We hooked up. But I swear to God, man, she said she was old enough, and it was *definitely* consensual!"

"When you say you hooked up … does that mean you had sex?"

"Yes."

"The three of you had sex?"

"Yes, but it was one hundred percent *con-sens-ual.*" He lengthened the word, emphasizing its meaning.

"And what happened next, Mr. Anoki?"

He sat back in his chair and looked skyward, thinking of the order of events. "She left. By the way, the only reason I haven't asked for a lawyer is I got nothing to hide." He opened his hands, palms toward the sheriff. "Yelena can back me up on that. We just had … a *consensually* good time. Then she left."

"How did she leave? Did she get a ride?"

"Maybe hitched? I don't know. She walked out and that was it." He felt satisfaction in his testimony. "So, I did nothing wrong, and if I'm not mistaken, this is where I get to leave now."

"How about Michelle Holmes?" He held up a photo.

"Yeah. We knew her. Partied with her a few times. Real nice lady. Pretty."

"Do you know she is also deceased?"

"Yes." His throat tightened. "But I swear to God, man. I had nothing to do with no one's murder. Swear … to … God!"

The sheriff grilled him about his encounters with Michelle, similar to Lilith's. Yet, Yelena's liking for Michelle resulted in more discussion about their meetings.

He watched the sheriff finish his notes. "'Bout time," he grumbled.

But when the lawman flipped the page to another sheet already filled with scribbled text, he flinched at the possibility. "You gotta be kidding me."

"Mr. Anoki, were you in Boulder Creek on the night of January 30th?" He peered at him, dogged and unmoving.

"We've been here a few months."

"Did you come into contact with Pat Hilgard at the hardware store on January 30th, and inquire about drugs?"

The sheriff had led him down an uncomfortable path, prompting him to lean back to create space.

"And did you, thereafter, go with your accomplice and linger around his house?"

He scoffed and rolled his eyes. "We aren't stalking anybody! I asked some dude who *looked* cool if he knew where I could score some 'shrooms. All he had to do was say no and we would've left. But he pulled a total dick move and knocked me down. I was the victim in that case!" Feeling as uneasy as a small field mouse catching glimpses of patrolling wings, he felt a flush of heat wash through him.

"Mr. Anoki, we got a report that you asked for a wallet after the drug inquiry and insinuated harm upon the female at the scene. Then, sometime later, you loitered outside Mr. Hilgard's home. In the morning, he found someone had vandalized his car. Does any of this ring a bell to you?"

"No, no, there was no vandalism! And the other stuff was just a joke. I swear. Jesus! It looks like I *do* need a lawyer here?"

The door opened. Another stoic officer entered and stood silently at attention while the sheriff finished his interrogation.

"That's all my questions, Mr. Anoki. You are welcome to leave."

He stood up, ready to bolt. "Thank God! I'm clean, folks. Don't know why all the shakedown."

"We just had a couple of questions. You can hire an attorney if you feel it's necessary. I need to know how I can reach you though. Do you have a cell phone or an address other than Jay's Timberlane?"

He begrudgingly gave the law his cell number, then got the hell out of the building.

"Jesus!" he said, shaking off the tension as he strode for freedom through the parking lot.

Meeting at their car, fresh from their individual interviews, they both felt like they had been through the ringer. A silent sulking filled the car as Yelena drove them back toward the Timberlane.

A short distance down the road, he rehashed his experiences with the authorities. "We gotta be more careful. This has gotten way out of hand! We don't need cops on us, and here they are! What's with these small towns where everyone knows goddamn everybody?" He glared over at her. "Michelle was *your* pick. We both knew she … and Lilith, were probably underage."

Yelena quietly nodded her head.

"And forget about the two at the diner!" Even though he favored the strawberry blonde who he had seen around more often—the crystal shop and cliffs—the small town and its inhabitants were turning out to be big trouble. He also remembered his beat-down at the hardware store with the brunette's guardian. "Plus, I don't want another ass-whooping from wannabe Chuck Norris!"

Yelena kept her eyes on the road enduring his ranting. But seldom did he explode like this, so she could just deal with it. Nevertheless, he lowered his voice to a reasonable volume. "What did they ask you, and what did you say?"

"I said we met Lilith and were worried about her being downtown by herself so wasted, and she stayed the night with us and left the next morning."

"Did you tell them we sexed up?"

"No."

"Did they ask you?" He felt an indignance rising again.

"Yes."

"Then you denied it?"

"Kinda. I just said we hung out and smoked. I didn't tell them we had sex."

"Well, that's fuckin' great, cause I did. And now, one of us looks like a liar! What about Michelle? Did they ask you about her?"

"Yes."

He waited for the story, and none came. "Well, what the fuck did you say?"

"I told them we partied with her. That I had set her up at The Lily and that's about it," she said, becoming defensive. Then, snuffing her sheepishness, she took her stand against his scolding. "Because that's the truth, Jaxon!"

"Listen, we have to get our shit together and our stories straight. I don't know why these chicks keep getting murdered after we meet them, but … frickin-a!" He pounded on the dashboard. It was Yelena who had the voracious appetite for sexually active young women, and she also enjoyed the search to find them.

"So, are we in trouble because they think we killed them?" she asked.

He shot a glare over to her, irate from the incredulous question.

.   .   .

Jay's Timberlane operated as a rustic establishment in Ben Lomond, just a few miles down the winding highway from Boulder Creek. It held the perfect setup for Yelena and Jaxon in between permanent housing prospects. Its décor reminded them of an earlier time—knotted-pine walls, avocado-green shag carpet, and sheer, pink floral curtains that covered a putty-colored blackout shade.

Beyond the aged textiles, they had the basics covered. The kitchen had a two-burner stove that could serve up buttered-crisp grilled cheese sandwiches. The shower ran warm water, and they could watch television on a forty-two-inch screen, though they rarely did.

With the local law enforcement keeping tabs, the two agreed to keep a low profile. But ever anxious, Jaxon could not stay grounded for long.

"Where ya goin'?" Yelena asked coyly as he emerged from the bathroom, freshly showered.

"I'm gonna run to town. Big town, not these crackerjack-box villages with all the heat. Explore a little more. Get some weed. Maybe something else." He accompanied his insinuation with a raised eyebrow.

"Remember, Lilith was from the *big town*. Why don't you just stay here with me?" she asked, patting his empty side of the bed, "and we'll go out together later?"

He held his hand up for all the talk to cease. "Wait … do you hear that?"

She intently listened and noted only the slightest hint of a radio.

"That's one of my tunes." He belted out a few lyrics from a Johnny Cash classic, full of elemental reference, while he swayed, wet hair freely swinging.

"Mmmm," she hummed, closing her eyes with a dreamy swoon. The corners of her mouth drew up into a sensual smile. "I love when you do that."

He knew it. She found great amusement in his love of old country hits, especially when he would sing and dance with her long after the music had ended.

Yelena rolled on to her stomach, exposing a voluptuous mountain of a behind, and purred out an audible sigh to capture his attention. She glanced over her shoulder at him. "Let's have fun before you go."

He ogled his favorite sight. Her alabaster skin showed a drastic contrast to her blackened, magenta hair. Even more splendid was the artwork that spanned the width of her solid feminine shoulders. A composition of brightly colored moon phases, a dazzling ombre-gold pentacle overlapping the three, and a scripted *Blessed Be* beneath it. Spanning the entire design, were ivy vines cascading to a tapered point, mid-back.

He could never pass up this offer, and pounced down upon her.

. . .

Outside their room, an unsupervised and barefoot lass traipsed around singing to herself. Capturing the sight of a ladybug on the weird couple's window, she came over to study the little red and black-dotted insect. Carefully plucking it from the glass, she heard noises coming from inside the room. She tried to peek through a small sliver of darkness beside the shade.

"Sarah!" her mother hollered from their room, six doors down. She waved her away from the couple's door.

The strange sounds coming from within the room would remain a mystery. She returned to her original aim while her ladybug took flight. She looked back at her own room and saw her mother's irresponsible half-eye on her while she walked over to the parking area. There, her mom's gray Prius had sat dusty and unused for weeks. She peered into the locked car and wished for her worn stuffed rabbit laying on the seat.

"Mom," she called out, hoping she could retrieve it. Looking back, she noticed her mother had disappeared into their room. No use asking again, she had been ordered to go play and her mother did not like repeating herself.

When she saw nothing else of interest, she turned her sight to the giant blue car parked next to their own. She skirted around to the back of it, and sounded out the words on its trunk, using her finger to break out the syllables.

"Cut … lass … su … per … reem. Cutlass … Supreme.

CHAPTER 25
TOO MANY CREEPS

"Thank you so much, Mr. Nguyen," Vivi said, as they exited their personal chariot ride in Tiffani's dad's luxurious pearl-white Tesla. He had offered his chauffeur services to ease the possibility of tardiness from the transit ride, and, as of late, avoid the additional worry of a serial killer.

Tiffani mumbled goodbye to her dad and shut the door.

The two coeds stepped onto the curb and started their walk across campus.

"Tiffani, what's going on? Your dad keeps trying to relate to you, and you're so cold to him." With no immediate answer, Vivi added, "Actually, you seem *really* quiet today. Are you okay?"

"He only talks to me when I ignore him."

"Oh, come on. Don't say that. He tries to talk to you every time I've been in the car."

"He mainly talks to you and throws me the occasional questioning look."

"Why don't you thank him for the ride to school?"

"He'd be surprised if I thanked him," Tiffani said. "Plus, it's on his way, so there's no inconvenience factor."

"How about tonight, when we get in the car, you make an effort?"

How about Vivi keep her advice to herself.

"Hello?"

Tiffani kept quiet and stared at the ground as they walked.

"And silence for me now? Okay, when you're ready, let me know."

On they walked along meandering paths, complete with manicured emerald lawns and gray-trunk trees bursting with buds resembling lime green popcorn balls. The glass structures mirrored the bright spring-time sunlight, while the cool breeze served as a reminder that summer remained distant.

With classes still in session, they arrived at Innovation Plaza, and took a seat on a comfortable bench that the sunlight had warmed. She enjoyed the sensation of the heat radiating into her lower back and chilled butt. For a moment, her concerns settled.

"Remember, I have my Psych study group tonight. What time is your dad here?" Vivi asked.

"Let's just meet at 7:30p.m. He should be here by that time, and if not, we can chat with each other before the silent ride home."

"Tiff."

"I'm just kidding. I guess I could tell him about my day."

"Yes, that sounds good." Vivi changed the subject. "So, what's going on? Why *are* you so quiet?"

She sighed. "I'm not sure if it's a big deal or not, but it's bothering me."

"Okay?"

"Early last month at the cliffs, this loser guy in all his leathers asked Hailee where to get some pot. I swear, I hate hanging around her ... it's the attention that she attracts."

"Okay, and?"

"Well, now that there's rumor of a serial killer, I am wondering if they saw the parking pass on her car. Because yesterday, I saw an old blue beater cruising the lot. It seemed out of place and gave me a really bad vibe. "

"Was it the same car?"

"We never actually saw their car. The leather guy was at the bathrooms by the lighthouse, and, later, when we saw the two of them together they were standing by Hailee's car."

Vivi twisted her lips, about to ask another question.

"I know I have a tendency to obsess, but the first one actually tried to block us from leaving the lighthouse bathrooms. Hailee thought it was funny but …" She paused, remembering her discomfort. "I didn't."

"Okay. Why haven't you told me all of this?"

"Like I said, I didn't think it was a huge deal. But the car yesterday triggered me. Also, when we were on the beach and saw them by her car, they were waving to us, like…" her voice turned to mockery, *"Hey there … here we are. We see you."*

"Seriously? Same guy from the bathrooms?"

"Same guy, plus the new one. Anyway, we went and told a worker about it, and he accompanied us to the car in his little cart. But by the time we got there, they were gone."

"Wow, that's messed up. But you're saying it all happened about a month ago?"

"Yes, over a month now."

"A lot of time has passed, Tiff. You sure the car yesterday was something to worry about? Was he checking you out or something? If it was an old guy, it could've been someone's dad, lost or something."

"I don't know … but what if they saw the parking permit and now they're stalking us?"

"No wonder you're distracted. You're ridiculously scaring yourself with all of this. Have you talked with Hailee about it?" She paused briefly. "Honestly, I'd probably be freaked out, too. Just let campus security know. They eat this stuff up."

A ping begged Vivi's attention, and she grabbed her cell to check her text. She quickly tapping out her response, then looked up again. "Okay, I've got to meet David before class. Luckily, he's close to the lab, but he needs to borrow my calculator." She situated her belongings, ready to leave. "Tell me you'll let security know. I can go with you, but it'll have to be later."

Vivi began walking backward, keeping eye contact, while getting further and further away. "Promise me, Tiff."

"Okay." Her confirmation held a non-committal mood, but Vivi seemed pleased enough, and hustled off to lab.

"By-eeee," she mocked, hurt by the abrupt departure during a vulnerable moment. "Yeah, no worries. You go ahead. I'll just walk to the other side of campus by myself."

She sighed, stood up and began her walk over to the next quad, passing through one of the smaller lots. Quiet and empty, there were only sporadic signs of the student body. This one darting to her car. That one disappearing around the corner. Taking a deep breath, she looked up to the expansive, clear heavens and decided that maybe Vivi was right. She should stop scaring herself. When she brought her eyes back to her path, she noticed the same large blue sedan pulling into the lot.

No way! She shrunk into the unease. The aged auto stood out amidst an army of eco-cars, Elantras and Civics.

It stopped a short distance before her, and she could see the stilled silhouette of the driver in his seat, looking in her direction.

She tightened her grip on her books and walked a little faster toward the next complex.

The car picked up speed, but pulled down the next row, heading in the opposite direction.

Whew!

But the relief became short-lived. Within moments, she heard the same whine of the car's engine coming up from behind her. A lump swelled in her throat.

The driver's voice beckoned from within the cab. "Hey, can you help me with directions?"

Her heart raced. Too many creeps lately, and one of them is a serial killer. *Please do not let this be him!*

She broke into an awkward, book-laden jog, praying for the bell to ring for a release of students and eyewitnesses. The upcoming quad offered safety if she could just get to its left turn.

Quickly, the car lunged ahead of her. The stranger's door flung open wide.

She dropped her books and ran faster. But wondering how close he was, she looked back. He reached out and grabbed onto her. In a second, he constricted her within his arms. The beast's brutish squeeze crushed her scream, and even her smallest breath. He wedged his inner elbow against her petite throat, locked her neck upward, and tugged her toward his car.

As she stared at the above blue heavens, her fading cognition no longer grasped their meaning.

CHAPTER 26
THE MOMENT'S AFTERGLOW

Arista counted down the minutes for her first solo visit with Shane since the snake incident. The painful infection from the bite had cleared. Finally, the two of them could catch up on events from the previous weeks.

She heard his arrival in the driveway.

Showtime!

She scurried around the kitchen with last-minute tidying.

After the sound of his knock, joy and relief bubbled over as she greeted him at the door.

Her happiness replicated itself on his face.

"Shane!" She practically flew into his arms, squeezing him so tightly.

He smiled and flinched, simultaneously, holding his healing hand up and away from the embrace.

"Oooh. I'm so sorry. Come in!"

They moved into her den and took a seat on the small loveseat, prompting an already alarmed Royal to retreat to the bedroom.

"How are you? How's your hand?"

"It's good. The chronic pain is finally gone." His bared hand revealed two innocent-looking red dots.

"Seriously?"

"Yeah, who could believe these little spots brought so much agony?"

"Oh, that must've been so painful. I'm so glad you're better!"

"You know, Riss, I gotta tell you … I've hugged you a dozen times over the years. Sad times like when our pets have died, celebration of football victories, and that time you got all sensitive over my remark on your purple hair." He laughed, reached over, and took her hand. "And I know our little jaunt to the cliffs took a disappointing turn …"

She nodded in agreement and grimaced, remembering all too well.

"But since you came to visit me, when I was all miserable in my room, I can't stop thinking about you."

She lunged at him with an enormous hug and nuzzled in for their first-ever passionate kiss. The energy held an intense connection that made her head spin.

She fell back into her place and they both sat enthralled in the moment's afterglow.

"That was nice." He looked at peace.

She giggled. "So, is Kenny going to be okay?" She visualized Kenny's wry expression, a trait she now missed.

"So, his mom told mine that he had two bites, so a lot of venom." He motioned at his own body as a guide. "One hit to the foot, followed by a strong hit to the wrist, and that's what attacked his bloodstream. Add to that, an extensive subdural hematoma from his head injury on the backstop. They think he may have laid there for a while before I even saw him."

"Oh no! Is he awake yet?"

"Yes, but he's very weak, and they're fighting another infection." Shane reverently lowered his head.

She mirrored the gesture but followed it up with encouragement. "Well, he has many prayers going his way."

He perked up with her statement and changed the subject. "So, what's been going on with you?" Relaxing his posture, he turned his body toward her and sat back for a good listen.

"Hah! A whole heck of a lot. Of course, you know me. Lots of crystal stuff, and I asked Analina if she'd do Ouija with me, but she actually tried to contact the goddess, Hel … and I wouldn't even try to do that … but she said, no. So, I'm *still* looking for that fourth participant since

Maddie had to leave town and Auntie will be back soon to hold the ceremony." She grinned at him, hoping he would bite, but caught herself. "Sorry, it was just a thought." She shrugged her shoulders.

"It's okay, Riss. I'm getting used to it. I love you just the way you are." He raised his chin as he smiled, before lowering it and reminding her, "but seriously, no Ouija."

She chuckled in relief. "Got it."

Smiling, he reached down to briefly hold her hand, then returned his arm to the upper cushion.

She paused. *Wait a minute, did he just say he loves me?* Shane had just said that he loved her, right? She regained her thought process and continued.

"Well, in a nutshell ..." She took in a deep breath and spewed forth a flurry of friendly gossip, including a watered-down version of Evan's shenanigans in magick. She didn't want to spoil their friendship with the true details, so the gist of it held sufficient.

Finally, she got to the grand finale of her spiel. "And Evan thought the murders happened because of him ... 'cause who knew that he had such dark moments in his me-time? He also tried to do the Ouija with me, and—"

"Wait a minute, Evan tried to do Ouija with you?"

"Well, a little try, but supremely disorganized. I've got to get the planchette from Auntie."

"That Ouija? The big, ominous Ouija table over there?" He pointed toward the cumbersome kitchen table with his eyes hosting an incredulous expression.

"Yes, just a few days ago. It worked, but I lacked the know-how to make it ... you know ... do its thing. Plus, we didn't have it's real planchette."

"You and Evan?" Shane looked flabbergasted. "What the heck has been going on while I'm staring at my crystal all day?"

She laughed. "I know, it sounds crazy, huh?"

He sat upright. "A bit, yeah! I'm just scratching my head that Evan, of all people, would do Ouija."

She realized she had hit a nerve. "Why so surprised?"

"Come on, Riss. Evan is the most Catholic guy I … *we* … know, and you're telling me right here … right now … that he's sitting in salt circles *and* did that Ouija board with you?"

The stark reaction on his face looked funny. Maybe even a little jealous. What a good momentum, and it excited her how easily he inquired about formerly forbidden topics. She had to ask one last time. "You want to try it? I finally had my four participants, but like I mentioned, Maddie had to go out of town because her poor grandma passed."

"Why is this so important to you?" he asked, cocking his head.

She felt the interest and latched on to the slightest chance. "Because, according to Auntie, the board has a rich history of helping identify serial killers."

"Does it really?"

She stood up and led him over to the rustic relic.

"Seriously, it does." She pointed to the dates. "My grandfather informed the police about his session's information in the 70s. All valid!" She looked up at him. "And wouldn't it be the most wondrous thing to bring justice for Michelle and Lilith while keeping the rest of our community safe?"

He eyed the board.

"Well, you want to try it with us?"

"Hmph. Maybe so."

CHAPTER 27
NO CHIRPY EXCUSES

Only days after Shane's half-commitment to a Ouija session, Arista had other rituals to consider. Since Auntie would return the following day, in time for a New Moon-scheduled Ouija session, the Dark Moon would need to suffice as far as her planning her own intentions. Hopefully, Mother Moon understood her predicament with timing.

With the afternoon still abundant in light, she introduced her plans to Royal.

"An aromatic cup of brewed chamomile and scraped vanilla bean tea and sliced, garden strawberries. Yummy! Look how plump and robust-o red they are."

Her disinterested feline sat perched on the kitchen windowsill.

"Hey!" She tapped the tip of his long, black tail.

Royal glanced at her but held more interest for the ruddy squirrel with its bouffant tail romping through their yard.

While filling Royal in on all the details, she slid forth a dark purple candle. "In case you forget, the Dark Moon is one-to-two percent visible. And since Shane will be here tonight, we're going to get start now—daylight. Weird, right?" In reality, it really did not matter since the moon held the same phase, whether the sky shined light or brooded dark.

She lit the candle and focused on its soft scent of heliotrope for relaxation. Then she reached for the young chlorophytum she had picked up at the nursery that morning.

"Like my baby spider plant?"

With the squirrel gone, Royal stepped from the sill to investigate the tender addition to his space.

When she returned from fetching a pen and paper at the far kitchen drawer, she found him chomping on a taper-ended leaf of her new perennial.

"Noooo." She gently tapped his jet-black nose.

But he remained quite interested in the new flora. The fascinated feline again stretched his neck out and chomped down on a tasty tendril.

"Hey!" she said, firmer this time. She snapped her fingers in his direction, "I said, no."

Royal's neck sank back into his shoulders, and he froze, staring at her.

She crankily turned her focus back to her paper and peered out of the corner of her eye, waiting for more mischief. Though it did not come, she swooped him into her arms, eliciting a quaint protest in mew-form. She put him to the ground, and watched him sashay just out of reach, where he sat down, and began his cleaning session.

"That insults me, Royal." Her thoughts turned to other matters. "I have to admit, I'm a little sad for Maddie right now. I wanted her to be part of our Ouija team. Hopefully, I can count on Shane." Her attitude lightened. "But he seemed pretty committed … and he hasn't called to cancel yet."

Mew.

"Anyway …" Coming back to her ritual, she lifted her pen. But instead of a thought, she met with the most concerning of distractions. It had been a while, but now she recognized the oncoming sweep of the vision.

Before she could set down her pen, her arms collapsed onto the counter. The ominous tattoo faded into sight, and a new urgency consumed her. She could feel herself running, and breathless and so very desperate. Her path from Auntie's house to her own cottage hosted a threatening sky above her, different from its usual rich blue. It glowed in a neon orange sunlight dimmed through noxious gray air. The greatest distress came from her pursuer as he relentlessly closed in on her.

Dingledeedo. Dingledeedo.

Shane's ringtone beckoned her to break free of her anguished trance. She could not, and the frantic pace of running down Hoot Owl Way kept its hold.

Dingledeedo. Dingledeedo.

At last, she crumpled upon her forearms and slowly opened her eyes. Only moments since the initial onset, her exhaustion felt more like an hour's worth of physical exertion.

Realizing she had caught the tail end of his last ring, she knew she could not return the call so quickly. Tiredness and worry chewed at her. The vision had become more exhausting each time. She grimaced as she pondered the scene, still vivid in her mind. The idea of the newly added chase terrified her, and this time she offered no chirpy excuses to keep herself upbeat.

With her heart still pounding, she noticed witch's best friend had been sitting beside her, though now he turned and jumped off the counter.

"Well, thank you for keeping an eye on me. You don't have to leave." She gathered herself and reached for her phone. "I gotta let Auntie know."

She first tapped on the voicemail left by Shane.

'Hey Riss, Bad news. Tiffani's been missing since Monday! Be careful and call me!'

"Oh no! Not Tiff!" She had to reach her learned Auntie, her confidante, her maven, and most revered. As she awaited the connection, thoughts rushed through her head.

The first ring—*Was Auntie still coming back tomorrow morning?*

The second ring—*Please, please let Tiffani be okay!*

The third and final ring had her dreading the usual transition to voicemail.

Auntie answered with a congenial *hello.*

Thankfully, a comforting voice! She lamented to Auntie about the dire news of Tiffani's disappearance, so fearful she would end up like Michelle.

"Settle dear, set-tle." Auntie said with soft assurance. "Fear will not help you, it only clouds your rationale. Choose cautiousness instead. Keep a low profile, stay alert and lock your doors. You have Analina, Shane, and the law, if you need help. My sisters and I will hold a special session for your friend tonight and send forth the energy. I'll let Margaret know as well. Hang tight, and I'm home tomorrow."

Calmed and encouraged by her mentor, and hearing that she would be returning, she decided hashing out the vision could wait a little longer.

CHAPTER 28
ALL ABOARD THE OUIJA

Though the temperate breeze hinted at the warmer summer nights to come, the hovering dark shroud of the New Moon made for an appropriate setting to hold a Ouija session.

Indoors, Arista had transformed her living room into a magickal ambiance for the long-anticipated event. She took an appreciative look at the double strands of purple-and-white miniature bulbs hung in the front window. They twinkled above the séance area and emitted a pleasing, cool glow that further set the mood for the mystical pursuit.

Quickly, she finished readying her house while Auntie took one last trip to the ladies room.

The gravel outside her cottage crunched as Evan and Shane pulled into the driveway, sparking her nerves. Showtime was upon them, and while the thought of this gathering brought excitement, it represented a most awful circumstance. What the town thought of as a rogue criminal who murdered one young woman now exposed itself as a menacing threat. Not only was the killer relentless, but he also chose women of her age and stature, and too many within her own social circle.

Hearing their car doors, she also thought of the other unusual disturbances. How horrible that Shane and Kenny were both bitten by a rattlesnake, and worse, Kenny still struggled to recover from the ordeal. Did this factor into the chaos? And her presence. And the recurring vision. How did these elements play into the entire state of discontent?

Within moments, she let go of the swirling suppositions and greeted her guests. When Auntie assumed leadership over the guys, she confirmed Royal occupied his post and shut him in her bedroom. Then, she went to the kitchen to ready the ceremonial tea and candles for their gathering.

In the living room, the guys disassembled the tabletop, another benefit of its multi-dimensional usage. They placed it on two sturdy cinder blocks atop a large, black velvet coverlet on the floor. Now the Ouija sat high enough from the ground, so that eloquently folded knees could slip easily underneath it.

From the kitchen, she carried her heavy tray of supplies and began setting places, while glancing at the guys' earnest participation to Auntie's further direction. So much support for a worthy cause. Shane had joined despite his hesitation, and temporarily set aside his beliefs in order to help. Evan, having so much guilt, expressed relief for his chance to atone. Their presence more than made up for Maddie's absence.

On each side of the table, she placed a lighter, a small stool and a squishy floor pillow for the relief of the participant's derriere. Comfortable recruits ensured uninterrupted proceedings. Next, she furnished an espresso-sized cup of freshly-brewed elderberry tea with hints of nutmeg and chamomile. The scanty amount represented ritual purposes only. Finally, she placed two votive candles—one black and one white—at each setting. Beneath all of them sat a single three-by-three-inch concave tile to catch the inevitable wax drippings.

The Ouija Team stood attentively present and beheld their workspace. All the luxurious special touches would have taken months of her sporadic part-time pay. Luckily, Auntie had an abundance of ritual supplies and loved to share.

She and Auntie buttoned on their finest magick cloaks. She wore black brocade with rich, wine-colored lace accents. Auntie, in black as well, had a deep, plum-purple satin lining within her cloak. Shane and

Evan had come in comfy black sweats, after she had told them black represented protection when dealing with the spirit world. After hearing about Analina's unpleasant experience, she decided the important detail would further safeguard her friends.

"Royal?" Auntie asked.

"In my closed bedroom."

"Okay, I love your furball as much as my own, but I guarantee the minute we start, he'll be right in the middle of everything. In fact, it's a good thing he's not my WallyCat, because he'd be *raowing* the whole time too."

She had heard many stories of Auntie's talkative Snow Bengal living largely at her Sedona refuge.

Auntie led the foursome to the floor and plunked down the previously missing link. "The planchette," she said, with a twinkle in her eye.

"There it is." She tittered, then quieted.

The guys nervously chuckled, also privy to the joke.

Auntie looked at each of them with a pleased expression. "First, I *must* tell you, it is not often that we have each element covered. Evan, you are earth, hence your placement on the north end of this table. Shane, you, being air, will note that you are on the east side. Our lovely Arista is fire, at south … which leaves me at the west side … Scorpio, that I am." She lifted her chin and cocked her head. "Yes! This is quite a favorable arrangement. I have great faith in this session."

She gazed at Auntie with sheer appreciation. She had listened to many lessons a greater portion of her life. Now, she sat here again … this time, with friends … learning something entirely new. It took her back to the innocent days of grade school and prompted a beginner's mind.

Auntie reached for her lighter. "Please take the lighter in front of you and illuminate your candles."

Soon, the room abundantly glowed from luminous little flames. She drew in the magick that dazzled her senses—the sight of warm-lit candles, the aroma of the spiced tea, and the feeling of her soft, warm cloak. But her love for those around her mattered the most.

"Now, set your candles on the small stool behind your pillow. Make sure that it is far enough away to prevent any … chaos."

They reverently followed the directive.

"I want you to take a few deep, cleansing breaths. We inhale for one, two, three, pause … and exhale three, two, one. This is the first breath. The second breath we do counts of six, and the third breath, we aim for a count of ten … that's ten seconds to inhale, a ten-second pause, and a ten-second exhale. Choose what makes you comfortable. But, deep … make it deep."

The group began their ritual breathing.

"Remember, your breath fills the stomach first, followed by your chest rising, and the shoulders rise last." Auntie tapped upon her body to associate the word to the area. "Breath activates spirit, so this is fundamental to a successful start."

They synchronized for three full cycles.

"Okay, my dears. So, we begin." Auntie's demeanor turned serious, and her voice grew more firm. "Take your tea in your hands." She lifted her cup toward the center.

They duplicated her action.

Firmly and audibly, she incanted.

Offered to the night, we shed all fear,
To reach you, and heed you, our intention we hold dear.
Bring it to the light, as you see it best,
For with clear mind, wide open, the answer manifest.
So may this be.

The group echoed the last line.

Next, everyone brought the tea to their lips in a reverent gesture and inhaled in the aroma of the scented steam. When Auntie took a sip, they mimicked her, tasting the pleasant witchy elixir. Then, each placed their cup down to the side of their black candle.

"Going forward, keep your breath slow and focused. Stay in the flow of what happens. Put your mind at ease that whatever transpires won't hurt you … though it could be frightening … depending upon the energy of the spirit. Do, you, understand?" Her choppy words came out in more of a command than a question.

The three apprentices murmured in accord and continued their focus on breath.

"Fingertips," Auntie announced.

The foursome put their hands forward, to lightly touched the authentic wooden planchette with its centered eye of glass.

"Spirit, we call on you tonight for your help. We call on you for insight and ask that you communicate with us in the ways of your past, through a medium that only you can navigate. We ask your help in discovering the evil behind the death of beautiful young women in our community. Spirit, we implore you. Are you with us?"

Without hesitation, the planchette began an efficient journey of truth. Lightly it scuffled to arrive on *Yes*.

Shane became nervous, biting his inner cheek as he watched the little plank move. But with the session delving deeper, it was important to stay focused, and she would not look his way again.

"Spirit, we seek to find the person responsible. Please allow us the initials."

Evan shifted on his pillow as Auntie made her inquiry, but he stopped as the planchette began its route.

It scuffle-scuffled to the letter *J*, paused, and followed the action with another scuffled-scuffle to the letter *A*.

Auntie had always mentioned one set of initials, so she watched a look of surprise cross her face when the planchette continued its travel on to the letter *Y*. It finally stopped after one more route to the letter *S*. Now it sat, as if idling at a traffic light.

She looked at Auntie. *Could there be two killers?*

"Thank you, Spirit. Are there two people committing these crimes?"

Scuffle. Scuffle. Scuffle.

The planchette disclosed its answer—*No*.

Auntie let out a small huff. "Spirit, we seek the date associated with this person. Please allow us the date of birth."

No movement came.

"Spirit—,"

A loud shriek stole the show, as Evan cried out in an inconsolable fit.

The shock of it grabbed everyone's attention, and a growing light rose behind him, flickering more brightly by the second.

He flapped his arms and batted at his head like a lunatic, his hoodie now aflame, the fire growing larger. "Get it off! Aighhh!" he cried out as he haphazardly sprang away, knocking the table off its block.

They dove into action, pushing him to the floor. Each grabbed their pillow and pummeled at his flaming sweatshirt. They battered him over and over, pillows thumping and thrashing to a booming percussion of sound.

Evan's feet kicked, knocking over candles, and spilling tea as he flailed around the area.

Continuously, they thwapped at him.

Finally, with all signs of fire on Evan extinguished, they relaxed to catch their breath.

But now the many embers and lit wicks from toppled candles ignited the floor covering.

The Ouija Team beat at the floor and its once-dazzling velvet coverage. They pounded again and again, snuffing out the embers, down to the last struggling flicker.

Shock and silence filled the room.

She looked around and gasped at the chaotic upheaval. "Oh, My, God!"

The family heirloom sat crooked on only one block. Wedged upward, its aged wood now gouged with fresh scars. The planchette was nowhere to be seen. The pillows suffered burnt patches and the velvet textile beneath them lay rumpled and scorched. Tea spills and bits of ceramic from the chipped and broken espresso cups dotted the canvas. Candles, misplaced holders, and wax spatters covered the entire, once-luxe surface.

Auntie mashed her hands into her cheeks. Her mouth gaped, and the spectacle stupefied her. Speechless, she began mindlessly picking up the remnants of their session.

Looking at Evan, perhaps to verify his state of being, Shane decided to follow his leader, keep his focus on cleaning, and his mouth shut.

"Good grief, Evan!" she exclaimed. This spectacle far overshadowed Ghost's dancing throw blanket atop her and even the prickly stroke up the back of her bare neck.

"I didn't freakin' set myself on fire on purpose, Arista!"

"No, I just mean …" She instantly felt guilty for her outburst. Of course, it wasn't Evan's fault. This fiasco was par for the course of the current happenings, and surely another disaster meant to derail their progress.

"Look, you two, the damage is done," Auntie declared. "We actually got pertinent information. Yes, we got initials! I think that's enough for Sheriff Michaels. I'd say a visit first-thing Monday morning is very appropriate!" She placed her hand on Evan's arm and spoke compassionately. "Evan, dear, we know you didn't do this on purpose."

Evan nodded in understanding to Auntie, then flashed a glare over at her, prompting her to soften. To see him return the forgiving gesture brought instant relief.

Auntie further scanned the damage, then tilted her head with an accepting smile. "We definitely have some cleaning to do. But, with all of us, it should go quickly. Evan, you and Shane take the tabletop back to its base. Arista, dear, the fabrics … my beautiful fabrics," she whimpered. "We'll keep what is salvageable. I'll work on all the breakage and spillage and …" her voice trailed off, clearly deciding it better to get busy.

While the team worked diligently, the new data swirled in her head. Four initials, yet the board indicated only one culprit. "*J, A, Y,* and *S,* right?"

"Yes." Her cohorts answered in sync.

"What if it's not initials at all? What if it's just Jay's?" She posed the question to herself as much as to her team. "Like, Jay's Timberland … in Ben Lomond? Creepy people stay there sometimes."

"Really?" Shane asked. "Our relatives have stayed there a few times while here on vacation. They liked it. I thought it's mostly families."

"Nah, man, there's major sketch who live there for months on end," said Evan.

"Well, it's never given a location before." Auntie pursed her lips. "Not that I know of, anyway."

"Yes, but it usually gives a date, and there was no movement when you asked for one." She glanced at Evan. "Even if we didn't have a commotion, I don't think a date was coming."

"You could be right." Auntie pondered a moment before expressively holding up her hands. "I'd call our session a real success! Yes! This mess is simply a minor inconvenience. Our real trouble … he's out there."

•　　•　　•

With the room restored to pre-chaos state, all signs of an event-gone-awry had faded away. Freed from captivity, Royal cruised the vicinity, sniffing for clues as to what had transpired. The members of the Ouija Team celebrated their overcoming of ambiguous feelings that preceded the ritual, and their united efforts, both on the board and post clean-up, lifted their spirits as they joked with each other. With all tasks completed, Arista followed the guys outside, leaving Auntie to brew fresh tea.

Evan waved as he got into the car, allowing her and Shane a moment of privacy in the darkened yard.

"Thank you so much for being part of this."

"Well, I've got to admit that was pretty intense, and not something I want to do every day."

She looked away. It definitely had not gone as smoothly as she would have liked.

"But ..." Shane drew her attention back to him. "That was crazy! In a good way." His eyes bulged as he let out a solid, "Wow! I gotta say, it got the adrenaline flowing." His thrilled demeanor became serious. "Not every day though ... but, yeah ... maybe we *can* stop this guy."

The couple united in an appreciative squeeze before Shane walked to the car.

She turned back toward her door and caught sight of two familiar orbs glowing from within one of her trees. "I see you there," she softly told the owl, before returning to the warmed interior of her house.

The night was not over. Now, she needed to bring all deferred information into the open. She sat down by Auntie who poured two cups of piping hot, sweet mint tea for them. They took a united sip.

"There's something I've been meaning to tell you, but I keep forgetting or I put it off for some other reason. Anyway, I've been having recurrent visions. Each time adds a little more detail."

Auntie tensed up and set down her mug. "What did you see?"

"Well, first, just a grubby hand and tattoo."

"What's the tattoo?" Auntie asked without delay.

"An upside-down pentagram."

She gasped. "What! What else?"

"Well ... it disappears into an inked slit on the hand."

Auntie clutched her cheeks for the second time that night, then dropped them again for further interrogation. "Were you in it? Does anything happen?"

"I think I'm running. Most recently, it was definitely daylight, but the sky looked weird. What's most concerning is the location. It takes place on our street."

Her face lost color, and she squeezed her eyes shut as if to will away the drama. "No, no, no!"

Now verbalizing it and seeing Auntie's response made it even scarier. But the urge to alleviate Auntie's mounting worry overshadowed her concern. "We'll be careful, though," she sputtered unconvincingly.

"My dear child! That is a *dire* warning for you … from you! We have got to keep you safe. I knew it! I just knew it!" She looked in all directions, as if making sure the threat had not already infiltrated the home. "And that I did not know this … did not detect it … tells me you are surpassing my own abilities to care for you."

She came closer and hugged into her. "Don't worry, Auntie. I know we can work on this together. Everything will be alright. And now we've got the Ouija info, too."

"Is there anything else?"

"Well, usually the vision comes at the same time the presence does. So, they usually happen together."

"Okay, I am thinking the spirit of this house is working with you. I know it's our family. Our ancestors are with us." She paused and shook her head. "Arista, I knew this day would come." She closed her eyes. "I can see it, what you envisioned … the tattoo … the ugly hand … and our street."

"But—"

"One moment," Auntie snapped, clearly still focused inward. She opened her eyes with a stern expression. "I need to know everything, from the very first vision to the very last."

For quite a spell, they sat, and she recounted each episode—the before, the after and a full description. Deeper into the night, Auntie stayed transfixed on her intrusive encounters, and the nerve-tingling experiences within the walls of her cozy cottage. The wise teacher became the enthralled student.

"And that's it," she announced, capping off the information. "I haven't felt unsafe, but it is scary. I realize the vision is a warning, so I've been more aware of my surroundings."

"I have a good mind to lock you in my own bedroom and not let you out of my sight. And I'm only half-kidding."

"But my sweet feline would be so lonely." She looked down at Royal, who peered at them from the very center of where their Ouija session had taken place.

Auntie held up her hands and offered an interim plan. "I won't lock you in my bedroom. You're an adult, and I know Shane has been hanging around more."

She laughed, feeling self-conscious, and wondered how much Auntie knew of their blooming romance.

"You also have Maddie, and Evan … and all your friends, so I will not smother you. But, Arista, please … please heed this warning and be extra careful."

"Of course." She accepted the caring demand with a nod.

"But we are here together now, and we are strong!" Auntie pumped her fist. "So, let's start with a united banishing spell. It cannot hurt. A bit of chanting, too."

After they settled on the floor, maiden and crone readied a few remaining supplies that had survived the earlier melee. While Arista arranged a few crystals, Auntie tinkered with the candles and holders, and even Royal got to join in the magick.

Still, she observed the unusual bewildered behavior of Auntie. While working with spirits, fire and the Underworld never truly stirred her, the knowledge of the visions and the tattoo completely derailed her. As if she knew what it all meant. And it was suspicious that she had always been forthright on all subjects over the years, except for one. Could Auntie's rising anxiety be because of that long-held taboo? Could it be a clue as to why her parents had abandoned her so many years ago?

CHAPTER 29
DISGUISED IN GORE

Cold, bruised, and in the crunch of pain, Tiffani faded into consciousness. The repeated brutal strikes from her captor left her hopeless and broken, and often being knocked unconscious skewed the sense of time. With the blindfold always on, the days blended into nights.

Not only was a violent death surely her fate, but the wretched existence leading up to it fell nothing short of grueling agony. She struggled with the painful sensations nagging at her. The gag in her mouth caused a constant ache in her jaw, while the tight blindfold restricted her circulation and tugged on a single strand of hair. The smallest inconvenience further tormenting her. Mentally, it bound her wits, and physically, it manifested as cuts and raw skin at her temples. Similarly, her wrists were bound to her ankles, and the tightly wound tape gave her little range of motion.

She tried to remember the face of her kidnapper from the initial abduction, but she had been too busy trying to evade him to notice. Now she sat in silence, imagining the beast who kept her captive.

But who he was and what he looked like did not matter. She had long accepted that *he* had caught her. The monster who killed young women and dumped their bodies into the icy river. She felt another sinking feeling wash over her and wept.

Her head dropped in defeat. Despite the crude blindfold absorbing most of her tears, a few found their way through the cracks and caused her face to sting.

From the acoustics of her muffled whimpers, and the smoothness of the cool fiberglass wall where she rested her cheek, she believed her cell was a small bathroom, more specifically, the tub.

She estimated her captivity at about a week now, but there was no way to be sure. Whatever time had lapsed, she could not bear it any longer. She re-situated herself toward the facet and leveraged the eye wrap against the stopper pull. Jerking upward, she slipped the blindfold up to her forehead.

In her otherwise darkened room, she caught a sliver of light from beneath the bathroom door. The blindfold slid back down, its coarseness burning as it blended with salty tears.

Suddenly, she heard movement beyond her darkness. Her muttering tormenter swung open the door. He hastened toward her, his pants swishing.

She knew the violence to come, and her body tensed in dread.

He grabbed a wad of her hair and cranked her head backward, her chin toward the ceiling, and her throat tight.

"Do you want to die?" His voice came at her in a vicious hiss as his lips touched her ear.

She sobbed, and tried to tell her captor *no*, but the gag and her lack of breath stopped her.

"Then shut ... the fuck ... up!" He thrusted her head out of his hand.

She sobbed and wished she could say please or reason with him, but the gag stopped her.

All her rushing thoughts ceased when a hard blow cracked down upon the back of her skull and the silence returned.

. . .

The slamming door startled Tiffani awake. The chill in the air indicated nighttime. Possibly the next night, as her lips had become crusty, and her thirst overwhelming. Had he let the others live this long? Since he had kept her alive this long, maybe he would spare her life.

Outside in the distance, a slow buildup became a wail of oncoming sirens. Her hope grew. Could they had traced her whereabouts?

But the envoy sped past her prison and faded into the distance.

She deflated and considered her predicament. Since she frequently heard traffic, she knew her prison bordered a main road. She just needed to access it.

A sudden inkling of hope filled her. With stillness beyond her room and the slamming door that awakened her, he had probably left. She desperately tried to yell out a plea for help. Or if the menace *was* around, a plea for mercy, or water.

With her bound hands and ankles, she banged against the fiberglass tub, hoping someone could hear her. She waited for confirmation that she existed at all and tried again.

Without a response, she repeated her proven method of slipping off the blindfold. This time, she successfully freed herself from it completely. In the darkness, she hoisted herself over the tub and onto the cold ceramic tile. She inched along the bathroom floor to the door. From the sliver of light that came from underneath it, she could see brilliant lime-green tile meeting a dingy tan shag carpet. The contrast in color offered her a new perspective. Blindness no longer held her captive. If she had to guess, she suspected this passage opened into the living area. Except for times when he left altogether, her kidnapper inhabited the room, belching loudly with the television blaring. Perhaps he held her in a motel room or a studio.

Her adrenaline rushed at the possibility of escape. Encouraged by the freedom from her blindfold, she tried to dislodge her gag in the similar manner by the door stop. The knotted tie proved too challenging. Switching to her tight bindings, she twisted and tried to make some kind of progress in releasing their hold on her. They too endured, impossible to tear apart.

From the parking lot, she recognized the whining engine of his car. So quickly, he had returned. She feared the worst. She frantically seesawed her body across the floor and retreated into the tub with a loud thud.

Excuses ran rampant within her mind. There might be less violence if he saw she did not try to escape. She could say that she was thirsty, or the blindfold hurt so badly, she tried to relieve her pain. After all, she had stayed in the room where he had placed her, proving she knew he was in complete control, right?

The keys jingled, the deadbolt snapped, and she heard the main door open. She held her breath as a long creak punctuated his entrance into the lair. He shut the door and approached, his pants always making that horrible swishing sound.

She hugged into the wall, wishing she had kept the blindfold in place and dreading the consequences.

He opened the door and flipped on the light. She looked into his eyes as they widened in shock. Then, a tremendous rage washed over him.

She squeezed her eyes shut, sobbing, and braced for more violence.

CHAPTER 30
HE ALREADY KNOWS

Bright and early Monday morning, Bethie marched into the sheriff's office with Arista and Evan right behind her.

"We need to speak with Sheriff Michaels, please."

"He's not in the office yet. Would you like to leave him a message?" asked the polished police receptionist.

"When might you be expecting him?"

"Oh! That's him pulling in now," the receptionist said, gesturing out the window with a feisty grin. "Looks like you have pretty good timing."

She led her troops to the sitting area. After all, who enjoys coming into a loitering mob insisting on an impromptu meeting? She spoke in a hushed tone to her cohorts. "There was a short time that I babysat our dear Sheriff Michaels when he was just a boy."

"No way," Evan commented.

"Yes, way," she confirmed, eyes wide, mirroring his expression, and adding a nod. "He was a real sweet boy. His parents were nice too, but I think they were a little leery of my eccentricities. Eventually, I got edged out by Mavis Boynton." Auntie sneered.

Arista giggled at her competitive streak, a hint of her shadow side that she rarely let her see.

Sheriff Michaels walked through the door and bid his coworkers a good morning. He threw a glance toward the Ouija Team, then strolled into the hallway and out of sight.

"Hmph. I don't think he recognized me."

A moment later, she re-approached the receptionist. "This is real important business. How long does it take him to get situated?"

"After his morning pit stop, he should be good to go."

She grumbled her way back to the seat.

A few minutes later, the sheriff emerged from the lavatory, its squeaky hinges echoing down the hallway.

Her eyes darted to Arista then over to the receptionist, who reached for her phone and waited before buzzing his office.

In stereo between the speakerphone and his open door, she heard the entire conversation.

"Yes, Patty," he answered, before eliciting a short groan as his chair creaked under his weight.

"Sheriff Michaels, you have visitors in the lobby."

"Is it the same group that I passed when I first got here?" he asked in an annoyed tone.

"Yes, it is. Sciatica or hip bothering you again?"

"Yes, and yes. And I couldn't get into the chiro this morning. Patty, it's okay for you to tell me I have guests when I walk through the door. I'm good with that."

"I wanted you to get comfortable first."

The sheriff sighed. "Okay. I'll be up there in a minute."

Watching Patty hang up and walk over to a distant file cabinet, she sprang up and walked toward the hallway. Peering down toward the sheriff's office, she watched him grab an over-the-counter pill container from his bottom drawer. He read the label, set it on his desk, then arose.

She darted back over to join Arista and Evan as they waited.

His footsteps preceded his emergence in the lobby. A congenial smile crossed his face when he looked at them.

She launched up off her seat like a pup released from its *Stay* command.

"What can I do for you folks today?"

"Well, Sheriff, we have some very important information bearing on the murder cases of these poor women in our community. We'd like to talk in private, if possible."

The sheriff gave Arista a once-over. Surely, he noticed the similarities.

"Sure, come on back."

When he closed the door, she jumped into her presentation.

"Sheriff, we believe we have a lead on the killer's initials, and possibly their location."

He cocked his head and nodded.

She took out her written note from the Ouija session, and put it on his desk, facing him. "My name is Bethie Spiritbrite. Well, my legal last name is Kelly. But folks around here know me as Bethie Dandelion Spiritbrite." *Surely, he remembers me!*

The sheriff gave a humored, acknowledging smile. "Yes, ma'am. I am familiar with you and your kin. In fact, if I remember correctly, you used to babysit me when I was a young boy."

"Oh yes!" Her voice rang out in delight. "You *do* remember me. Well, isn't that a hoot! Hah!"

"I remember a lot of foliage information. You taught me about our local plant life. I use it even to this day."

She felt enlivened by the recognition and filled with joy, until she noticed Arista staring at her with a glint of amusement in her eye. She returned to the serious matter at hand. "Well, anyway, this here is Arista Kelly. She's my grandniece … the child of my nephew, and has been in my care since she was eight years old."

Arista politely smiled at the sheriff.

"Also here with me is Evan Navarro."

"I'm a local too," Evan said with a quick smile.

"Well, it's real good to meet all of you." The sheriff looked directly at Evan. "Evan, I know your father. Ray Navarro … real nice guy."

"Oh. Cool," Evan said with a sputter, not expecting the acknowledgement.

"Anyway, Sheriff, our source is not a usual avenue, but we believe it gave us this pertinent information."

"Yes, ma'am. What have we got here?" He looked at the small note with her handwriting.

"Well, we have initials. We have a sequence that includes *J, A, Y,* and *S.*"

"Uh-huh. Is this copy for me?" He pointed to the four-by-four-inch pale yellow sticky note.

"Yes."

"Okay. Might there be anything else?"

"Well, we believe it is one, or maybe two persons, responsible."

"Or it could mean the killer is staying at Jay's Timberlane … that place in Ben Lomond," Arista said.

"Yeah, shady characters stay there sometimes," Evan added.

"Noted." The sheriff flipped open his large desk pad and taped her note onto a page. He penned additional information beneath it. "Anything else I need to know?"

The trio looked at each other.

"No, I think that's about it." She assuredly nodded her head and sat back with folded arms.

"Okay. Thank you, Miss Bethie, Dandelion, Spiritbrite." He looked up and smiled. "I know my father knew a Kelly family member or two way back when. A mighty fine, law-abiding family, and I like that."

"Oh yes, Sheriff," she cooed. The sheriff had become such a handsome man. "Anyway, these letters … I hope they help you catch him."

He ventured into the inevitable question. "Can you reveal your source?"

She straightened her posture—her shoulders dropping back and her chest jutting forward. She smacked her lips and spoke matter-of-factly. "Sheriff, you are a long-time resident here in the mountains, are you not?"

"Yes, I am."

"Then you *do* believe in its mysterious ways?" She knew he must have his own stories to tell.

"You know, Ms. Spiritbrite, I have seen an unexplained thing or two in my lifetime. Why do you ask?"

"Well, I would like to ponder whether to disclose my source a while longer. I just wanted to know your thinking about the nature of things."

She stood up, leading Arista and Evan to follow suit.

"I'm thinking that your source is of a ... unique nature," the sheriff confirmed, his eyebrow raised.

She smiled "You might say that."

"Okay, ladies ... and gent. I thank you for coming in today."

Before letting the group leave, he jotted down their contact information on his pad, shut it, and led them to his door.

"Oh, and Sheriff," she turned and lightly touched his arm, "I *do* hope that pain of yours promptly diminishes." She gave a steady squeeze and her voice inflected, "Gone, gone and moving on." She swung around and jetted off before he could fashion an appropriate response.

• • •

The sheriff walked back to his desk, looking forward to an afternoon without interruption. He thought of this random new lead. He suspected Jaxon was up to no good, and he lodged at Jay's. How ironic that his prime suspect and Bethie's first set of initials were *J* and *A*.

"Jaxon Anoki," he said aloud.

Patty's buzz interrupted his thought.

"Sheriff, I have Dr. Kessler on the phone."

"Yep, that's my chiro, ring him through."

He dropped his chin as a moment of illumination hit him.

"Wait a minute." He shuffled through the files on his desk, grabbing the murder case of Lilith Grainger. He flipped it open. "Yelena Summer. *Y* and *S*. You've got to be shittin' me." The deputy interrogated Yelena, and he had not paid close attention to her last name until now.

The chiropractor's call rang through to his desk.

"Jaxon. Yelena. And I know that source. It's that Ouija."

He energized from the notion of puzzle pieces fitting together and grabbed the call of his beckoning chiropractor. But as he heard the friendly greeting of Dr. Kessler, he noticed his sciatic pain was completely gone.

· · ·

The trio hustled to Bethie's car, and she could not wait to hash out the session with her troops.

"So, there you see it. While I'm not ready to share Ouija as our source, I like that Sheriff Michaels is a local. Most locals have their own eerie experiences to share, and he admitted, in his own tough-guy way, he does, too."

"Okay, I was wondering about that. I mean, it was pretty impressive in our mysterious setting to watch the planchette do its thing. But addressing it with the sheriff seemed to fall totally flat," Arista said matter-of-factly.

"Oh, no, dear, not in the least. He has his own stories. I'm sure of it."

"I bet he does," Evan agreed. "The plot thickens."

"Yes, it does. Anyway, I believe our dear sheriff will take the info seriously."

"You sound so sure of that, Auntie. Why?"

"Because Sheriff Michaels' father was the sheriff in charge during the 70s. And *that*, my dear children, is the significance of our Ouija's dates and initials—Hah! His father helped catch a few of the county's most notorious serial killers."

"Damn!" Evan marveled.

"Oh, wait. I think I remember you mentioning a little something about that when you first showed me the table."

She started the engine and continued her story while the car idled.

"In the 70s, they simply knew my friends and I as hippies. That was a good thing, because had they known we were a coven, well … folks weren't as accepting back in those days. Anyway, I was away that whole year in Arizona with my friends, Margaret, and Pearl." She turned to Arista. "You know Margaret …"

Evan interrupted from the backseat. "Is Margaret the one who shuffles around town?"

She whipped around to face him. "Evan … my friend does not *shuffle* around the streets. She is *not* some kind of hobo, for goodness sakes."

Arista flashed a wry look back at Evan, who shrunk down in the backseat. "His mom has a thing about Margaret."

"Um, you are good witches, right?" he asked, hesitantly reminding them, and squirming before two sets of piercing eyes. "Because, I'm just saying … it looks a little wicked right now."

She looked at Arista, then back at him, and released an exaggerated cackle. Arista contributed her own genuine chuckle.

Evan looked at them with uncertainty.

"Oh, I'm just kidding with you, Evan. Anyway, a couple of my coven members, including my brother had taken their Ouija findings to the elder Sheriff Michaels each time they came available. He did not deem the tip noteworthy, because Declan was very honest about the Ouija being his source. However, after they caught the killer, the elder Sheriff Michaels compared the information and found all the details valid. Hah!"

"Okay, well, good. Because as we sat there giving him nothing but a few initials … it felt anemic," Arista admitted. "But hopefully, his dad told him about all that."

Evan nodded vigorously. "Yes, I felt that anemic-ness, too."

She eyed him in the rearview mirror.

"But I believe it! I do. The whole thing," Evan said with his most convincing expression.

"This sheriff is a good man. I have a real good feeling that he is going to take us seriously. But it must unfold as it will. Today was not the right time to talk Ouija magick with the law. He will realize the importance in his own time."

"You know what, Auntie? I think he knew we were going to say something like that. You could see it on his face. He already knows."

CHAPTER 31
AN AWFUL NIGHT'S SLEEP

Sheriff Michaels endured the awful night's sleep. Tossing left, he felt stifled by his own covers. Tossing right, the streetlamp glare shined too brightly. Switching to his back, his legs cramped. He opened his eyes, realized his failed attempt at sleep, and stared at the ceiling.

To have the town's chaos play in his head like a movie at this hour created more angst. An endless loop of the stark recollections of young women dead before him, the murderer still on the loose, and his county full of frightened citizens. He had no control over it. Could he find Tiffani before it was too late? And word had it, the problems branched further than just his county. How many more would there be?

"J, A, Y and S," he said aloud, trying to drown out his morbid thoughts and unanswered questions.

The new kidnapping victim did not fit the murderer's usual demographic. She attended a reputable college, had been reported missing the day it happened and did not lead the life of a wayward young woman. Authorities also believed that she had disappeared from campus, not inconspicuously in the late hours. However, he had learned two things from research. One, when serial killers get comfortable, they can branch out into fresh territory. And two, sometimes they just want to get caught. Either way, the murders would continue until they found him.

"Well, shit!"

He flung his covers in frustration and bolted out of bed like go-time at an army barracks. He checked the clock—three a.m. Frustrated, he lumbered to the fridge to grab a packet of squeeze applesauce, since he knew his late-night anxiety usually led to hunger.

Seated at the table, he envisioned the perkiness and quirk of his former babysitter and her minions from earlier in the day. A certain charm came from the earnestness of their faces and the seriousness they gave their tip. Their faith in the provided initials brought forth a memory from his childhood.

He could still picture his own father that memorable night in February 1973. He made the jubilant announcement to little Pete's mother at the kitchen table as he burst through the door from work.

"We caught that son-of-a-bitch, Mira, and wouldn't you know, those crazy hippies and their goddamn Ouija board were one hundred percent correct! We didn't take them seriously, but they nailed it!"

Despite the late hour, he had heard his father's commotion, jumped out of bed, and listened to the exuberant announcement from upstairs.

Now alone in the stillness of his kitchen, he fondly recalled a young Bethie Kelly. In her twenties, she represented the lighter side of life. Playful, bubbly, and always smiling, she was a beauty to behold with long strawberry-blond hair. Regularly, she blended her melodic singing with Margaret Troxel's tambourine. Together, they harmonized while freely celebrating their bohemian lifestyle in the park.

Now, decades later, an awakening washed over him as he slurped his last bit of applesauce. He could not ignore the wisdom of the Ouija. Not when his father, a grounded man of the law, gave it merit.

As mentioned to Bethie, he had his own stories of bewitching *aha* moments after a lifetime of mountain-living. The centuries-old church bells rang late at night with no one around. Lights flickered and doors closed with no sign of a breeze at the Brookdale Hotel. And, heard mostly from drunkards and deranged vagrants endured the story of a shapeshifter who transformed into an animal at will.

He sat back in his chair. With his movie and incessant questions now subdued by reason and fructose, he decided he might need to have another talk with Miss Spiritbrite. He also needed to check on that pending search warrant for Jaxon Anoki.

CHAPTER 32
AN ILLUMINATED BEAM OF SPRINGTIME

Sheriff Michaels' voice rumbled through the radio. "Make contact. On my way, over and out."

The commotion outside her cell awakened Tiffani. She heard the police radios closer than ever. This very second she had to act. Despite having a severely bruised head from almost two weeks of abuse, she used it against the fiberglass wall.

BANG! BANG. BANG.

To attempt a scream served no use as her gag resisted, causing her to become light-headed. The exertion also took what little remaining energy she had after weeks of saltines and water. She let the dizziness pass and pounded again.

BANG! BANG. BANG.

She did not care if her captor came to deliver another brutal strike or even the final, fatal blow. The possibility of rescue lay before her, and she thrust herself over the tub. Used to the routine, she slipped her blindfold and flipped around, situating her feet on the door. Then, she pounded her heels as hard as she could.

•　•　•

The early morning knocking on their cabin door startled Jaxon. He pried himself from Yelena's clutches and stuffed himself into his briefs before walking toward the rude intrusion. On the way, he bellowed at the nuisance, "Hang on!"

The moment he opened the door, the deputy began his arrest script. However, the onset of a loud knocking interrupted him, causing him to stop and listen.

"I got 'em," the fellow officer assured seeing the deputy's distraction.

"Don't try anything foolish, Mr. Anoki," the deputy said in a threatening voice, before warning Yelena, now sitting upright. "And you stay right there!"

Yelena nodded.

"That knocking isn't from in here," he said defensively.

The deputy ignored him and stalked over to their bathroom door.

"I said—" The deputy's partner firmly shoved his face up against the wall, stifling his comment.

"Save it," the officer said as he cuffed him.

The lawman addressed him from across the room, "Mr. Anoki, what's in this bathroom?"

"A big mess." He snorted as he watched the deputy turn the knob.

Upon opening the door, he switched on the light and beheld an unpleasant scene, a windowless eyesore of dingy caulk and green tile. Their self-care products littered the tub and sink, some empty bottles, and some half-filled. Dirty, odoriferous clothes cluttered the floor, accompanied by wet towels and worn shoes. They had tried to control the smell with an ocean-breeze air freshener. But really, it only blended into a tainted scent of repulsion.

"Like I said," he snarked.

The banging resumed with less intensity.

"It's gotta be the next room over." The deputy motioned for his partner to watch them both. He flashed a quick glare over to Yelena, still hugging the covers against her unexposed nakedness. As he hustled out of the room, a stern warning, "Not a move, Mr. Anoki!"

"They're not going anywhere," the deputy's partner declared.

. . .

KNOCK! KNOCK!

"Hello, County Sheriff's Office!"

She could hear the officer's voice thundering outside and gathered her energy to kick. But faintness quickly overcame her, and her legs slid down the door, back to the ground.

"County Sheriff! We'd like to have a word with you!"

Why couldn't they hear her? She hoisted her legs upon the door and drummed her feet loudly and rapidly. The thought of missing her chance horrified her. Using all her strength, she rallied her effort and drummed even harder. With more intention she kicked and kicked to the sharpest point of a building rage. How could they not hear this?!

Her legs collapsed to the floor in sheer exhaustion. With her heart racing from the exertion, she recovered her breath, and began again, a fit of anger fueling her last-ditch effort at freedom. *Please, please, please don't leave me!*

But the booming voice had gone silent.

She heaved for oxygen. She could barely lift her spent and bruised legs. While she still heard muffled voices, they were no longer at her door. With her chance of rescue drifting away, she heavily sobbed and kicked again.

. . .

"Mr. Anoki, do you know who rents the cabin next to you?" the deputy impatiently asked.

"We don't know him that much. We hung out a few times when we first got here, but he started getting way too weird toward my girl." He motioned to Yelena. "So, I told the freak to stop tailing us or I was going to bust his ass. He followed us everywhere! Then—"

The deputy stormed out, leaving him mid-sentence. He looked to his sleep-worn beauty shielded by their covers, prompting Yelena to bless the tension-filled room with a nervous titter.

.　　.　　.

Sheriff Michaels approached Jay's Timberlane and noticed what appeared to be a sizeable bird perched atop the sign. As he got closer, the great-horned owl became clearer, and he felt a grand discovery unfolding before him. Amusing to consider the tip when its written down on paper, but impossible to deny when presented as large, bold-yellow letters—*J, A, Y,* and *S*—on the lodge's sign.

Kkkkksssshhhhh!

He skid to a stop within the lot, sending a charged dust storm through the complex. He jumped out of the cruiser and hustled over to his awaiting men for the debrief.

"Sheriff, I spoke with Mr. Anoki and checked his unit. It's clear. But there was a heavy banging coming from this room … comes on strong, then fades out. And Anoki mentioned something about this tenant stalking them. I think we should get in there but wanted your input."

"The warrant's for Anoki." The legalities troubled him. "But this is right next door. Have you checked with the management office? Can they get it open?"

"No answer."

"Dammit!"

"It was loud, Sheriff, I seriously think someone's trying to get our attention."

"Well, someone's in trouble, and we need to help. We're going in!"

He took decisive action just as the banging began again.

"Sheriff's Office, we're coming in," he announced and with the help of his deputy, busted through the entryway.

Soulless and vile with a stench of sweat, the room reeked of dread. With nothing catching their attention in the main area, he rushed over to the bathroom door. He could hear rustling on the other side. *It's her!*

He tried opening the door but felt a resistance up against it. He also heard the muffled cries of a woman.

"Sheriff's office, please move away from the door," he said calmly, and waited a moment, before he tried again.

.   .   .

The lifting of her own bodyweight beleaguered her. Moving another inch seemed unbearable. This was too good to be true. It was almost as crushing as the hope for survival that had kept her alive while suffering the violent hits, the crushing kicks, and the degrading verbal abuse.

She could barely breathe from the audacity of rescue, as she weakly pushed herself back toward the tub and collapsed to the floor.

The door opened with the silhouettes of efficient agents, and she watched as the room filled with a brilliant ray of the springtime sunlight, shattering the most barbaric darkness she had ever known.

CHAPTER 33
PRETTY LAIDBACK GUY

"APB on a 1985 blue Cutlass Supreme, driver's name is Henry Maxwell Wallish. Alias Mack Phearson. License plate is …" Sheriff Michaels barked orders into his radio with a renewed enthusiasm. Sure, they got Tiffani, but they could not let this piece of crap get away.

At the front step of his unit, a handcuff-free Jaxon stood with Deputy Hendrickson. They watched as the ambulance rushed Tiffani off to the hospital. Her name, confirmed by her own admission.

"Man! Thank God you guys found her!" Jaxon shook his head in disbelief at the crisis.

He knew it was his nerves and emotional investment in the case, but it grated on him that Jaxon assumed the victim to be Tiffani. In fact, with momentum on Jaxon being the suspect, he still wondered if he had anything to do with the crime. But all details would eventually be known and for now, he checked out clean.

Most importantly, it was nothing short of a grand triumph in finding her. And now he had a lot to do. "The suits are arriving soon. Hendrickson, get this place taped up. Hopefully, we find this dirtbag before he leaves town?" He turned to Jaxon. "Mr. Anoki, I need to ask you some more questions."

"Sure!"

With Yelena now dressed at the foot of the bed, Jaxon told him all about his felonious acquaintance.

"When we first met him, he was a pretty laid-back guy ... real smart with computers. He gave us a ride a few times when our car was in the shop ... to the city, Big Basin, The Timbermill. It was weird though. Anytime we'd hang out, he'd take off, and finally ... sometimes hours later ... he'd be back."

"Did you ever notice anything suspicious in his car?"

"Nope."

"What else can you tell me about him?"

"Well ... we hadn't hung out for a while 'cause he'd gotten so shady. But one day, I see him at the cliffs, and he was friendly. So, we took a ride and checked out some chicks." Jaxon glinted his eyes. "Ya know, at one point, we were at Natural Bridges, and he insisted on harassing this chick and her boyfriend. I'd seen her around Boulder Creek, so I just wanted to be friendly. But this guy was just doggin' on her ... and the boyfriend was getting all pissed at me, 'cause I'm the one in their face. I'd had enough! He took me to my car, and I just left."

"You're talking West Cliff Drive, Santa Cruz?"

"Yeah. Locals call 'em *The Cliffs*. Anyway, the guy just had no smooth moves. I could tell he didn't truly appreciate the beauty of a woman." Jaxon looked over at Yelena, who blew him an air-kiss. "It's kinda hard to explain. He's just blunt. He'd gross me out if I were a chick."

"What about the banging?"

"First off, it was *nothing* like today. Otherwise, we mind our own business. There's banging coming from our room sometimes. So, we'd hear it, but it always stopped. I thought he was just getting' it on with someone." He released an exasperated huff, shook his head, and looked over to a bored Yelena alternating between intently listening to his story and picking at her nails.

"We'd like you to describe the suspect to a sketch artist."

"Yeah, whatever! Thankfully, I'm on the right side of the law this time."

"Yep," He eyed Jaxon.

"Ya know, the more I think about it, you guys have been harassing me and Yelena while ..." He grimaced toward the ground. "Man! Did he really kill the others, too? Michelle and Lilith?"

"We don't know yet, Mr. Anoki, but we'll surely look into it."

"Man, that's so messed up! That freak must've taken Lilith the minute she left. No wonder you were on our case so hard."

The more Jaxon talked, the more he appreciated the brief information he had gathered from Tiffani, including the description of her captor, and that he had worked alone. Otherwise, he'd surely wonder if this incessantly jabbering sexual deviant standing before him had something to do with it.

"Okay, Mr. Anoki. I'd appreciate you at the station sometime today. I figure you two are clean, but for good measure, I'd like your story on record. Can I count on you two?"

"Yeah. I'll be there."

"I'll drive him Sheriff. Don't you worry," Yelena said, surprising both of them with her sudden verbal engagement. "We want those beautiful ladies vindicated."

"Well, thank you Ms. Summer, because we'll need your statement too."

"You got it!" she said, smiling flirtatiously, leading Jaxon to furrow his brow in slight irritation.

"Alright, I'm going to check on the team. We'll be back with you."

"Yeah. You know, those girls were real cool." Jaxon gazed at the ground, shook his head, then spit out the door. "That guy is seriously fucked up!"

"Yes, Mr. Anoki. He surely is."

•   •   •

Henry inconspicuously drove past the police car parked in his complex. He sat behind the wheel of his Cutlass Supreme, the same *tuna boat* that had projected catcalls while driving past young women, passed mountain bikers in the parking lot at Big Basin and also the car that notoriously ended the lives of two women and altered that of a third. And that was Santa Cruz County alone. His roster of kills included more victims state-wide, still left undiscovered.

Within the cab of his ominous ride, he drove on, spitting mad. He furiously slammed the steering wheel while fleeing on Highway 9 into the mountains. This marked their last night together, and they had stolen his final thrill.

Spittle dotted the windshield as he yelled obscenities. Had Jaxon figured out everything and ratted on him? Or was it that frickin' kid always snooping around the complex? "My ritual!" he psychotically yelled. "Mine!" He despised the injustice. After investing so much time and effort in refining his process, a far cry from his haphazard ways in SoCal, still he came out on the losing end.

He thought of how his life had electrified since his coven days, when he wreaked havoc with burglaries and assaults, all for the cash easily taken. The company he kept with Fergus and his stupid black magick and childish belief in fairy tales bored him. And his palm tattoo of an inverted pentagram, remained an inconvenient reminder of the affiliation.

He recalled arriving in Boulder Creek and discussing the area with Fergus, who promised him a nice finder's fee.

"All I'm asking is for you to hang around your dad's house," Fergus said. "I know she's in those mountains somewhere. Bay Area, Santa Cruz, maybe San Mateo. And if you see a chick that looks like this," Fergus texted him an old picture of Keira in her twenties, "call me. Arista is in her mid-twenties by now."

Henry scowled at the picture. "Brunette, huh? Fine, I'll hunt down some brunettes."

"I want her alive! Don't pull your criminal shit with my niece. I have a greater purpose for her."

"Then why don't you get her yourself?"

"I need another set of eyes. I've come up empty-handed each time. But I know Keira left her in that area. Now she's off in Arizona, withering away without her."

Henry came present and scoffed at the interaction. Fergus could conduct his own manhunt. Nothing mattered now, except his own greatest desire—the thrill of killing a soft, young woman.

·   ·   ·

"Okay, I'm out," Arista said.

"Thank you, Arista. I really appreciate you coming in today. I figured it would be a busy weekend." Analina squeezed her with an appreciative hug.

"Sure, anytime."

She left the chime of the door behind her and hopped on her bike.

Cautiously peddling to avoid the traffic on Highway 9, she made her right onto the north end of her neighborhood. Her surroundings seemed okay, no sign of danger. And since her next sharp right lay just ahead, she did not bother to look at the traffic coming up behind her.

·   ·   ·

Henry hit Boulder Creek and saw emergency vehicles tending to a car accident. Ever the fugitive, paranoid, and not wanting to risk capture, he took a shortcut and found himself in a small neighborhood.

Then he saw her. The madman who craved young women saw the familiar, beautiful nymph pedaling her bicycle from town. While youthfulness and sexuality initially attracted him to his prey, with this one, he saw happiness and hope, and he loved to destroy those virtues the most.

He slowed down and strategized his next move, his car nearing this angel, who he had seen regularly. Yet, with her back to him, she stayed oblivious to his approach.

A small thought crossed his mind. Why didn't he notice it before? Perhaps he had eyed too many brunettes because of Keira's dark hair. What if Arista wasn't a brunette and took after her father's side? Ian had dark brown hair, but an anomaly amongst his rumored family of gingers.

Fifty feet away, he stilled his mind and focused on the timing. Well within his grasp, he could take her right here.

Thirty feet away, it lined up perfectly.

Ten feet away, time to act!

By chance, the nymph took a sharp turn, at the same time a potential witness walked out of his front door. He had no alternative but to continue straight ahead, a necessary measure to flee from the law.

With his real time vision of the nymph gone, he danced her lingering image seductively in his mind. She would be worth the wait. He calculated the radius between The Timbermill and other areas he had seen her around the main strip. She had to live somewhere nearby.

"No, Fergus, this one I will not report to you. This one will be mine. I don't care if she's your niece or not."

He would not brainstorm a strategy today. His getaway remained the priority. But he would return, and when he did, he would come for her.

CHAPTER 34
SCRY INTO LAVENDER

It had been two months since they rescued Tiffani from the killer's grasp and the community sighed a breath of relief with no further sign of kidnappings. Vivi had even texted Arista and Maddie to join her at a small, girls-only gathering in the park with guy-talk and hard seltzers, which Arista graciously declined.

She also did not feel as alarmed when Auntie announced her summer crystal fairs in Sedona, promptly jetting off thereafter. With Shane by her side as night fell, she could let her go. Everything flowed with normalcy again in spite of the missing culprit that surely must have sought out safer territory since his cover had been blown in the mountains.

With summer settling in, she woke up to the glorious morning sunshine and went about her delightfully mundane life. Though, her usual routine proved a little different, as she found a wonderful surprise waiting for her on the front porch.

These are for you, Beautiful Girl.
As blue as your eyes, as blue as the sky.
Love, Shane

A thin blue ribbon held the note onto an extra-large, lead-crystal beveled vase containing a freshly-cut bouquet of Magda's gorgeous cobalt blue hydrangeas, complete with accents of dark green leaves.

"Aww. He must've stopped by so early, so it would be the first thing I saw!"

Mew.

She brought the vibrant arrangement over to her inconspicuous table, reverted to its most practical purpose. She took a step back to appreciate the esthetics.

"It looks perfect, Royal. I know he won't answer, but a quick message is in order."

She dialed Shane and brainstormed a clever message. If she remembered correctly, he was enjoying the outdoors with his Sports Summer Camp. An activity where he taught a group of rambunctious elementary kids the basics of flag football, basketball, or soccer, depending on the day of the week.

"Hey, Jesuit Boy! Just wanted you to know that I love, love, *love* these beautiful flowers! Please make sure your mom knows too, because I know she takes great pride! Anyway … very thoughtful … can't wait to see you."

She ended the call and set her phone on the table. She appreciated the effort more than anything. It brought back the fresh joy of their relationship that existed before the lethal seasons.

However, as she contemplated the past, a lingering question surfaced. Obviously, she embraced the cessation of murders, but where did he go?

She groaned, and immediately stopped herself. "I will not dwell on that," she avowed, snuffing the unpleasant ruminations out of her head.

With her stout companion weaving between her knees, she playfully grabbed at his long tail and jiggled it.

"Okay, enough. It's garden time."

Once outside, she heard the summer rush of downtown Boulder Creek beyond her own quiet street. A hectic time of year for the locals, many out-of-town drivers were simply passing through on their way to the county beaches in Santa Cruz, Capitola, or Aptos. Convertible BMWs and eco-conscious Prius drivers honked if someone took too long at the four-way stop sign. Frequently, it brought out self-righteous attitudes and high-strung tendencies.

"Jeesh! Hope Margaret steers clear of the chaos." She chuckled as she pictured an animated Margaret playing Frogger with beamers, but she meant it all in good fun.

Summer meant tending to gardens, and more than just her own. Besides her lovely array of flowers and shrubs, she also oversaw Auntie's flora while she peddled her wares and read tarot in the desert. But she would head over there in the coming days. Today, her own fragrant English Lavender needed trimming.

Snip. Snip.

Kneeling on her foam squishy pad, she gathered the heads—some still showing hints of vibrant purple—so she could macerate them with coconut oil for all manners of purpose. Aside from calming rubs, she liberally used the dried buds in diffusers for her favorite blueberry lavender tea.

She eyed the nature around her, then looked at Royal, who mewed for her attention while peering out from inside the kitchen window. She cast another snip at her lavender and felt the jarring approach of an interruption.

A sensation crawled up from the base of her spine and wrapped around her shoulders, as if strapping her in for a reckless and fierce ride. Knowing it inevitable, this time she welcomed the vision with new proficiency and looked forward to the insight it would give.

Her lavender bush faded to her own Hoot Owl Way. A shaky scene running from Auntie's house. Her heart fiercely raced, and the force that pursued her had her in a panic. And the tattoo. She could see it, too. Suddenly, its owner took a mighty swipe at her, causing her to lose footing. She crashed to the ground.

With her heart pounding, the image of her street slowly faded away, and, again, she stared at lavender. A familiar call beckoned her.

Meeee-ew.

She looked up at Royal behind the window screen, annunciating his meow—worried and unable to help her.

"It's *still* here," she uttered in defeat. She shook her head in disappointment and worked to settle her heartrate. "Can't that asshole just be gone forever? I don't want to hide in fear or let terror consume me to the point of madness."

Royal put his forepaws high on the screen and hooked in his claws, allowing for a fulfilling stretch. His white whiskers splayed out as he emitted a garbled yawn.

"No, honey, you cannot come out because I cannot risk you getting eaten by critters." Her breath recovered, and she looked for the resolution. "There must be a good reason for having this, since I haven't had one in a while." She twisted her mouth and bit the inside of her cheek. "I've been complacent. Too lax. But that is definitely me running …" The reality sunk in. "Running for my life."

Regardless of the subject, she found strength in her gift. "Well, I rode it this time. I know you saw me, Royal."

Aside from the panic it contained, the thought of her ability to scry fascinated her. She reprised her extended journey. This time, she had sensed its oncoming prompt, and accepted it with purpose and control. Plus, she felt much less drained after the episode. "Hmph."

She also knew she needed to bring the newest development to Auntie's attention. At long last, this version brought her into frame with the pursuer. Of course, it worried her, but as long as she prepared for the oncoming assault, maybe it, too, was something she could control.

"While Auntie's on her trips, at least I can count on Shane to stay with me."

Perceiving safety while immersed in the daylight, she resumed gardening. The sun continued to rise as she trimmed and harvested her lavender, and within an hour, she wiped at her brow and looked forward to her blueberry lavender tea over ice. She stopped to pull a strand of hair from her mouth when Royal spoke up again.

Mew.

She turned to see him peering toward the pines. "What do you see?"

She estimated his trajectory of interest, then adjusted her view up into the canopy. Deep inside the branches, amongst the pinecones and needles, she could barely make out the resident great-horned owl.

"Oooh, I see him … or her," she said, correcting herself in a hushed voice.

Not wanting to disturb the owl's presence with a trip to her refreshing pitcher, she hummed, and continued her work in the spiky garden of fragrant silver and purple sprigs.

CHAPTER 35
DON'T BE CRUEL

Henry sat at a worn metal desk in a small but tidy living room strategizing his next move.

His terminally ill father lay on the couch with his steel tank's thin rubber hose transporting oxygen to his shriveled mouth. Its hissing sound created a rhythm that could soothe a mentally-healthy person to sleep or drive a lunatic to his last frayed nerve.

"Hen … ry," his father rasped.

"Hold on, Dad." Busy jotting down his observations of the places he had spotted his sweet nymph, the request could wait. On the wall in front of him he had hung a small, dog-eared map of Santa Cruz County and pinned it with red thumbtacks and yellow stickpins.

"Hen … ry," the voice rasped again, no difference in tone nor volume, repetitive like the oxygen tank.

He ignored him, continuing to study his laptop. For over two months, he had kept a low profile. First, driving up to Oregon to ditch his Cutlass in the Upper Klamath Lake, erasing the last sign of Mack Phearson.

He checked his reflection in the window and took pleasure in his new disguise, which included a freshly grown beard and a fifteen-pound weight gain.

"No more pocket-protector engineer. This guy's a flannel-wearing mountain man." He looked over his shoulder at his father. "Right, Dad? You like my new look?"

"Hen … ry."

He refocused on his goal, and supposing that she could be Fergus's niece, he opted to call her *Arissa*. He also thought of Fergus's smug stature standing before him and sneered. No more chasing sticks like a dog for him. Arissa was his. He didn't care if she was Fergus' niece or not. The brunette looked a little more like him, anyway.

"Hen … ry."

He cringed. "What, old man!"

"P-p-lease …"

He slammed his fists down on the desk and stormed over to the source of irritation. "What? What do you want?" he shouted into the face of his needy father.

"Can … I … have …" His father stopped, exhausted from the rigor of talking and defeated by the maniacal stare of his son.

He raised his hand, the tattoo in full display, and lightly slapped his father's head. "Spit it out, you old coot!" He laughed at his own behavior.

His father's head sank in defeat.

"Well? You got my attention."

At a standoff, the silence persisted.

He stared down at the old man, wanting him to verbalize his need, despite the difficulty. But he already knew what he wanted. "I suppose you want some water?"

His father nodded, with downcast eyes.

He scooped up the glass and went to fill it. When he returned, he found his father looking at his marked-up map.

"Hen… ry … don't … be … cruel."

He scoffed. "You wondering what kinda whirlwind I'm creating, Pops?" He set the glass on the side table and squatted down to peer directly into his father's face. "Listen, Pops. You need me here. I know that 'cause you can't do shit for yourself anymore. So why don't you just stare at the boob tube, like you do all day … every day … and mind your own damn business?" Smirking, he pinched his father's chin between his thumb and forefinger and raised his eyebrows. "Ya got me?"

His father's eye twitched, but he held still from the leverage on his chin.

He pulled away abruptly, jolting his father's neck, and walked back to his calculating corner. "Face it, Pops. You're at my mercy now. In this house," he thumped his chest, his voice booming, "I'm the man! In fact …" He whirled around, staring squarely at his father, and hushed to an eerily calm voice. "Maybe I'm a monster."

CHAPTER 36
THESE MAGICKAL RITUALS

"That's a handsome plaque there, Hendrickson." Sheriff Michaels nodded in acknowledgement at the award given for his deputy's leadership in rescuing Tiffani.

"Thank you, Sheriff. I learned from the best. I wish we could have caught him, too."

"Yeah, well, we're not giving up. We're on the job. Suits are on the job. We all just have to keep a good lookout, follow up on leads, and make sure our town stays safe." He gave the deputy a firm pat on the back. "I'm headed out for the day. You have a good one."

"You, as well."

Another summer workday had ended as he buckled into his civilian car and headed south on Highway 9. He winded along, passing Brookdale Lodge and its haunted presence, on through Ben Lomond, where firefighters hosed down their new, red pumper, and set his aims for Felton.

As he approached Highlands Park, he heard a familiar voice.

"Hey there, Sheriff!" Yelena bellowed from the parking lot of Jay's Timberlane. Unpacking a bag of groceries from the trunk of their metallic black Mustang, she accompanied the greeting with a flirty wave and her ear-to-ear grin.

He checked his rearview mirror and, with no drivers in sight, slowed to a crawl. He gave a friendly flick of his two forefingers.

"S'up, Sheriff," Jaxon flatly acknowledged as he slammed the trunk.

"Jaxon." He gave a respectful nod before accelerating again.

He found it ironic how these two oddballs were settling into the community when they were so close to facing charges. Their legal sexual vices aside, they meshed well with most locals. Jaxon had even gotten a job at the local tire shop.

But, as he drove on, his mood turned. The couple also served as a reminder. Despite putting up a strong front to his deputy, he felt immense regret for failing to capture the violent criminal. Even with all the data—his real name, aliases, several sketches from different witnesses, and prints from his unit at Jay's—still, the demon roamed. Further, after authorities found his torched car in an Oregon lake, he suspected that he may have altered his appearance.

Then he recalled the day when two good witches from his county visited him. Dutifully, they brought knowledge from an obscure source. Similar to his father, now he knew that leads taken from this family were to be treated respectfully. Could their 'undisclosed source' provide more information?

And what must Arista be doing this evening? Hopefully she had not settled into complacency with the killer still on the loose.

•   •   •

"Here, kitty-kitty." Shane attempted to gain acceptance from a smug Royal, sitting pear-shaped in the hallway and peering at the inconvenient human.

Arista watched with amusement and knew the approach married with the generic term did not work. "Oh, come on, Royal. Be friendly." Since he did not budge, she went to him. "Please, be more welcoming to Shane. He's our protector, you know."

The fussy feline turned away and walked toward his new bed, a chocolate-brown, velour-ridged beanbag in the living room. He had sheer disinterest in this new human with which he had to share his beloved.

"Okay, let's take it outside," she said, hoisting her tote bag full of amenities.

They walked onto the front porch into the cool air, and a very special night. For her, the Full Moon arrived as a celestial wonder each time it occurred, and now Shane, willingly, had interest in her eclectic lifestyle. She would make this a ritual for him to truly remember.

He looked up and scanned the sky. "Where is it?"

"It hasn't risen yet. That's the most fascinating part, and we get to watch it happen." She dug into her tote and withdrew a king-size, fluffy red blanket, and spread it out before them.

"Cool." He helped her straighten the corners of the sizeable ground covering nearest him.

They both dropped down onto the plush bedding atop the pea gravel.

"Comfy?"

"Truly, and my contribution ..." Shane stretched out to grab the two bottles of hard cider, pilfered from his mom's wet bar that he had set on her steps upon his arrival. He twisted the lids off, handed one bottle to her, and they clinked to the night ahead of them.

"Ooh, here it comes!" She pointed to the swelling aura surrounding their darkened hills. "Watch."

Slowly, the indigo night sky illuminated with a cool white, luminescent glow shining through the redwood valley.

She eagerly gazed without blinking, determined not to miss the magickal moment when the bright white sliver of the moon appeared over the mountain's silhouette. She also felt thrilled about the other event of the night. Shane did not know yet, but her plans held something much more engaging. On this night, she could not wait to be fully united with him.

Out of the corner of her eye, she watched him ping-pong his gaze between the moon and her hair. Each time she would guide his view back to the sky, as another generous portion of the white orb exposed itself, further reaching up toward the heavens.

They took another drink, and he glanced over at her. "So—"

"Look at Mother Moon," she softly interrupted.

He peered upward and playfully mocked. "She loves these magickal rituals."

"Sshh. Just look at it … so beautiful."

She secured her drink in the pea gravel at the edge of their blanket and laid down.

Shane copied the action.

Together, they watched the full moon complete its ascent while lying side-by-side.

"It *is* pretty," he offered genuinely. Then he took her hand and rolled toward her. "*She* is pretty," he said, gazing into her eyes. He cupped her face, and they merged for a loving strawberry-flavored kiss, compliments of her natural lip balm. With his arm draped over her, he pulled her closer toward him.

She felt the urge and pressed in, dizzy with her increasing arousal. But she giggled, pulled away, and laid flat again.

"Mmmm. So, is this a love ritual? Have we begun?" he asked before taking another swig.

"Oh, you mean the ritual with warm candlelight glow under the aura of a full moon?"

"Yes."

"And rose petals sprinkled all around us?"

"Sounds great to me!"

She sat up with a humored smirk and lifted the tote. She took out a tall, blood-red pillar candle, wedged it into a sturdy Himalayan salt base and lit it. Next, she held up a chunky hand-sized Rose Quartz heart and moved it across the flame. She brought it close to her heart with her palms placed one atop the other and closed her eyes. *May this love be true and blessed.*

She held it a moment longer, opened her eyes and placed the crystal on Shane's heart. "Close your eyes and feel it."

He closed his eyes, and within a second, opened them. It would do.

She placed the Rose Quartz at the base of the burning candle. Then she finished the canvas of their plush bedding with a lavish scattering of dried rose petals along the entire border of the blanket.

"You weren't kidding, were you?" His eyes followed her every movement, and his smile grew with each dropping rose petal.

He started to sit up, but she playfully pushed him back to the ground and straddled his hips. It felt powerful, owning so much confidence in this moment. "Did you know you're in the presence of a goddess?" she seductively asked.

"That is evident."

"Mmm-hmm." She removed her soft cotton tee, exposing her stomach and peach-colored lace bra.

Shane stroked at her tenderly.

She looked down at him. He was so beautiful.

"How'd you do that?" he inquired in a whisper, pointing to the dotted white scar on her abdomen.

"It's been there as long as I can remember."

"Yeah? How'd you do that?" he asked, his finger now at her solar plexus.

When she looked down, he quickly stroked her lips.

She came down upon him and smothered him in more sensuous, fruity kisses.

Gradually, he flipped her to the ground and pressed up against her, while she absorbed his love, his kiss and caress. Bustling with each other's remaining clothes, she inhaled his scent, his strength, and, finally, his slow, rhythmic dance. It swept her away. She consumed the sensation that radiated throughout her body. The dizziness, and the complete surrender to her intense new lover, fully satisfied her.

After years of waiting, this moment of unity bound them together.

Time flew, and the chill set in, prompting them to get dressed and retreat indoors.

"I'll be right there. I'm just going to get some moon tea ready for steeping tonight."

He left her in the kitchen and ambled toward the bedroom.

She filled her glass pitcher with fresh filtered water, but the elation of true love and sensation caused her to lose focus on her mindful ritual. She giggled when she realized her completed elixir sat basking in the glow of moonlight on the counter, yet she had no recollection of preparing it.

When she walked into her bedroom, the air felt stifling. "Well, I'm glad you're here, cause otherwise I'd just swelter in this room all night." She opened her bedroom window to allow the cool breeze entry.

"Hmph, looks like I didn't drive him completely away."

Royal sat at her bedroom door.

"Hah! Only because he wants to keep an eye on you."

She went to her bedside and eased in beside Shane as she had done at least once a week since Tiffani's rescue from the madman. They had agreed this overnight arrangement would be especially true when Auntie traveled. Sure, his nightly visits were great, but she considered the sleepover a veritable treasure, when they would talk for hours before falling asleep.

"It's stuffy in here tonight." Shane flung the covers off himself, exposing her lower leg.

"Okay, thank you, but no." She pulled the covers back over the both of them.

"Come on, Riss." Once again, he flipped them.

"Please, I get a little chilled, especially as the night goes on." And once again, she pulled her floral cover back upon her. Although this time, she kept his skin exposed as much as possible, with only his feet covered. She paused for reaction, but none came, so she rolled over and prepared to sleep.

Shane moved his feet atop the blanket. After a few seconds, he whispered, "This is not about blankets. What if I wasn't here tonight? What if you were too hot and opened that window and …" He stopped the flow of worry. "I just want you safe."

"I wouldn't have opened it. It's only open because you're here, and I know you'll keep me safe." She smiled to herself and nuzzled into her pillow.

He stroked her hair.

Suddenly, her phone rang out with tones of a witchy hum. She'd alternate this ringtone between the original by a Scotsman and the redo by the more angelic voice. Either way, it always represented priority.

She jumped out from under the covers, now leaving them double-layered upon Shane, and hustled toward her dresser. "It's Auntie," she said, quickly bringing the phone to her ear. "Hello?" The late-night call not only surprised her but brought forth a bit of worry.

"Arista, dear, it's me. I'm coming back—unexpectedly, I know."

"Okay, great! What's going on?"

"My friends and I have just completed a very thorough ritual. We prayed, meditated, and incanted many good blessings upon each of our members and our families. Now ... I don't mean to frighten you, especially before I am back ... but that old feeling is creeping up again."

"Oh, no." She knew she had been lax on her intuitive practice. This was especially undisciplined of her since her scrying proved that the danger still existed.

"I must get back to you."

"Great! I'll be glad to see you."

"They haven't caught that damn beast yet, have they?"

"No, but they found his car in Oregon. Maybe they'll find *him* there, too."

"My dear, I do not want to put you in a panic, but my feeling is similar to past revelations. About you ... as a child, way back when. I sense that urgency again. And honestly, my intuition is always stronger ... I'd say even more accurate, when I am at a distance from you."

"Really?" *What does she mean by that?*

"Yes. How can I say this?" Auntie paused, choosing her words carefully. "Your optimism and upbeat presence, while a breath of fresh air and sweet to the soul can ... well ... they can sometimes be a barrier to my intuition. Perhaps your optimism gets in your own way as well."

"Hmph. Okay. Well, I'm being safe. But it will be good to have you back." *What the heck is that supposed to mean? Optimism is one of humanity's most valuable assets.*

"Okay, dear, I'll—"

"Auntie? Hello? Hello?"

She looked at Shane, then down at her phone and saw the call had ended. She quickly tapped Auntie's number. After two rings, a voice. "Auntie, what happened?"

"Well, I don't know. It just went dead. It does that to me sometimes. Pearl says my cheek is to blame, but I don't know about that."

"Okay, so you were saying ..."

"I'll be back tomorrow. But it won't be till later in the night."

"Okay, great! Safe travels!"

Disconnecting, she set her phone down and relaxed the façade she had maintained for Auntie. She felt the intrusion of reality upon her night's previous elation. Not only was it a downer, it also worried her.

"Well, what did she say?"

She took a breath and spoke with a tone of logic. "It's not so much what she said, it's the urgency with which she said it."

She grasped at the fading bliss—her glorious full moon ritual and the passionate memories of her evening with Shane. She settled back into the heavy burden she knew all too well.

"He's coming back ... and he's coming for me."

CHAPTER 37
ALLIED WITH THE STORM

It happened to be a rare occurrence for Boulder Creek to release a mid-August storm. In fact, a nourishing relief from the drought remained absent for the entire Bay Area, where brooding clouds only teased. Though, on this eerie, warm summer night, thunder rumbled in the distance, warning of its oncoming electrical surge.

As it picked up strength, the gusty winds harassed even the sturdiest trees. The crashing and clanging of loose garbage-can lids sparked worry in outdoor pets causing them to cower in the safest, hidden places.

Bethie felt accompanied by the storm while returning from the airport.

"Here you are, ma'am," the courteous driver announced.

"Thank you. Your driving was quite satisfactory."

She fussed with the confusing app, finally finding the tip screen and generously gave. Then, she pulled the handle, only to have the wind thrust her door wide open, hinges strained, leading the driver to bristle.

"Oh, rats. Sorry about that."

She hoisted her bags and shut the car door with a swift bump of her behind. Hurriedly, she approached her mountain abode as the wind howled about her and vigorously blew her hair. She struggled with the bulk of her luggage and found the deadbolt extra fussy when trying to gain entrance. Finally, safe inside her home, she used her foot and gave a firm slam.

"Sheesh!" she cried out, exasperated from the fury that howled outside her cozy shelter. "Like fighting off rabid dogs."

Once she had placed her bags in her room, she aimed for the kitchen. There, she grabbed an oblong cardboard box from her unopened mail pile and took it, along with her baggage, to her bedroom to unpack.

A few minutes later she heard the rumble of a vehicle in her driveway, followed by Arista and her positive energy bursting through the door.

"Hey Miss Sedona!" Arista walked toward with her arms prepped for a big hug. "I've missed you so much!"

"Me too, dear. Just remember those trips help both of us. Have you kept with your practice?"

"Nightly prayers, of course, but not much spell work. I did miss Midsummer, but I paid homage to Áine for summer's sake. Oh! And I charged my crystals on the full moon. Twice since you've been gone. I believe you taught it is only the lunar eclipse to forego charging and the one in June was solar, so yeah ..."

"Not bad. Maybe this Shane fellow is not such a hindrance to your practice, after all."

"Oh, I've kinda recruited him into a few of the moon rituals as well," she said, with a sparkle in her eye.

"Well, it puts my mind at ease that you two are together. He's a big strong one, he is. And I can see your eyes light up when his name is mentioned. Now, what about your presence? Your ghost?"

"There's been nothing since you left."

"Interesting. Perhaps Shane's presence has scared it off?"

Arista shrugged.

"What about the vision?"

"Just after you left, I had one."

She peered at her, awaiting the story.

"I was in my garden. I think I scried. Instead of it bowling me over, I recognized its onset. I had better control this time and relaxed into it."

She hesitated and scrunched her nose. "There was a little more detail. I was running, and then I fell … because someone grabbed at me."

She drew a breath to calm herself. "It is as I feared. I knew I needed to be here. Anything else?"

"No. Old news."

"Well, I don't want to believe it, but my intuition has brought me back because that vision is merely waiting for the next prompt."

"What do you mean?"

"This is not over, Arista. We must make safety our priority, and you know what a strict teacher I can be when holding you to your commitment as a gifted witch. I know you can beat this!" After spending time with her coven, she always felt braver, and clearer with intention due to the plentiful encouragement from her peers.

A sudden crack and rumble beyond the cottage walls made them jump. The storm drew closer. It held a three-second count from the time the jagged lightning flashed beyond the sheer window panels to the time it sounded its percussive war drum.

"Okay, we start now. My group and I can send many good vibes from the desert. However, being here—with the redwood scent, fresh air, and the mountain's energy—that will enable us to work together for a positive outcome. Come with me."

Arista followed her into her bedroom, where she zipped open her carry-on bag and took out a cape. With a mighty thrust, she shook it and released a cloud of Sedona dust. Then, she handed it to Arista. "I wore this in multiple ceremonies over the past month. It is rich in process, and I want you to have it."

She walked to her wardrobe and put on her sturdiest jet-black satin cloak with a stiff collar that jutted to her ears. Seeing Arista's expression, she realized its ridiculous vampire appeal, but drastic times called for drastic wear. Then, she clutched the blessed gift for her dear grandniece and tucked it under her cloak. She turned to face her.

"Arista, the danger has merely been dormant … not dead. So, I have something for you."

She walked over to her, and from beneath her wrap, she revealed her ornate athame and began a dissertation of its usage. "I am called to pass this on to you. Like the table, this athame has been in our family for almost a century. For me, it has carved many a symbol in sand and on candles. It has cast circles during rituals, both private and with family, has charged amulets, and has been a source of meditation for me. Perhaps you will scry into it? I give it to for these purposes."

"Oh Auntie, no. I can't."

"You must, dear."

"Why would you give away your beautiful athame?" Arista held her gaze on the gift but did not reach for it.

"My trip had a few important purposes." She stood up tall and proud and momentarily lowered the gift. "First, you are now looking at a regular vendor for the Cosmic Prisms Metaphysical crystal shop in Sedona, Arizona."

"That's great news!"

"Yes, indeed. Pearl has grown her business enough to buy my inventory outright and only takes twenty percent of any tarot readings that I do."

"Congratulations! I'm so happy for you!"

"Thank you." She pursed her lips for a moment of gloating before shrinking back into her collar and readdressing the athame. "But there were more important matters. We thoroughly blessed this through my coven's most potent rituals and protection spells. We did the bulk of it amidst the powerful vortices of Sedona … all four of us … and put all our energy together. The shipping cost of the back and forth was outrageous, but worth it. By the way, thank you for getting my mail!"

"Of course!"

"Anyway, a whirlwind of power lies within this blade now." She gazed at the athame glistening in the night's lighting, emblazoned flashes bouncing off of its shiny steel. But it belonged to Arista now, and she held it out to her. "This relic usually stays with one until death, but I know I must give it to you now, for a greater purpose than adorning your altar. Keep it safe and keep it close."

Arista reverently reached out to receive the gift. To be so much more than a simple moonstone-bejeweled accessory awed her, apparent by her wide eyes and careful handling. Like the table, she had not disclosed its true intrinsic value in familial history to her. But she had seen Arista frequently eye its intimidating beauty—the girth of the Celtic-knotted handle, the sharpened double-blade that curved to a lethal point, and the worn leather sheath that held its influence in check.

After a visual rundown of the ornate dagger, Arista held it to her heart. "I don't know what to say. Thank you? It's one of the most beautiful things you own, and I seriously feel bad taking it from you."

"Remember to acclimate it to your altar and bless it with an oil of your choosing." She cupped Arista's hands and closed them over the athame. "This is a necessity, not a whim. It is another element of safety that comforts me to know I did all I could to keep you safe."

"Well, I will definitely treasure it for a lifetime."

She saw the excitement in Arista's eyes, but noticed she kept her usual giddiness in check. The fact that she maintained her poise was surely a sign of her maturing as a witch. She would do right by the exotic artifact.

"You said your trip was for a *few* purposes."

She paused and contemplated the question. "Well, the rest can wait for another time."

"Are you *sure* about that? I've got time."

Arista seldom questioned her and must have sensed the secrecy. The only surviving mystery—her missing parents. And she wondered if she had any memory of her uncle as well. The time neared to address it all, but tonight the focus of passing the athame to a new generation held strong. "I'm sure for now."

"If it's okay, I'd like to stay here tonight. I've gotten used to having Shane around, but his mom and sister definitely want him home on this stormy night because his dad's on a business trip."

"Of course, dear. Anytime."

They chanted softly in unison for some time. Finally, deciding they had covered all bases on verbiage and intention, they celebrated with a mini cup of piping hot lemon and ginger root tea.

Arista's yawns increased, and with her own energy flagging from travel, she announced the end of their night. "I am comforted by the shroud of night since your vision is a daytime pursuit. So, off to bed you go!"

After their *good-nights*, she went to her altar. She sat alone, many thoughts brewing about that undisclosed matter for her Sedona trip.

In the quiet solitude of her room, she whispered at her reflection, "I hope they can locate Ian," but resolved to knowing the search would take time.

CHAPTER 38
A NEEDLE IN A HAYSTACK

Sheriff Michaels carefully parallel parked his cruiser at the front of the Boulder Creek hardware store. He gave a respectful nod to the town oddball, Margaret, as she shuffled past his cruiser on her way to who knows where. When she received his gesture with an ornery smirk, he knew she meant no ill will.

With his windows down, the soft morning breeze refreshed him as he listened to the spirited voice coming from inside the store. He could hear the bellowing of his long-time friend, Pat Hilgard, conversing with his niece.

"Hey Maddie, I appreciate you helping today. I know you'd rather be with Arista 'bout now, but Thanks!" Uncle Pat stopped, and his subsequent silence begged a response.

"Sure," Maddie said, "you mind if I take a quick break?"

"Yeah. Go for it!"

He hoisted himself out of the cruiser and leisurely strolled toward the door. As he neared, he noticed Maddie's focused attention on her phone. He readied for the avoidance as she obliviously barged at him narrowly missing the human impact of his solidly-armed body.

"Whoa, Maddie. Take it easy. Don't mow down our good guys," Uncle Pat said, harassing her from the counter.

"Mornin'," he said, and stepped back to create space.

"Oops, sorry 'bout that." Clearly a little embarrassed, Maddie gave a quick smile, flashed a glare to her uncle, and hurried off down the sidewalk.

"Good to see ya, Sheriff." Pat kept to formalities when he visited in uniform.

"Heya Pat! How's life been treating you?"

"Well, life's been real good this year … other than my mom passing a while back, but we knew it was coming. She's in a better place."

"Sorry to hear."

"Ah, no worries. Hey, any new leads on that whack job? I still don't like Maddie staying out late, and it gets a little cumbersome to corral a twenty-three-year-old."

"We have a couple noses in the air in Oregon, but—"

The dispatcher interrupted their small talk.

Pat gave a nod of understanding, and he strolled over to the battery aisle to take his call. "15U15. Go ahead."

"Sheriff, the station got a call from Yelena Summer. She says she thinks she has an urgent piece of information and wants you to call her ASAP."

"Copy that. You have the contact info?"

After obtaining the phone number, he picked up a lithium-ion battery from the shelf and approached Pat at the counter.

"Don't they furnish this stuff for you guys?"

"They do at the county building, but it's fritzin' on me a bit, and I'm not running to Santa Cruz just to pick one up."

Pat chuckled. "Yeah, I got ya! So, helluva storm last week. What's the story with that fire up north? Should we be concerned?"

"Yeah, it *is* a bit concerning. Evac may be coming."

"Damn! Well, thanks for the heads up."

As he left the shop, he pondered the possibilities of Yelena's call. Although he had spotted the unusual pair occasionally, her urgent message had his attention.

"Hey Sheriff," Yelena charmingly greeted through the phone.

"Ms. Summer."

"Sheriff, me and Jaxon were talkin', and I thought I may have some helpful information for you."

"Go ahead."

"I went through my text messages, looking at all the group chats of me and Jaxon and Mack ... Henry ... or whatever his name is. But anyway, way back when we first met in January, he said he had to run to his dad's house real quick before he went out with us."

He sat up in his seat.

"Any contact information with that?"

"No. And I'm tellin' you, I scoured. But, yeah, he just said it. Now he could've been full of it and just had something else to do, but I thought you'd want to know."

"That was real wise of you, Ms. Summer. We'll surely check into it."

"Alright." Yelena held silent for a second. "Well, that's about it."

"Okay, thank you. Just let us know if you find anything else."

"You bet."

He disconnected and fastened his seat belt. It may have been a needle in the haystack, but something worth researching.

CHAPTER 39
LAVENDER TEA ... AND CHAOS!

Setting aside her troubling foresight, Arista enjoyed the comforting warmth of the summer morning at her altar. She sat sky-clad and focused on her intentions.

KNOCK! KNOCK! KNOCK!

She startled at the solid rapping and reached for her robe, as Royal perked up on his cat post, eyes wide and alerted.

Who on earth knocks like that? She hastened toward the source. As she neared her caution eased, seeing sections of a familiar town deputy—hat, badge, and holster—through her many-paned front door. She tightened her robe and dreaded the news. Was it Auntie? A friend? Was it *him* back again?

"Good morning ... Deputy Hendrickson. Ms. Kelly, we're just giving warning that there could be evacuations coming and the sheriff asked that I let you and your aunt know. I'm sure you heard of the fires that started about a week ago?"

Great-aunt. "Yes."

"There's been some change in the wind conditions. It's beginning to fuel our local fires closer to the one up north. Hoping they won't merge, but we have to be prepared. We're just giving our citizens notice that evacuations could come soon."

"Okay. When might we know for sure?"

"We'll keep you posted."

"Okay, I'll tell her. Thank you for letting us know!"

"You take care." Hendrickson respectfully nodded beneath his law-emblazoned cap and left.

She closed the door and worriedly looked around her kitchen, envisioning the cozy ambiance succumbing to a furious blaze. Just as quickly, she stifled the thought and scanned her countertops. So much to pack—jars of teas and herbs, colorful salts, and spices. She saw her hanging crystal so generous with its glorious morning prisms, and her favorite celestial-themed mug. The fear of loss grew. What about the magickal table? In an emergency, how would they transport the large, cumbersome piece? Such an important part of her heritage would have to be saved.

Royal came into the kitchen and mewed at her feet, his tail coiling up and around her knee, a feline hug of reassurance.

"I don't know about all this, Royal, but you and I will be fine." She picked up her lug of fur and flexibility, smooched his head and set him atop the counter. Then, she grabbed a pop-top jar of loose lavender tea and mindlessly created her second cup of the calming elixir for that morning.

But, what the heck she was doing?

"Lavender tea … and chaos!" She huffed at the irony and dumped the crushed blend back into its container. This was no time for tea. She had to tell Auntie right away, and with Shane already gone, she would need to go alone.

"Maybe biking is safer than walking." She looked at Royal and pictured her escape. "That way I can get away really, really fast!"

Mew.

Her neighborhood bustled with activity. Finally, she rode out in the open again, biking down the street, experiencing the windblown freedom of the ride. She listened to the debates of the wrens and the chattering of the warblers, and pictured scenarios of birds in courtrooms and tea houses. She appreciated the buzzing of honeybees gathering nectar for their hives as she pedaled past the jasmine hedge of her neighbor's yard. All of nature's busyness surrounding her showed no sign of fire, nor disharmony, and no loose ends of a murderer.

The freedom fleeted, as thoughts of the roaming demon barged back into her psyche. Not only did the town have a hovering possibility of *him* lurking, but Auntie had revealed dire warnings of a certain impending doom. If not bad enough, a raging fire now loomed, threatening to destroy everything in its path. Sheer chaos, without a doubt.

She rallied within and picked up speed, focusing on the luminary sun and its vibrant morning glow warming her back and bare shoulders. This freedom would be short-lived, as she needed to get to Auntie's without delay.

When she reached the entrance of Auntie's shrouded driveway, a creeping sensation of her previous visions came to her mind. She stayed grounded and conscious this time. Perhaps intuition at its finest. From this point forward, she would no longer choose idealism over reality. She had to listen to her gut, and at this moment, it told her to look over her shoulder.

She stopped at Auntie's entrance and stabilized her bike. Setting her right foot to the ground, she scrutinized her surroundings, and scanned all directions, searching for the flaw. She saw an abundance of natural beauty.

Unnerved but satisfied, she entered Auntie's property and found her working in her garden, enthusiastically tending to her mint. Now in its straggly phase, the leaves had lost their fresh succulent tinge and become coarse to the touch.

Auntie looked up as she approached, and made brief eye contact. But she did not greet her and went straight back to gardening.

"Good morning." She felt happy to see her wise one and a little hesitant of the cold shoulder.

Auntie kept her gaze down and offered no response.

She gave a kindhearted hug to her back and delivered the latest news. "Deputy Hendrickson just left my house, and he says that we may need to evacuate."

"Hmph. Well, that's troubling. When will we know for sure?" Still, she focused on her mint.

"He wasn't sure. They just wanted to give us an early warning. Probably to pack our valuables."

"Thank you for letting me know."

Auntie appeared to be as snippy as her lubricated clippers. "Sooo, the mint smells very lovely."

"Mmm-hmph."

When the small talk fell flat, she realized it was time to go. Auntie would open up later. "Well, that's about it for me." She turned to leave.

"Arista!" Auntie whirled around and spoke with sharpness.

"Yes?" She came to full attention, as her great aunt stood up and stared at her with furrowed brows and a reddened face of anger she had rarely seen on her.

"You just told me of your vision a few nights ago! Where's the safety of coming down here unannounced? You told me Shane offered to drive you places, yet here you are ... alone! Riding the streets without a care. What are you thinking?"

The latest vision spooked her too. And she dare not mention the eerie moment earlier on their street. Worse, it would give *him* power, striking terror into both of them. So, she went with reasoning.

"It's just down the street, and Shane's at work. I was careful, and it's barely a block."

"Listen to me. I am back early because I have a horrible feeling! My ladies and I know it's coming, and you are *not* taking it seriously!"

Despite being admonished, she saw the panic and worry consume Auntie's face and regained her compassion. "I'm sorry. You're right."

"The tattoo that you saw has serious implications. It's just another piece of this awful puzzle." She shook her head in frustration. "Tell me when you are on your way over here. Can you do that?"

"Yes. I'll call next time. I promise! And I absolutely agree with everything you're saying!"

"Fine!" She huffed and looked away briefly. The tension eased on her face, and her complexion returned to its natural color. The only red remaining were her rosy cheeks. "I don't want to be angry with you. I am sorry for flaring up." She transformed back into her ditzy self. "Whew! That all just spewed out of my mouth in such an unloving way. I'm sorry, dear."

"It's okay. I know it's because you love me. And I love you too. But Auntie, please … you have to tell me what you are withholding. I know there is something else. Please, I can handle it." She hung by the moment.

Auntie let out a deep sigh and placed her tools on the tiled, purple, mosaic dragonfly adorning her small table. She dusted off her light-green gardening apron and smacked her lips. "Well, Arista, maybe there is." She looked off into the distance. "Are you interested in why your parents left you here with me?"

The question shocked her. Yes, she had just placed the invitation, but the long-abandoned topic also brought a sense of fear and sadness, ambiguity, and loss. Her desire to know had waned as she grew, and she decided not knowing might be better. She wanted to forget the pain of abandonment. In not reliving it or having the void from it, she could pretend everything was fine. But now, with the question posed, and the offer accepted, she honestly could not answer.

Auntie studied her face. "It's up to you."

"Umm … sure," she answered unconvincingly. Then, remembering her need to let go of the resentment over her parent's departure, she confidently answered. "Actually, yes! Yes, I do."

"Arista, your parents loved … they still love you dearly! But your uncle is a bad person with a …" Auntie pinched her fingers together as if holding a green pea, "little bit of power. And while this power cannot do much, aside from torment your poor mother, it gained him a bit of popularity with a darker bunch."

With the revelation at hand, emotions flooded her. At first, she numbed, bracing for the drama to unfold. Then, she felt the urge to cry, and ached for her inner child, who still grasped the stuffed animal, while watching her dad drive away without her. But all she could do right now was listen.

"Your birth brought great hope you would be more powerful than any of your preceding family members. This includes me, your great-great-grandparents … all of us. You had the potential to inherit abilities from both of your parents, even though they both *avoided* their gifts. But for as long as I can remember, my grandfather swore that one day you would be the gifted one."

Auntie took a breath, looked her in the eye to gauge the interest and continued.

"Ian aimed for normalcy and refused to use his foresight through dreams. He had suffered a few bullying incidents in childhood. Then, as a teen, his classmates beat him up because they mistakenly believed his foresight of their vandalized car was admission of guilt. What he had tried to help them avoid got blamed on him."

She stared at Auntie, telling the story of Ian, her father. She listened as if hearing folklore, and he, merely a fictional character.

"After that, he would take a pill. Something like zoa-pine, or sera-sine."

"Melatonin, maybe?"

"No, not that one. I'd recognize it if I heard it. Anyway, he wanted to make sure his sleep stayed dreamless. We believe it was because of that, he missed the signs."

She felt regret for the man in this tale.

"Your mother also has a power, one to attune to her brother. From a very young age they were inseparable. Synchronized with each other's emotions and, later, their locations. When your mother and father met, your uncle became very jealous, and angry at the perceived competition. Their eventual marriage only made it worse."

She could hear Auntie talking as she gazed down at the mint. Sections of it were still green and velvety, and she could smell the earthy fragrance.

Auntie noticed the distraction. "This is a lot to swallow. Let's sit." She led them over to the comfy, cushioned patio furniture. "Are you okay with this conversation?"

"I am." Still, she felt annoyance at how easily the story flowed out after all this time. Maybe she wasn't ready. She had already endured, processed, and healed from this immense childhood pain. And this inconvenient reminder only stirred up more distressing emotions.

Auntie needed little encouragement. "Fergus grew more and more spiteful. It hit a tipping point when they announced your coming arrival, further securing the bond between your parents. Keira stopped attuning to, and from, him as best she could. Finally, with you inside her womb, her mother instincts kicked in and she told him enough was enough."

"I think I remember Uncle Fergus."

Auntie cringed at the mention of his name.

"Yes! I remember him babysitting me. He was very tall and would give me shoulder rides." She found glimpses of real people emerging from this folktale, a reintroduction to her former life.

"Yes. That was him." She spoke with derision, while reaching for her cup of melting ice water to take a sip. "Anyway, your mother cut all ties."

"I expect that made him even angrier?" Now, she began to experience more compassion for the mother of this story.

"Absolutely! He physically disappeared from their life for years. During that time, he created an inner circle of black-magick, and she noticed an increase in his intrusions, this time, physically. Sometimes, his members would loiter outside their house in L.A.. They'd be gone by the time your dad got home. A couple different times, Keira ran into one of his followers at the grocery store. They said nothing to her, just opened their palm. They all carried the same mark."

"The upside-down pentagram!"

"Yes."

"Wow. So, my visions hold more than a general ominous threat." She sensed the same creepiness percolating within her as earlier on her bike. She kept it to herself.

"I'm afraid so. Meanwhile, your parents saw the gift in you. And I felt it! A very precocious child you were. So brilliant in your speech, your love, and your little abilities beginning to show." Auntie tapped her thigh. "I've always had a bit of attunement to you, my dear! While I seldom saw you, I knew what you looked like. I'd know if you fell from your bike or if you felt elated over a new friend. I'd verify it when I called Ian … on an actual phone, mind you, not these baffling things we have now!"

She snickered, knowing Auntie's disdain for cell phones and appreciated the humor injected into this challenging moment.

"Anyway, my attunement to you was not so invasive as what your uncle holds over your mother."

She glanced at Auntie's aging face. So dear was her relationship with this woman and the honesty pouring out of her produced mixed emotions. A little resentful for the long-time secrecy, but endless appreciation for rearing her with so much love. Everything appeared so confusing.

"Near your eighth birthday, Fergus weaseled his way back into your family's life promising he had changed. And of course, your mother loved and trusted him, so she believed him. But he had them fooled."

She groaned. Experienced time and again by the masses, the classic story of betrayal prevailed. How sad that it happened in her own family.

"He returned so he could experiment ways of gaining your predicted powers. And with him, he brought criminals who jumped when he commanded. He may not have had true magickal power, but his ability to manipulate weak minds made him a very dangerous person."

"What do you mean—'experiment'?" She sat up and grit her teeth, absorbing the detailed exposé. "I thought he was pretty fun. How bad does this get?" Since she alive and well today, it could not be too bad, right?

"Fergus started a blood magick ritual on you … stupid, awful man." She lowered her head in regret. "Because your mother refused to attune, she too, had missed the signs of his malice."

"Blood magick! What kind of ritual?"

"I phoned your father and told him of my worry. It was his knowledge of the bond I shared with you that lead him to sleep naturally. No pya-zine or whatever it was."

"Ambien, maybe?"

"No, not that either. Anyway, over the next couple of days, a dream came to his clear mind."

She held her breath.

Auntie's eyes squinted. "In his dream, he saw Fergus take a heated blade to your innocent little tummy," her voice broke, and she teared, "and cut you horribly."

Stunned, she felt a cold lump in the pit of her stomach. The thought sickened her. How despicable to do that to a child! Worse, she really liked that guy!

Auntie's eyes teared, prompting her to reach over and stroke her arm.

"Thank goodness the act was only foresight. But, when your dad investigated, he saw Fergus had already started the ritual with you— practice, for lack of better words. He had scratched your tummy with his athame, leaving little bloody scabs ... an inch-long. The only way this was possible, without you waking ... or knowing ... was that he had drugged you. When you told your father of the almond milk that made you sleepy, it confirmed everything."

She lifted her tank top and examined her ages-old scar, the same insignificant mark Shane had recently noticed. The discovery of its origin disheartened her. How could she have forgotten this?

"When your father saw the wound, he went and brutally attacked Fergus. He feared Fergus had hurt you in other ways. He beat your uncle and kicked between his legs so much that he will never bear children."

She gasped. "So much violence." She gently traced the faint white, dotted scar, shrunken over the years. It seemed such a small effect for so much madness.

"Your father had no regret. He felt the act itself, the mark on your body, and the drugging was enough to validate his rage. We thought he would kill him, but he stopped short of it … for you. He did not want you to bear that legacy."

Auntie took a drink followed by an exhale of relief. "Arista, I tried to tell you when you were eighteen, as well as twenty-one. But we didn't want you to go searching. The status quo had worked so well for years, nobody wanted that protection to end. Powers don't just go away. If you reunited with your mother, your uncle would know."

"Wow, what a mess." She surprised herself by uncharacteristically kicking at a dandelion by her foot. Slowly, it came to her. The heightened energy of a late-night escape so long ago—an unusually tearful mother and an edgy father with an unexplained busted lip.

Auntie briefly raised her eyebrows very matter-of-fact. "I was ready to talk if you asked, but you were such a happy young girl, and—"

"Yes, I am a happy person." She interrupted in an attempt to motivate herself with positivity. But the spark fell flat. "Actually, I don't know. I'm feeling removed from the whole thing. I think I now understand what disassociation means." She paused and searched for meaning. "Wouldn't they want me even closer after all that?"

"They didn't know what that spiteful uncle and his followers would do. They surely didn't want his beating taken out on you. He had already exploited you. The dream signified his potential, and nobody wanted to chance it."

She hummed in understanding.

Unexpectedly, Auntie spoke from the side of her mouth. "And the Kelly clan doesn't bring law into family drama. The loopholes can fail the victim. From the oldest days, we deal justice in our own way."

She remembered the earlier dates on the Ouija, and the explanation of her great-great grandfather taking matters into his own hands.

Auntie's mood lightened. "And all of this brought you … to me! They wanted you completely out of harm's way." She gave a small, spiteful chuckle. "Fergus hated your father so much he never got to know him. He knew nothing of Ian's magickal abilities. He also had no clue that our family has a rich history in this nourishing place we call home!"

She contemplated how much she loved her mountain sanctuary, Royal, Shane, her friends, her upbringing, and the fulfilling life that she lived. "I would have wanted nothing else."

"I promised I would always protect you ... with my own life, if necessary. I also promised to school you in magick, and no better place existed than these abundantly fresh redwoods. Plus, I had the help of my friends ... well, just Margaret now. Everyone else moved to Sedona."

She harrumphed at the mention of Margaret.

"I know you don't see her, but she's here for you if I am not."

"Okay, I know you keep saying that. But I don't see her ... like, ever."

"No? Not even in town?"

"Well, yes, but she's very quirky. She's never uttered a word to me, not even a *hi*."

"Arista, she's mute. Didn't I tell you that?" She looked off to the side trying to remember the telltale moment.

"No, I don't remember you saying that at all."

"Oh goodness, my oversight! She lost her voice many years ago. It was a very complex ritual. Rumors abound of whether it ended up a complete success or an epic failure. She was never the same."

"Really?"

"Yes, she's quirky, but I know I can rely on her."

She still had her doubts, however, the unplanned conversation about Margaret's oddity and the disclosure of her muteness provided a fresh perspective.

"Anyway ... I've blathered long enough. That is the story, in its entirety. You may grieve or be angry." Auntie looked at her with empathy in her eyes. "I just hope you can see it as the only option we had, and ultimately, forgive us all."

"So, where are they now? Are they alive?"

"A triple-layer intermediary exists. I have to admit, it is an immense challenge to reach them, but possible. Just please remember, it may put everyone at risk again."

"Whew! Well … I *truly* appreciate all of your honesty. This is a lot to process."

An accepting embrace preceded a few minutes of comfortable silence. Then, pondering the exhausting tale, and feeling her weariness, she longed for home.

"I think I need a nap now." She laughed, only half-joking. "Do you mind seeing me off?"

"You bet."

"Shane will be here later, too."

"Good, I like that."

Accompanied halfway, she waved at Auntie standing diligently at the Brooks' jasmine hedge, an equal distance between their two homes.

Lost in thought and astonished by her history, she pedaled onward to her driveway. Upon arrival, she barely remembered the ride. She dismounted her bike at the porch, recalled her promise of caution, and quickened her pace to the door.

Chapter 40
Behind the Jasmine

Henry crouched behind the Brooks family's fragrant jasmine hedges. The aromatic flowers masked his disgusting stench, a side effect of rising heat blended with his predatory anxiousness. He watched as the old bag loitered, making sure his Arissa got home before she returned to her own house.

Lucky for him, the Brooks Family were on vacation, and their absence had enabled him to follow up on unfinished business. After tracking Arissa, he had inconspicuously frequented her quaint neighborhood. He loitered to establish the women's routines, the schedules of the neighbors, and got to know more about his next victim. She made frequent trips to her aunt's house, spent a lot of time by her kitchen window and, unfortunately, had a frequently-visiting boyfriend. But considering the factors and proper timing, an evacuation could eliminate the obstacles.

While he waited for the biddy to toddle back to her house, he applied his ugly memories to his plans for Arissa. He saw his approach upon her lithe sexual body, his heart racing, followed by an adrenaline surge when he lunged and seized her. How exhilarating over the following weeks—his dopamine release while he tortured her, starved her, beat her, and watched her sense of humanity vanish to pervasive fear and groveling. Finally, as the last shred of the attraction had faded, he would clench her fragile neck and squeeze, watching his reflection in her dying eyes.

"Frick!" He winced, trying to contain his volume. A fierce sensation of bee venom interrupted his wicked thoughts. He flicked the insect away, squeezed out the stinger and smeared it on his jeans. The anger of pain transitioned to his loss of Tiffani. The incomplete ritual held great offense for him. He would not let that happen again.

Arissa was his focus now. She was exciting to covet. He recalled the first time he saw her, two young women walking by The Timbermill on that chilly day in late winter. Though insignificant now, he still believe that brunette friend of hers could be Fergus's niece.

To have Arissa keep appearing in his life teased the pursuit. Losing her as he fled from capture only created greater craving. More determined than ever, he devised a new plan. Her sun-kissed shoulders on that bike ride over to her aunt's house had him fantasizing about the devastation he would bring upon her.

He stood up and peeked past the hedge. The aunt was still in view. He bided his time, considering his options. Arissa had an oversized boyfriend, but he was only around half the time. She had a protective aunt, but the old bag was spacey, no physical threat and acres away. There was also that witch thing, but only if he bought into ghosts and fairy tales, and he had ditched those beliefs long ago.

After the old lady disappeared from sight, he emerged from behind the jasmine. He hustled out of the neighborhood, zigzagged the side streets, and arrived on the main drag of Boulder Creek. He hopped into his new ride, his father's aged Chevy pickup, that helped him blend in with the locals.

As the motor turned, a sense of progress aroused him. She was well within his reach.

CHAPTER 41
I KNOW THAT TATTOO!

The ashes fell in an eerie silence. They were a soft whisper to warn of the impending panic and fury that lay over the ridge. Flames approached from two directions, merging in the middle to ignite and destroy. The sky transformed into a shroud of doom as they merged, a kaleidoscope of red, orange, and slate gray with the smoke particles allowing only the longer wavelength colors to breach. The merciless had snuffed out the blue.

The town declared an evacuation five days after Hendrickson's warning.

Bethie packed for efficiency, adamant about securing her finest Egyptian tapestries and material swaths first. Next came every item upon her altar. Now, she sifted through the remains of her ritual room, down to its bare minimum. She sighed at the barren walls and stared at her empty altar.

"No! I refuse to believe this is the last time I see this room." She avowed this notion and abandoned her mental image of smoldering ruin.

Toting the last box into the kitchen, she surveyed the area and felt less of a dramatic connection. The bulk of her better culinary items stayed at her Sedona refuge. Nevertheless, she carefully tissue-wrapped a few geodes and other small trinkets from her windowsill and set them atop her tapestries.

"Ugh … feels like moving …" She groaned, before hoisting the bulky container of collectibles to her bony chest and heading for the car.

Lack of sunlight and ash flakes served as a constant reminder of the approaching fate. Gone was the scent of her garden, now muted by the harsh smell of smoke. No birds chirped and no neighborhood children giggled or taunted one another. She heard no voices, only silence, except for the occasional fleeing of another family car.

She wrestled with the box, situating it into her trunk and wedging it perfectly between her other belongings.

Out of the blue, she heard a familiar, delicate noise calling from within the trees.

Woot. Hoooo.

She stopped to appreciate the familiar sound for a moment. The owl in her yard was not just an amazing, beautiful creature, but also a friend.

The call's purpose quickly washed over her. The hoot came as a warning. The reality of the moment struck her. Although she could not see him, she felt his presence.

"Hi there." A voice coming into her driveway broke the silence. The bundled-up man made his way up her drive, a demon rising amidst the tumultuous firestorm. "It's a tragedy, you know! This fire. You need any help?"

"Stop, I don't know you!" She felt the danger enshroud her. He was no helpful stranger. Within her mind, she saw his cold, calloused, guilty hands, though presently he buried them in his pockets. She sensed him grow beyond his stature as he made his way toward her.

"I said, *stop!*" She moved backward toward her porch, putting the car and its open doors between her and this devil, upon which she kept a focused eye.

He shook his head and chuckled. "Oh no, no. You've got it all wrong. Hey, it's okay!" He reached out his hands, palms open to calm her, exposing the tattooed sigil of Fergus's coven.

"I know that tattoo! You stop right there!"

The man studied his hand before looking her in the eyes. A malevolent smile crossed his face.

SSCCRRREEEECH!

A blur of force followed the battle-cry bearing down hard on the stranger. The owl swooped, flogging with intention.

He screamed and batted at the bird.

Again, an air assault. A deliberate strike from the talon, opening the flesh on his bearded cheek.

To witness such an encounter momentarily captivated her. Just as quickly, she sobered to reality and knew this encounter could only mean one thing. Arista's fate drew upon them.

She ran into her house, hoping to keep Henry distracted and away from Arista. If only she could find her phone!

•   •   •

While battling the raptor, Henry grabbed a small rake from the garden bed. He met the last attack from the owl with a counterstrike to its underside.

With one of its extended legs now injured, the bird retreated into the trees.

He dabbed at his cheek wound, looked at the blood on his fingers and glanced up into the obscurity of the branches and needles. With the threat gone, his eyes shot toward the interior of the old biddy's house.

He clenched his teeth and angrily flung the rake aside before stepping onto the whimsical porch of inanimate animals. Lining the area were a hedgehog, a turtle, and a smiling cat, all carved out of large stone. Further, he stalked toward the door, bypassing the huge chunks of green, waxy rock and a stack of various wind chimes.

"Fuckin' nutcase," he said, scoffing at the inventory at his feet.

He stepped into the house and cautiously proceeded. "Hell-oo-o …" With a melodic taunt, he stalked into the hall, approaching the first room.

·   ·   ·

In her ritual room, Bethie abandoned her search for the phone and sought something to protect herself. Was there anything sharp or long enough to keep him at bay? Anything to whack him over the head? She had already packed all such objects into the car.

Frantically, she pulled open the drawers of her antique altar. Maybe she could use a drawer? Ridiculous! Wasn't there anything for protection? Grasping at straws, she realized her sobering predicament. Why had she come to this room? She could've gone out the side door!

"Hell-oo-o," he said, his voice beckoning down the dimmed hall.

"Be strong, child." she said aloud, not caring that it was audible as long as it sent the intention to Arista.

With no other option, she smashed the mirror of her altar, wrapped her hand with the hem of her long skirt, and secured the largest shard. Maintaining courage, she held it determinedly and readied for the battle of her life.

CHAPTER 42
PLAYED OUT IN REAL TIME

Just a short distance down the road, Shane had finished packing his mom's SUV with Arista's most valuable items. Unfortunately, the Ouija table was too hefty for transport. Regretful at leaving the magickal masterpiece, she hoped that a sprinkled, salted protection spell on the perimeter would make a difference.

Most precious to her, she had packed her newly-cherished, inherited athame, along with her favorite crystals into her small, tan-suede satchel that she wore across her body.

When Shane crammed Royal's crate into the floor area of the SUV, she poked two of her fingers through the wired door and gently rubbed his forehead. "Remember … we're going to be fine." Her crated feline stared wide-eyed into the distance, mortified in the luxury. "You have your favorite fur-ridden blankets and infused, calming kitty toys. Plus, how about this deluxe room you're in?"

"I don't know, maybe it's *too* much space for him." Shane eyed the girth of the plastic kennel. "Maybe more appropriate for our Schnoodle."

She gave a little laugh. "He'll be fine." She gave Royal one last rub. "If you don't mind, I'll ride with Auntie. Phone communication is not her strong suit. And that way, Royal can have the seat. I think he loves you now anyway!"

"Are you sure she'll have room for you?" He scanned the limited remaining space in his ride.

"Yes, I know for sure."

"Okay, you ready?"

"Yep!"

Shane got into the vehicle and backed onto the empty street, with her taking the lead at his front bumper. After he righted the car's direction, he trailed after her toward Auntie's house.

As usual, with his attention upon her, she felt playful and skipped, hips exaggerated in their swinging.

"I see you, dancer girl," he said, bellowing out of the window.

She giggled, self-corrected to maturity, and secured her satchel before breaking into a slight jog.

He pulled up beside her. "By the way, it looks like this disaster distracts us from your b-day, but don't think I forgot it."

"Aww, thank you." She leaned through his window and gave him a quick peck on the lips, then waved him onward as she stepped into Auntie's driveway.

He took a generous look into the yard, with its overt signs of packing and gaping car doors and away he drove.

She sang out the self-given name by which Auntie loved to be addressed. "Hey, Dande-lion Spirit-brite! Are you ready?"

Silence.

Inside the car, she saw the stacked belongings. Again, she called out, and walked toward the house. But as she neared the porch, a suspicion emerged within her.

She heard nothing.

The smoke that had inundated her senses, she no longer smelled.

Her surroundings became a soft blur.

Stillness.

Here it came on a conscious level, the reminder of the inverted pentagram tattoo. And, in this instant, she truly noted the sky ... her vision made real.

From the darkened interior of Auntie's house, a man appeared, his quick pace coming straight for her.

Her view sharpened, seeing only his maniacal eyes. The expected presence had come. A magnificent moment of sheer horror befell her … to meet him … to see the demon … he, who had terrorized the community throughout the year.

He lunged off the porch and grabbed her, slamming her to the ground.

She fiercely kicked at his shins. She dug her feet into the earth, attempting to thrust him off of her, and scratched with all her might into the flesh of his face, aiming for a bloody slit already gouged into his cheek.

He struck at her again and again.

She rolled to the right, her satchel wedged between their torsos, and created a barrier from his assault. Their grappling had inched them closer to a small pot. She grabbed it and smashed it into his face.

He flinched, the soil abrasive to his eyes.

She brought her knees upward and gave a mighty thrust, sending him a short distance away from her. She scrambled to her feet and ran up Auntie's driveway.

Her house! If she could just get to her house!

Faster she ran. Her attacker's pace keeping time with her as the two jetted past the Brooks' jasmine hedge. Breathless and fighting for her life, she looked for signs of awareness. Was anyone still around?

Suddenly, he took a mighty swipe at her. She lost her balance, and tumbled upon the asphalt, her vision complete, playing out in real time.

Henry dove to tackle her but lost his own advantage when he ended up landing beyond a firm hold of her arms.

She sprang up and sprinted towards her driveway.

Running, she screamed, but the verbal effort only slowed her down. She would not attempt it again.

She grabbed her hedge for leverage, swung around the turn and bolted toward her door, blindly rifling through her satchel for the key to safety. Finally, she grasped the coolness of metal.

It was too late! He caught up and struck her with his hammered fist to the side of her head.

The impact effective, she fell to the ground, and the man dove atop her.

She struggled, slapping away each pawing strike upon her. She locked out her arms to hold him up and away from her body, and violently bucked.

"No use, bitch," the man hissed, but he, too, seemed to tire from the intensity of their battle, his sweat dripping down upon her face.

Without warning, he rose like a striking serpent, a vision of horror, before smashing down hard with his fist to the side of her chin.

And all went dark.

CHAPTER 43
A GRAND RELEASE

"Arista, where are you?" Shane grumbled, nervous that every attempt to reach her ended in voicemail.

Reaching Highway 17, he merged northbound with the traffic. Hesitant of proceeding to much further, he knew there were few options to change your course of direction once further up the hill. Maybe he could reach another.

"Hey Evan, are you guys home?" His anxiety rose, despite a calm voice.

"No, we're just passing Livermore. We're going to my grandfather's house in Stockton."

He heard Rose in the background inquiring about the caller.

"What about the Hilgards? Do you know if Maddie's still around?"

"Gone, too. They left last night. Maddie said you could see the inferno against the night sky … like something straight out of Mordor. Super wicked! Crazy that it's coming straight for us."

"Jeez, and I thought the smoke was bad! So, they're long gone too. Hmmm."

"Yeah, her uncle just pulled the trigger since evac was inevitable and fires are unpredictable."

"Okay, I'm trying to reach Arista. But I'll just talk to you later. Travel safe."

"Yeah, take care. Tell her I said *hi* and stay safe."

"Yep." He ended the call. The lack of contact with her unsettled him. He stepped on the gas. He just had to twist and turn up the highway a mile or two more before he could set his car in the right direction, back to Arista's house.

.　　.　　.

Arista came to and felt as if she were floating. Where was she?

Her dire situation and all its terror came rushing back to her. She struggled to focus from beneath heavy eyelids, realizing she lay in the arms of the killer. She fidgeted but felt little coordination to be effective.

"Now, now … you settle down sweet Arissa," he said, clutching her tighter. "Please allow me to introduce myself …" he sang in a dignified manner. "Henry, Arissa. Arissa, Henry." The psycho babbled his formalities while juggling her in rigid arms.

More she squirmed, prompting him to toss her onto the floor in her living room.

She struggled to stay conscious when her head struck the wooden floor. Focusing on the sound of her remaining crystals scattering to the ground from her satchel, she tried opening her eyes. Woozy, she could only see blurred shapes.

"And we don't need to worry about that fire. No, we don't, sweet Arissa. The county evacuates before the fire is close enough to kill. So, with everyone gone, well, you and I can enjoy the privacy. And no need to worry about that old battle-ax of yours either. I took care of her, too."

In her haze, she discerned the tail end of his psychotic innuendo. *Auntie?*

He kicked at her foot. "Hey! You in there?" Then, he turned and walked the short zigzag path into her kitchen. After turning on the water, he called out to her. "You know, I came back for you?" He chuckled. "You know, I'm thinking it *is* you who has all sorts of fans in Washington. But they don't get to have you."

The water stopped and he re-appeared in the doorway, ogling her defeated and limp body. "I have to say when I saw you back in the winter … mmm, so pretty you were, my little doll. And you know what … I don't care if you are the one Fergus is searching for. It wouldn't be worth his praise to let him have you."

She tried clearing the blood from deep inside her throat and struggled to decipher the meaning of his bantering.

He snickered. "But I am sorry, sweet Arissa, you won't be my last."

. . .

Sheriff Michaels pulled his cruiser onto Bethie's street. It would not hurt to check on his new favorite citizens. He wanted them safe from the rising possibility of flame and devastation. Hopefully, they had already left, as they were instructed.

Nearing Bethie's driveway, he slowed and noticed the bright yellow Volvo wagon, doors agape, in her driveway. He stopped and waited to catch sight of her, but after a couple minutes, and still no sign, he called to her. "Ms. Spiritbrite."

No response.

He backed up a few feet and turned into her driveway. By now, he realized that not only was there an extended absence of Bethie but also a lack of reaction to a car, specifically law enforcement, in her front yard. Something was awry.

"Ms. Spiritbrite, I see you're all packed up," he said in a friendly tone, masking his concern. After all, she could walk out at any moment, arms loaded and exasperated from the exertion.

He got out of his cruiser and circled her car, gathering visual information and noticing the eerie silence. Maybe she occupied the bathroom.

While scrutinizing the surroundings, he produced his first cough since the evacuation, a sign that smoke and the destructive force drew nearer.

"Hello, Bethie, you in there?" She could also be at Arista's place.

But his gut told a different story.

He approached the porch.

"I'm hoping this all passes real quickly, and we can get back to our homes soon." He knew he talked only to himself.

By his feet, at the base of the porch, he noticed a broken clay pot. An accidental misstep during packing? Or a sign of struggle? He carefully unsecured his gun, but kept it holstered as he walked up the first step of the porch.

"It's Sheriff Michaels, I'm coming in."

He ceased his friendly formalities as he passed the kitchen, drew his weapon, and readied for trouble. He crept down the hall, peering into each nook that he passed until he found himself near the last room. From outside, he could see a dressing table with an exposed pressboard face bordered by broken shards of a former mirror.

"Bethie?"

He peered around the doorway. His gut turned. She lay still on the floor with a small stream of blood trickling from her nose and her hand amidst a puddle of viscous red. With his worst suspicions confirmed, his thoughts turned to Arista. Bethie was not the draw for this violence, but merely the obstacle. And now Arista faced a life-threatening danger.

He bolted to his cruiser and radioed for help before he left his police car and its noisy radio behind him. Urgently, he ran to Arista's cottage.

Halfway up the road, he noticed the signs of a fresh struggle on the gravel—shed blood and a small pink crystal. He tightened his grip on his pistol, and onward he went, keeping alert of all directions.

As he turned the corner into Arista's driveway, he noticed the small, shattered pane on her front door nearest the knob. He rushed to the side of the house and crouched to observe the inside scene.

·   ·   ·

Arista's jaw ached, her body felt bruised, and the lengthy struggle of trying to keep her attacker at bay had vanquished all of her energy. Not a thread of fight remained after the ruthless knockout. She lay on the ground while he taunted her as he snooped through her kitchen.

In a moment of peace, she eyed Royal's catnip ball lying motionless under the Ouija table.

Henry spoke to her from her bedroom, but his words were unclear. With him out of sight, the idea of escape crossed her mind. She tried to lift herself from the floor.

Out of nowhere, he appeared and shoved her firmly to the ground. "No, no, you stay right there."

She whimpered. He had conquered her physically, and now mentally. Every inch of her felt pain and exhaustion. If she ran, he would catch her. If she tried to fight, he would hit her again. So, with the stakes set so high, she prayed, quietly … slowly.

"Great warrior Goddess, prepare me for this inevitable battle,
fight with me,
Justice, shine your light and judgement in this dire hour.
Protect me from him that would harm me.
Stay with me. Comfort me.
So may this be."

"Stop that shit, bitch!" Henry snapped, poking his head around the small hallway entrance. He glared at her.

A blessing in disguise, she noticed that her divine appeal had affected him and found solace in her sliver of control over the situation.

She began again, "Great warrior Goddess, prepare—"

"I said stop it!" He rushed toward her to deliver a joint-crunching kick to her hip.

·   ·   ·

Crouched outside Arista's house, Sheriff Michaels caught sight of Henry through the window. Despite the mountain man's beard, he could see through the attempted disguise. He had the same close-set eyes and hairline in the plentiful sketches from various witnesses. He even held a resemblance to his hapless father, who they had interviewed the previous day after investigating Yelena's lead.

Out of his sight, he heard the soft tone of Arista's incessant murmurings and noticed how they provoked Henry. He creeped up to the front door.

"I said stop it," Henry demanded with a hard kick. "Your witchy shit isn't gonna help you this time!"

"Who's to say?" he posed deadpan through the door's broken pane with his aim set at Henry's chest.

Henry startled.

"Freeze! County Sheriff!"

Shocked by the abrupt intrusion, Henry swung around, and readied to bolt.

He fired, intending to strike him dead.

When the bullet grazed Henry's shoulder, he jolted but his expression turned angry, and he attempted to run at him.

Again, he pulled the trigger. This time hitting Henry's neck.

Struck, he buckled and fell to the floor, out of sight.

Quickly, he acted to gain entry. He delivered a solid kick from his heavy steel-toed boot to the door. A sharp pain shot up his leg and back, but he would deal with that later.

· · ·

Arista found courage from Henry's distractions, and weakly shifted herself around on the floor.

She caught glimpses of him desperately assessing his shoulder as he tightly gripped his neck. As his panic consumed him, her strength and courage grew. With renewed energy, she had to act fast while he nursed his injuries.

She grabbed her satchel and pulled it close, furiously shuffling within it. Desperate to secure her new, most-treasured athame, its cross guard had caught on something.

"Goddamn you," Henry said, venomously spewing his words as he clutched at the gaping gory wound on his neck. He squeezed at it, trying to stop the arcing spurts of bright red plasma squirting from his carotid artery.

Flashing quick looks in his direction, she frantically contended with the cross guard and felt the urgency as blood oozed down his forearm, soaking his clothes.

Suddenly, Henry launched himself upon her, wrestling her face-up on the ground beneath him. He latched both hands upon her neck, now fulfilling his process.

Deprived of oxygen, and immobilized by the hold, her eyes slowly began to close. But in her last hint of consciousness, a translucent apparition swept down upon her and Henry. A painful jolt of sheer vitality hit her between the eyes, and an invigorating sensation overcame her. Inward she swept into a realm of dazzling luminescent neon shapes—a vacuum of sound, void of time … void of being.

.   .   .

The sheriff, on his third and final attempt, shot the doorknob. He rushed into the house and zigzagged towards the living room, drawn by the sounds of a struggle.

As he turned the corner, he watched Arista's eyes slowly closed as Henry absorbed her life force with his sickened state of psychosis.

"Freeze Henry!" He shouted with authority yet respected the proximity of firing so close to Arista.

In a shocking instant, Arista's eyes shot open, the look on her face hauntingly chilling. She looked up at Henry with a hardened stare he would swear was not her own. Then he heard a foreign utterance in a deepened voice release from her mouth.

"*Mothaigh crúb an chait.*"

"Henry! Freeze!"

But neither Henry nor Arista reacted to his warning.

With Henry's back toward him, his body made a sudden, violent jerk. Just as quickly, it eased into stillness.

With the threatening body posture ceding, and all tension gone, he walked up behind Henry, gun drawn to his head. "It's over Henry, hands up!"

Still Arista's piercing stare stayed fixed on Henry. Then, slowly, she shut her eyes, and fainted back to earth.

Henry's body sagged before slid sideways off Arista. He rolled onto his back, prominently displaying a wicked blade buried deep within his solar plexus. The two of them, evil and innocence, lay side by side.

Quickly, he knelt by her, and pulled her out of Henry's reach. He felt a pulse and briskly patted her face. "Arista! Arista! Wake up!"

Her eyes slowly blinked to attention. Drained of energy, she came to as he propped her up against the living-room wall.

"Hey … you okay? Arista, do you know where you are?"

The sound of sirens slowly rose in volume as the bustle of law enforcement infiltrated the neighborhood.

She looked over at the bloody body of Henry. "Is that him? Is he dead?"

"He won't be hurting anyone anymore."

He smoothed her bangs out of her eyes and glanced over to Henry, then back at her. The less regard he gave to that toxic waste, the better. Still, he would keep a peripheral eye on him until his cohorts gathered up the carcass.

"Arista, what do you remember?"

Her silence gave him time to think about the eerie way Henry had fallen to her. He saw it with his own eyes, yet it all felt displaced. The stern facial expression, the strength of the thrust and the voice, so different from her own. It begged the question—was it truly Arista?

CHAPTER 44
THE SIGHT OF HIM

Arista could hear the sheriff's voice but faded in and out of consciousness.

"Arista, what do you remember?"

Slowly, she floated into awareness. She remembered Henry's relentless pursuit of her, the falling and skinning of her elbow, which stung even more so now, as she probed at it. She remembered the mighty hits that he inflicted upon her, the kicks and praying on the floor … and her athame.

"Arista—"

"Yes … my house. What happened?" She eyed the madman, his dead body covered in gore laying by her sturdy Ouija table. On his half-opened, bloodied hand, she noticed the inverted pentagram tattoo. She shivered and turned away.

The awareness of her own hand became apparent. Bringing it closer to her face, the sight of Henry's blood and the tackiness of it drying sickened her. "Oh, no!" She anxiously and frantically looked around, now seeing the glutinous red pools covering her wooden floor, and felt her heartbeat quicken.

"It's okay. He's gone." He placed his hand on her shoulder, a gesture of reassurance.

"I was trying to get my athame." She eked out snippets of what had happened. "It was stuck … he strangled me. But …" She shook her head in confusion.

"You did it!" the sheriff said, half-smiling, before his expression turned serious once again. "You got him."

"I did? But I don't remember," she whimpered.

The EMTs rushed in and escorted her outside, where paramedics in latex gloves took samples of the blood upon her. At last, they cleansed her hands and forearms of the monster's residue.

The lawful crew strung yellow crime scene tape as had been done so many other times throughout this bizarre year. They scribbled upon notepads, and despite the need to evacuate, law and order prevailed on Hoot Owl Way.

She could hear mutterings about *Bethie Kelly* and strained to find out the importance. "Where's Bethie?" she asked to no one in particular. Still weak, she pushed herself to pursue this very necessary question. "Where's my Auntie?" she asked, a little louder.

Shane rowdily pulled into the driveway, heightening the chaotic environment. The officers stormed him when he dashed out of the car. But Sheriff Michaels quickly cleared him with a nod knowing that was her guy.

"Shane!" she cried.

"Oh my God, Arista!" he said, barging in for a hug. "Are you okay?"

The relief energized her. "Yes, where's Royal?"

"He's safe in the car. Jesus!" he exclaimed, darting his eyes at the scene and upon her.

"He's probably so scared right now."

"They're going to transport her. You may want to say your goodbyes," the sheriff informed them. "We'll talk soon. Until then, you take care." He walked away to allow them privacy.

She acknowledged his goodbye and watched the dutiful paramedics continue their process on her, while Shane tried to stay out of their way. "I heard them talking about Auntie. Please make sure she's okay," she asked of him.

"Got it! I will." Shane bolted toward the officers to fulfill the quest.

The EMTs checked her injuries and re-took her vitals.

"Bethie Kelly? Do you know if she's okay?" She felt herself beginning to hyperventilate again.

"No ma'am. We're here for you. Please, try to relax and let's get you stabilized. Just breathe. Look at me."

She looked at the EMT.

"Breathe. Nice and slow," she said, dragging out the words and guiding her in a calming voice.

Arista followed her lead.

"Good, that's good," she praised.

But what about Auntie?

After a few more minutes, they swooped her up and loaded her into the ambulance, where she lay on the gurney enroute to the hospital. Her accompanying EMT meddled with tubes and buttons and made sure she stayed reasonably comfortable.

"How are you doing?" the attendant asked.

"I'm fine, I think. I'm very worried about my great-aunt, Bethie Kelly. Do you know anything about her?"

"The ambulance transported someone else, but we have no further details."

She found an ounce of relief in the answer. It had to be Auntie, and at least she had professional care.

She played the scene of the showdown between her and Henry continuously in her mind. She recalled all the precursory actions, but the strangulation, and what happened next, persisted as mystery. Who stabbed him? And what did Sheriff Michaels mean by *you got him*? Was he implying that she was the one who killed Henry? Impossible! Even to save herself, she felt incapable of ending life in such a gruesome manner. What strength enabled her to plunge the athame so deeply through his jacket into his flesh and bone?

And yet, she overheard the sheriff recounting the story to another officer. He had said she was awake and talking, resolute in her words, and that the words she used were foreign and her voice, unusually gruff.

In a sobering moment, her anguish of finding meaning in her reflections eased and she felt a comforting lift. She didn't kill Henry.

Something else was present, and it became present in her. Perhaps the owner of the voice in her shallow dreams? The owner of touches and breezes, the dropped items, and the creaks in the night. The same occupying presence that had shattered her lavender jar, startled her awake with a hanging leopard throw, and alarmed her with many surprise visits throughout the years.

She felt a sense of warmth wash away her aches and confusion, and slowly a smile crept upon her face. Ghost had paid a visit … and saved her life.

CHAPTER 45
AGE THAT CREATES SUBSTANCE

Lazily, the sun eased into the desert mountains, casting hues of blues, purples, and a spectrum of yellow to red beyond its radiating energy. Faces of the red-rock cliffs absorbed the kiss goodnight from the already risen crescent moon, and the shadows cascaded down through the crevices, deep into the canyon walls. It provided the perfect backdrop for one's spirit to soar and healing to begin.

Bethie felt blessed to return to her sacred second home in Sedona. Head trauma protocol required a week-long hospital stay because of the severity of the blow to her head. Henry had struck to kill, but she held stronger than he could have ever imagined. A month after her doctor's release, she sat amongst mystical-minded friends, happily processing the lingering effects from her ordeal.

The Waning Crescent Coven settled on the back patio of her desert abode enjoying the dusk of summer's last night. Candace Bailey lifted the teapot and poured her a cup of steaming spiced chai. "It's wonderful to have you back at home with us, Bethie. We were so worried about you."

She basked in the energy from her circle of crones. The three beautifully aged women who graced her presence brought a balance of whimsy, calm and security.

Across from her sat Pearl Seaborn, with her silvery-white and purple-streaked hair tightly pulled into a bun. Her dark, purple-rimmed, cat-eye specs matched her lightweight sweater, accessorized with a hanging Scolecite medallion. Pearl had a sharp tongue, a quick wit, and kept very business minded. She easily manifested money when taking on new ventures and also made sure all witchy matters stayed on course for the coven.

To her right sat Candace Bailey, another silver-haired beauty, with a close-cropped cut atop cocoa-colored skin. A sought-out scryer and healer, Candace performed both white-magick and a select few hoodoo practices, and her schedule booked out weeks in advance. Her words were soothing yet wise, dispelling doubts long after she left. She could swear Candace's breath emitted a scent of rose.

And to her left sat Bridget Ciccone, the newest member of the coven and the youngest of them all by a couple of decades. Bridget would mostly listen to the chattering bunch taking in seasoned knowledge of the craft. During the five years with them, they discovered the middle-aged goddess with the flowing cappuccino mane had, not only spot-on intuitiveness toward strangers, but that she also served as quite a catalyst when the foursome got together. Her element of earth closing their circle.

"I am so grateful for your prayers," Bethie said as she sipped the aromatic tea, enjoying the invigorating scent of cinnamon, ginger, and clove. "What would I do without you?"

"We never stopped praying, Bethie, not since you left! We knew the severity when we all last gathered," Pearl said, with a raised eyebrow. "Your lovely niece, how is she doing?"

"She is chipper, as always. A little smoke damage to contend with and an extensive floor replacement needed. But Shane's helping her with contractors in both of our places."

"Oh, that's a shame," empathized Candace. "You never consider those aspects."

"On a much lighter note, the Navarro parents ... that's Evan's family ... hosted a birthday BBQ. While they held it for Evan, his mother included Maddie and Arista, since they had both missed their special day, too. It provided quite the update. Turns out her friend with the snakebite lost his forearm from the ordeal. The infection progressed and amputation became the only option to save his life."

A gasp of regret emitted from her sisters.

"He'll be fine, though, because he has a healthy attitude and is already learning how to throw a football with his prosthetic."

The group nodded in a reverent gesture.

"And Evan has a new girlfriend." She pursed her lips and tapped at her chin. "What was her name? Hmmm. Bree! Yes, Bree has joined their little group."

"Oh, that's lovely," Candace said. "He had so much angst sitting in the shadows for so long … darn-near pulled him to the dark side."

She chuckled. "While he was more than willing to atone, I overheard him say the next time he participated in a ritual, it would involve a Catholic priest and a cracker."

The ladies exhausted a round of cackling before Pearl moved to a more serious note. "You know Arista would be gone if it weren't for your blessed gift to her!"

Typical of Pearl to change the mood, but she found her footing. "Sheriff Michaels would have gotten him. He had already shot him twice."

Pearl stood firm. "You never know. That monster could have finished the job before the sheriff finished him off. It was your gift that empowered that sweet child!"

She wanted to stay humble about her intuition to pass on the athame. However, with Pearl non-relenting, she knew to appease her, lest she launch into a fit to have the last word. "Well, I guess he could have taken her from me had she not killed that horrible beast herself!"

A murmur of agreement arose.

"Actually, my friends, something else occurred during the melee. Something very peculiar."

"Oh, this sounds good," Pearl noted. "When Bethie's voice drops like that, it is of the most supernatural importance."

"Well, it takes something very peculiar to be labeled as such by a witch."

The group tittered in unison.

"Arista told me she wonders if her house spirit possessed her. She remembers nothing of the murder." She paused for effect. "But, the sheriff says she was wide awake, growling out a phrase that sounded," She air-quoted the sheriff. "… *foreign*. He also believes it unusual that Arista's thrust held so much power."

"Is it the spirit that you have mentioned over the years?" asked Candace.

"I imagine so."

Pearl nodded with confidence. "So, it is true. The Kelly ghost, and its abilities to connect with the mundane world. How fascinating that Arista potentially channeled it."

"It is true."

"Wow! This is amazing stuff," Bridget said, failing to contain her usual poise in front of her elders.

"Yes indeed, Bridget. So, Bethie, what is your plan now?" Pearl asked.

"I continue a next-level training with her, and we hope that not only her spirit stays virtuous, but that the Kelly ghost does as well! Murder is a bit tricky, and while Arista may not have intentionally done the deed …" Her volume trailed. "Anyway, I foresee it will be okay, as I believe the spirit is my granddad! Let's hope our kin remember us on visits from the Otherworld."

The witches united in an awed coo, followed by a united sip of tea.

"There's another issue at hand—literally. When the killer first came on to my property, he bore Fergus' sigil on his palm. As I had told you, Arista had several visions of that tattoo before all came to pass." She looked at them with a growing seriousness. "So, it confirms that he still searches." She sighed and shook her head as fatigue overtook her.

"Keira has been *here* for over a decade. How did he find Arista after so much time has passed?" Pearl asked.

"I don't think he told Fergus about Arista. Otherwise, he would have been there himself. So, it shows that he stays cowering in the shadows while others do his dirty work. I believe he fired a shot in the general direction where he thought Keira had left her—"

"Bethie, I think it's time you make the reintroduction, especially if their absence is no longer helping. It's important for Arista. She is an adult and has come into many powers—intuition, spirit world, scrying, and now channeling. She is still learning, but her bag of tricks has grown substantially. You don't have to be her sole protector anymore. Reach out. Find her parents."

She sighed, set down her cup, and gazed into the sparkling-orange glass pebbles of her fire pit. "Arista has always put *so much* faith in me. But my magick is waning, and it has been for some time now."

"Bethie, you are being too hard on yourself," Candace said in her kindest voice. "You and Arista just went through a terrible ordeal. You are going to have doubts. But you are both safe because of the foresight to give her the athame."

The kind words eased her glumness. "You only bequeath a family athame when you are dying." A spark of sass bubbled from her. "and I think I want it back!"

A boisterous laugh eased the tension, and the group sipped in unity.

"Of course, I'm joking. It's Arista's for a reason, and now it holds a more complex history with the killing of that awful monster. I'll work with her on a cleansing ritual but will research with an elder since I've never done that."

"Bethie, we are the elders," Pearl retorted.

She froze, pondering the notion. "Touché, Pearl."

Another united chuckle filled the air.

"Where is the athame now?" asked Candace.

"It's in evidence at the sheriff's office. I am not sure how long they keep it."

"Well, at least it's safe there," Bridget said.

Candace set down her teacup. "Bethie, I think it's important we address your concerns." She looked at each of the ladies. "I think we can all agree that youth reigns for its energy and beauty and vibrancy, and we dread aging for loss of the same. But it is actually age that creates substance! Many cultures and heritages believe this. It is the same with us. Existing within an aged crone is a significant source of wisdom, foresight, and fortitude. As Pearl said, we are now elders, and that is great!"

She could not find the reassurance within herself. "But how did I miss seeing that monster come to my house? I didn't protect myself and here I sit with a huge goose egg on my head and a sliced hand." Her shoulders dropped, and she shook her head and teared. "And I let him get to her."

"Witches are not superhumans. We are simply intuitive people with a little extra gift. Sometimes we are spot-on and sometimes we miss the mark. We practice and we believe, and above that," Candace opened her hands skyward as if releasing a dove, "we let it go. We give it to the universe and if it happens, we can claim it. Or we can just be thankful that things go our way."

"That reminds me … my dear friend from the trees swooped down on that monster. It allowed me time to get to my altar."

"Your owl swooped?" Pearl asked, gaping.

"Yes, my resident owl."

Pearl drew in a breath, and she smiled. "Well, that certainly worked in your favor. Listen Bethie, as you said, you still have quite a goose egg on that stubborn head of yours. You've been through the ringer! Your judgement will be dampened, and you may be mopey and doubtful of yourself while you deal with concussion symptoms. Remember that."

Candace further encouraged her. "If you have any doubts, just ask us. We'll keep you grounded. Or, if more appropriate, we'll take you astral."

The collective effervescence of cheerful humor echoed through the quiet neighborhood.

Only one thing did she miss at this joyful union, her dear Arista.

•   •   •

Arista finished her evening offering at her altar, then turned to face a patiently waiting Shane, stretched out on her bed. Royal sat tall by his side, enjoying the only man he had ever accepted.

"My Royal finally loves you."

"Well, he should. I'm a good guy." Shane stroked from head to tip of tail, prompting Royal to turn toward him. "And I love him too," he said, looking into the eyes of his new friend.

She reached down beneath her altar and pulled out her tarot cards. "Okay, it's been months since I've drawn tarot, and I think it's a good way to celebrate new beginnings."

"Dang! You do that stuff too? Oh, wait … of course you do." He said, feigning ignorance.

"Of course, I do." She wryly mimicked.

He came over and loitered beside her. "Will it ruin it if I watch?"

"No, it won't ruin it and, of course, you can watch. You want me to read for you too?"

"Uh, no, thank you anyway. Let's give me and the occult a rest for a while."

"Point taken, but a teeny bit of education?"

"Sure."

"Other religions have used the cards too. They can be a simple card game or a divination tool."

He squinted, looking doubtful of her claim.

"Seriously. Anything can become taboo through ignorance. And ignorance creates fear." She softened her tone. "But that's enough preaching. I appreciate your participation this year. You've been great."

"Well, thank you," he said, and dove in for an extended kiss. Pulling away, he nodded toward the deck. "Let's see what you draw."

She thrice shuffled the deck, then tapped the top of the cards—one, two, three. Making the most of her limited space, she carefully spanned the deck across her altar. She perused them, then made her choice, bringing it to her chest without looking. She looked at Shane, then the bed, and Shane again.

"Alright, I get it," he said, backing up to sit down on the mattress edge.

"I always let Royal look first."

They looked at Royal, now curled comfortably on the bed with eyes closed.

"Maybe not," they said in unison.

She lifted the card from her chest and looked at it. *Oh great, he's going to harass me about this one.*

"What did you get?"

She put the card back to her chest and pondered her response. *I'll have to fully explain it.*

"Well?"

"Okay, first glances can be quite deceiving." She braced herself for harassment.

"Yeah? Let me see it."

She turned her card to face Shane, prompting a chuckle. "Actually, this is a good card," she said defensively.

"Yeah? So, what does it mean? 'Cause that title is—"

"Hold up. Just look at it for a minute." She walked over and sat beside him. "See how he's vibrantly dressed? He's festive and confident. The butterfly and cute puppy are symbols of innocence, and yet also show the potential of growth. And The Fool—"

Shane laughed and poked her in her ribs.

"Oh, just settle down." She knew he was just being playful, but also wanted to convey the positive meaning of the card. "Listen to me for a minute. The Fool is a good card for a new start. Plus, if you were playing a regular game of cards, it's the ultimate trump."

She playfully glared at him and awaited his response.

"Okay, I get it." His eyes twinkled. "What other benefits come with being a fool?"

She rolled her eyes.

"I'm kidding. That's the last of it, I promise," He briefly put his arm around her for reassurance. "So, what else does it mean?"

"It means new beginnings and approaching the world with wonder, optimism, and caution. It might be wise, given the horrible experience I just had!" *There's no way I'm telling him about the naivety aspect.*

He quieted.

"And, yes, for future reference, it may very well ruin it if you watch me draw." She was just kidding, but he didn't have to know that.

"Come on, Riss."

Puppy dog eyes won't help you now. She took her cards back to their case, put them beneath her altar, and returned to her bed.

Shane scooched back to rest beside her, sending Royal retreating to his post with the bed becoming too crowded.

She remembered how happy she felt with her tarot draw the previous winter. *The Lovers* reading had come to pass, and he was still adorable, and easy to forgive, despite his teasing.

Peering up at her ceiling, she sighed. "Auntie's not coming back for a while. I can tell by the emptiness of her house."

"Don't worry. She always comes back, her words exactly."

"People don't always come back. They may mean it when they say it, but things happen, and they don't."

Shane studied her as she lay in silence. "Are you okay?"

She realized that moping in a pool of pity was not the behavior of a good witch, especially with her boyfriend present. "Uggh. Yes. I'll be fine."

"So this is about Auntie?"

"Maybe."

"Well, why don't you go visit her? You've never been to Sedona, right?"

"No."

"Well … you want to go?"

She paused and thought about Auntie on a backdrop of desert shrubbery and a spark of excitement grew within her. "I never considered it."

"Hmph, looks like my brainstorming is a success then!" He tenderly pulled her into the crook of his arm.

She cozied into him. What might the desert be like? Maybe too hot? Maybe a new start?

"Well, what do you think?" he asked with a tight squeeze.

"It would be nice, as long as Auntie to invites me." She shot a glance up at Shane. "I don't want to just invite myself."

"I don't think she'd mind at all. In fact, maybe we could go together."

The invitation struck her. "Really? You want to go with me? Like a couple's vacation?"

"Sure, I don't know when … and I need to ask my mom about the car. Hmmm. And my teaching commitments may limit time off."

She thought of her own commitments. "I really need to get a few counseling sessions in, but down the line I could totally put them on hold, but … yes!" She squealed and bolted upright.

"Oh boy, what did I just get myself into? In all honesty, I've never taken a road trip with anyone but my family or football, nor have I been out of Cali except by plane. But … my mom would probably help me put it together. Unless you want to?"

"No thanks. You can do it. But it sounds so fun!" She gushed with excitement before lunging on top of him.

"What about winter … when it's not so hot? We'll have to figure out the car, too" he said, reasoning as she started kissing his neck. "And where to stay … and … we'll just hash it out later."

CHAPTER 46
A GLIMMER OF THE JINGLES

"Hey Dustin, I've got to get home. You almost done?"

"Yep, almost done," Dustin said as he typed away at his terminal. "Thanks for staying!"

"Alright. I'm going to make a pit stop while you finish up."

When the female deputy disappeared into the hallway, he waited until he heard the bathroom door shut. After checking that the coast was clear, he hastily got up from his desk and darted toward the wall unit of keys. He punched in the code, grabbed a small silver key ring, closed the unit, and rushed to the evidence room down the short hallway. The first key failed, but the second yielded entry.

While the deputy piddled two doors down, he stared at the partitioned shelving system. "K … Ke …" he whispered, running his index finger along the file labels. "Kelly!"

In sync with the toilet flushing, he retrieved the small box from the cubby. As he secured the sturdy plastic bag containing the athame, he noticed it crusted with Henry's blood. He tucked it into his heavy jacket, before sliding the box back into place.

Carefully closing the evidence room door, he hastened back to the cabinet to rehang the keys. He could hear the sink's running water as he quietly shut the cabinet door.

The deputy reappeared in the hallway just as he reached his desk to shut down his computer. She noticed his haste. "Whoa, there. You don't have to rush that much."

"I've kept you here long enough." He grabbed his backpack and thanked the deputy again for staying late. With his final wave goodbye, he headed out but kept his hand gesture brief knowing by end of shift, the makeup had usually worn off his tattooed palm, revealing his inverted pentagram tattoo.

Diving into his car, he felt the thrill of success. With his heart still racing, he focused on his route to deliver the blade. And knowing of the henchman's impatience, he drove up Felton Empire Grade, taking the mountainous road's twists and turns with the precision of a professional driver.

· · ·

High above Dustin's getaway, a great-horned owl flew unnoticed. It flapped its expansive wings as it finished its circuit of familiar territory. It hovered in the streetlamp glow atop a telephone pole to peer down at Earth & Ocean. From there, it glided through town, stopping at the Navarro residence to urp up a tubular token for the lady of the house. Then, it headed to The Timbermill, followed by Hoot Owl Way. It glanced down on Bethie's garden of fading sunflowers prior to its flight toward Arista's cottage. There, it saw shadows of life socializing as silhouettes behind a closed semi-sheer curtain.

Onward it flew into the shrouded forest, full of wild creatures—a grey fox cuddling into its softly padded sleeping cubby, a bobcat softly footing through the brush, and plenty of prey seeking refuge from the night's predators.

Finally, it took a methodical plunge toward an old one-bedroom shack with crooked shutters and profusely peeling paint. Down it flew into an overgrown yard of broadleaf dock and orange marigold, of crabgrass and light pink aster, and further past the sizeable vegetable garden within a haphazard planter box full of bulky, bright orange pumpkins radiant in the moonlight.

The owl flew in through the front window, and everything became silent and still.

A small light illuminated inside the shack. The creak of rusty hinges on a cupboard, followed by running water, sent a gurgling sound effect through the yard.

A dim porch light flipped on and out came Margaret Troxel in her woven serape and hat that sported a handsome, new rattlesnake-skin hat band. No longer shuffling in her usual gait, she now hosted a significant limp from an injured leg, struck by a small rake.

She sat down upon her wooden porch swing and reached for her tambourine, the risen moon catching a glimmer of the jingles. She tapped it and softly hummed.

I truly hope you enjoyed the read!

For Reference and Inspiration

"A to Z Witchcraft | Terminology and Definitions"
https://witchcasket.co.uk/blog/a-to-z-of-witchcraft-terminology-definitions-glossary/

"Air & Fire Metaphysical Shop, Boulder Creek, CA"
https://www.airandfire.com/home.html

"Big Basin Redwoods State Park, Boulder Creek"
https://www.parks.ca.gov/?page_id=540

Book of Stones: Who They Are and What They Teach," by Robert Simmons, Naisha Ahsian

"Britainnica" www.Britiannica.com

"Collateral Damage" Eugene Anthony Chase
https://www.santacruzsentinel.com/2020/04/19/sculptor-e-a-chase-leaves-striking-santa-cruz-legacy/

Finding Appropriate Names -
https://www.momjunction.com/articles/

"Gayle's Bakery and Rotisserie," https://www.gaylesbakery.com

"Gilded Lily, Felton, CA" https://tattoshopsnearme.com/the-gilded-lily-tattoos/

"United Irish Cultural Center of San Francisco"
https://irishcentersf.org

"Its Beach, Santa Cruz, CA"
https://www.californiabeaches.com/beach/its-beach/

"Learn Religions" https://www.learnreligions.com

"Merriam-Webster Dictionary" https://www.merriam-webster.com

"Monarch Butterfly Garden, Natural Bridge State Park, Santa Cruz" https://www.parks.ca.gov/?page_id=26135

"Natural Bridges State Park, Santa Cruz" http://parks.ca.gov/?page_id=541

"Outdoor Apothecary" https://www.outdoorapothecary.com/goddess-of-spring/

"Sawmill Restaurant & Ale House, Boulder Creek" https://www.thesawmillbc.com

Scott Sipes, State of California Park Ranger / CAL Fire

"Serpent's Kiss, Santa Cruz, CA" https://www.serpents-kiss.com

"SolisRedhead" https://www.etsy.com/your/shops/SolisRedhead/tools/listings

"West Cliff Drive, Santa Cruz" https://www.santacruz.org/listings/west-cliff-drive/

"The White Witch Podcast w/Carly Rose" – Spotify – *Lots and lots of Witchy Love!*

"Wikipedia" https://en.wikipedia.org/wiki/

Witch's Book of Spellcraft by J. Mankey, M. Cavalli, A. Lynn and A. Mankey

WITCHY DICTIONARY

Áine – An Irish goddess of summer, wealth and sovereignty. She is associated with midsummer and the sun. Also, as the goddess of love and fertility, she has command over crops and animals and is also associated with agriculture.

Altar – The ritual workspace; a table, shelf, or other dedicated area where witches practice their craft.

Athame – A ceremonial knife or blade which is used to channel and direct energy and cast protective circles.

Besom – A traditional broomstick constructed of twigs tied to a sturdy pole. Used as a spiritual cleaner, the besom usually does not touch the ground, but is churned a few inches above it.

Black-Magick – Magick derived from evil forces, as distinct from good or benign forces; or magic performed with the intention of doing harm.

Brigid (var.) – In Irish mythological cycles, Brighid, whose name is derived from the Celtic *brig* or "exalted one" had two sisters, also called Brighid, and they were all associated with healing and crafts. The three Brighids were typically treated as three aspects of a single deity, making her a classic Celtic triple goddess, similar to the Triple Moon Goddess aspect. In addition to her position as a goddess of magic, Brighid was known to watch over women in childbirth, and thus evolved into a goddess of hearth and home. Today, many Pagans honor her on February 2, which has become known as Imbolc. The Catholic Church adopted Brigid as a saint.

Buzz Pollination – A technique used by some bees, such as solitary bees to release pollen which is more or less firmly held by the anthers. To release the pollen, solitary bees are able to grab onto the flower and move their flight muscles rapidly, causing the flower and anthers to vibrate, dislodging pollen.

Coven – A gathering of at least three witches who come together to practice witchcraft.

Divination – The art or practice that seeks to foresee or foretell future events or discover hidden knowledge usually by the interpretation.

Doppelganger – A ghostly counterpart of a living person.

Familiar – Familiars are a witch's helpful, guardian spirit. Familiars may take the form of a pet, a spirit animal, or even an obliging non-physical entity.

Fetch – The fetch is described as an exact, spectral double of a living human, whose appearance is regarded as ominous. A sighting of a fetch is generally taken as a portent of its exemplar's looming death.

Fortuna – A Roman Goddess, Fortuna is often represented bearing a cornucopia as the giver of abundance and a rudder as controller of destinies.

Hedge Witch – Also known as a Green Witch, their focus is on interaction with the natural world.

Harm to None – The concept of ethical reciprocity. Used to imply the Golden Rule in the belief that the spirit of the Rede is to actively do good for one's fellow humans as well as for oneself.

Hel – In Norse mythology, Hel features as the goddess of death / the Underworld. She was sent by Odin to Helheim/Niflheim to preside over the spirits of the dead, except for those who were killed in battle and went to Valhalla. She determined the fate of the souls who entered her realm and is often depicted with her skeleton exposed down one-half of her body. She is typically portrayed in black and white representing both sides of all spectrums. Daughter of Loki.

Hoodoo – a body of practices of sympathetic magick traditional especially among African Americans in the southern U.S.. Conjuring spirits and ancestors is prevalent in hoodoo, as is connecting with them for personal gain.

Inverted Pentagram – A five-pointed star without the circle, a symbol of the elements, that has been turned upside down to represent dark arts or the devil, in terms of Christianity.

Macerated – To cause to become soft or separated into constituent elements by or as if by steeping in fluid.

Magick – First introduced in the 1600's, it has more recently been adopted to differentiate stage magic and illusion, with the real magick associated with witchcraft.

Occult – Not manifest or detectable by clinical methods alone, but by astrology, card reading, palmistry, etc.

Otherworld, The – In Irish Mythology, it is described as a supernatural realm where there is everlasting youth, beauty, health, abundance, and joy, and where time moves differently. It is the dwelling place of the gods as well as certain heroes and ancestors.

Pentacle – The pentacle has long been used by witches as a symbol of protection; the points of the pentacle representing the five elements of earth, air, fire, water, and spirit…the five things essential to sustain life. The circle surrounding them contains and protects, and also connects the five points indicating that earth, air, fire, and spirit, are all connected. In white-witchcraft, the single point sits upright.

Pentagram – A five-pointed star.

Scry – Divination which involves gazing into a surface such as a crystal ball, a mirror, water, or flickering flames or even simply closing one's eyes. The images seen by the diviner can be fleeting, hazy, or vague, but their intuition helps them to discern and understand the scattered images and translate them into something tangible.

Sedona Vortex – Located in Sedona, AZ, the vortexes (the proper grammatical form 'vortices' is rarely used) are thought to be swirling centers of energy that are conducive to healing, meditation and self-exploration. These are places where the earth seems especially alive with energy.

Sigil – A symbol used to represent a desired outcome, charged during their creation, with the intent of the practitioner.

Sky-clad – To be naked, specifically during spiritual ritual.

Summerland, The – The name given by Theosophists, Spiritualists, Wiccans, and some earth-based contemporary pagan religions to their conceptualization of existence on a plane in an afterlife.

Tarot – Any of the set of 78 playing cards (divided into five suits, including one of permanent trumps), often used for mystical divination. Suits usually consist of pentacles, wands, swords and cups, with The Fool as an ultimate trump card.

Triple Moon – Also known as the Triple Goddess. Representing the Maiden, Mother, and Crone, and honoring each stage of the female life cycle, the triple moon symbolizes the three, united.

White-Magick – The use of means (such as charms or spells) believed to have supernatural power over natural forces, that forego the means of ill intent upon others.

White Witch – A witch of any race or ethnicity who practices white magick : a beneficent witch.

Winter Solstice / Yule – One of the eight sabbats, celebrated in December (usually around the 21st). A time when either of the Earth's poles reaches its maximum tilt away from the sun. Thereafter, the days start to get progressively longer. Yule is a celebration of rebirth, renewal, and the continuation of life. A perfect time for candle magick, rest, and self-care.

Witch Bells – Witch bells are a cluster of bells, designed to hang on your door as a protective charm, and ring whenever anyone enters, ensuring whoever is paying you a visit doesn't bring negative energy with them.

Widdershins – In a direction contrary to the usual, counter-clockwise.

ABOUT THE AUTHOR

Sherri was raised in Huntsville, Texas. Walking barefoot and catching crawdads as they swam the creek beds, she loved all things free and natural. Her childhood was rampant with talk of ghosts, demons, and back country folklore. This inspired her first "book" about a poisonous flower that shot toxins onto children as they smelled it. Her classmate bought it for all the change in his pocket. At age nine, her mother packed the two of them up and headed to California. She has ping-ponged throughout the area ever since. Her first professional step into writing was the fitness book, *Mom Looks Great*. Now, transmuting the grief of her father's passing, she delves into the world of thriller and paranormal writing, pouring forth in the form of *Murder Under Redwood Moon*.

Note from Sherri L. Dodd

Word-of-mouth is crucial for any author to succeed. If you enjoyed *Murder Under Redwood Moon*, please leave a review online—anywhere you are able. Even if it's just a sentence or two. It makes all the difference and would be very much appreciated.

Thanks!
Sherri L. Dodd

We hope you enjoyed reading this title from:

BLACK ✿ ROSE
writing™

www.blackrosewriting.com

Subscribe to our mailing list – *The Rosevine* – and receive **FREE** books, daily
deals, and stay current with news about upcoming releases
and our hottest authors.
Scan the QR code below to sign up.

Already a subscriber? Please accept a sincere thank you for being a fan of
Black Rose Writing authors.

View other Black Rose Writing titles at
www.blackrosewriting.com/books and use promo code
PRINT to receive a **20% discount** when purchasing.

Made in the USA
Las Vegas, NV
25 March 2024

87758080R00173